CROWN OF NIGHT AND RAIN

AN EMPIRE OF CURSES AND DREAMS

THE NIGHT AND RAIN SERIES
BOOK ONE

SUSAN PERSON

Author's Note

Dear Reader - Please be advised that this book series contains content that may be upsetting for some readers. Should you wish to learn more information for your best reading experience, please scan the QR code below for additional details and content notes.

CROWN OF NIGHT AND RAIN

PART ONE
NIGHT & RAIN

200 Years Ago
The Height of the Great War
Compilation of diary entries and personal accounts from the
War Museum

The king summoned her for an audience. She knew he loved her, but she never became more alive than when she was on the battlefield. She could have settled into a comfortable life of luxury, but she needed more. She wanted to leave her mark on this world, and she only hoped he would honor her request. If dying for all of faekind on a battlefield came for her, there would be no greater honor.

Daphina knelt at the base of the dais. The king rose and held out his hand.

"You are of a great house and ancestry. You

kneel to no one." He helped her to her feet, casting an adoring gaze on her.

"My king," she said, her voice full of admiration for the once-great monarch. Had he not been blind to the coming changes of the world, she might have still considered him the same great monarch she loved.

"I've granted your appeal to return to the battle." He held her hand and patted it. "But you will be returning as my general to lead our army."

Pride swelled in her chest at this appointment. She'd been at the top of her strategy class and had some of the most powerful magic in the kingdom. Now the king allowed her an opportunity to use it. "You honor me, Your Majesty."

"We are preparing the prison you suggested, but we will need you when the time comes to lock the magic in place."

"Of course. I will make sure I am ready. Is that all, my king?" No one else had her Nyx-given gifts, and although attempts had been made to keep the knowledge quiet, more knew each day.

He stepped closer and kissed her cheek. "Come home when it is all done."

A blush crept over Daphina's face for she knew he meant his castle, not the great house of her family. He was centuries her senior, but the fae didn't worry about the passage of time like some of the other far-off kingdoms. "Yes, Your Majesty."

CHAPTER 1
ARIANNA

A chill ran over my skin and melded with the sorrow gripping my heart. I covered the hollow place in my chest as if that could ease the ache and loss embedded deep inside me. Two distinct anniversaries marked the day, and neither deserved a celebration. I stared out at the Forgotten Forest, the greenery dense and lush like an invitation to explore, but not even the unicorns with so much power at the tip of their horns would enter. The castle loomed behind me, as it always had when I ventured out on this day, along with a future that wasn't meant to be mine.

Five years ago, my older sister, Gemma, and her bonded disappeared into the woods. Gemma and Cyrus never returned, and no one went into the forest to look for them. Ever. The anniversary never got easier, especially when it was the anniversary of my mother's death too. She had died ten and five years ago.

A great war had transpired more than two hundred

years before my birth where the forest stood. It had long been said no one survived who entered. Gemma thought she could reach peace between the kingdoms, and Cyrus refused to let her go without unicorn representation. That's what Marius had told me and Father. I never understood, still didn't, what peace was needed when no one from either kingdom dared to cross the Forgotten Forest.

Though neither Gemma's body nor Cyrus's were ever recovered, no one stood at the edge to call for them any longer, except me on this day. I'd called her name five times—once for each year since she'd been gone. The woods served as a barrier between the Court of Love and Prosper and any of the enemies who remained, but according to our historians, there weren't enough of them left to ever matter. They might have even died out by present day. Our people were safe. But my sister was gone and so was a piece of my heart.

Our great empire had stood apart from the other, if it was still there, longer than they ever had been one. Though I had never seen the other lands, my teachers said both kingdoms put up walls, even though a vast field once separated them. I often wondered if those left there wished to join us in a kingdom built on love. In the early days, the field had been barren from the many battles. That time was long before my birth. Trees blanketed the space in a thick forest now, and that was all I'd ever known. The wall on our side stood high with its white stones, and the historians said the wall on the other side was shorter, darker, and made of unicorn stone. The last thought made me sick to enumerate how many unicorns the dark side of faekind had to slaughter to build a wall from ground bones and horns.

A huff of warm air blew up my neck. "You're too close, Arianna."

I didn't even flinch having sensed him down our bond before he approached.

"As close as I can get," I said, laying the wreath of moonflowers at the edge. My magic coaxed them to bloom in these dusk hours, as if it, too, understood the importance of the day and cooperated. I'd lingered longer than usual, and I got closer to the edge each year. What if Gemma was still out there? Could she have survived years in the forest? The thought of her alone in the dreadful woods was a better outcome than dying at the hands of our enemy. Cyrus would have protected her. Their bond was strong like mine and Marius's. While Marius gave me space, you rarely saw Gemma without Cyrus, so I knew he'd do whatever it took to save her, including being separated from his great love—which only left one conclusion. An end my heart wouldn't let my mind consider. The notion my sister still wandered the forest was foolish.

"You cannot bring your sister back any more than I can bring my brother back."

I closed my eyes and let out a breath before turning around to face Marius. I expected to see a solid black unicorn with a golden horn behind me, but he had used his magic to appear in his humanlike shape. His golden-brown skin shimmered, and I admired how he glowed in this form. "I know. I just miss her, Marius."

A golden tear slipped from his eye, and I reached up to catch it. He mourned with me. Our losses were as intertwined as our bond. I studied the liquid that held so much power fae had been known to fight over them. "The price is high for these in the market. You need to keep them close."

"Only because I trust you, Arianna." Outside of unicorns, the circle of elves he engaged with was small. Most of them he seemed to barely tolerate. His faith in me with something so precious spoke volumes about our bond.

I held my hand out. His horn appeared, virtually transparent in this form but as deadly either way. He dipped his horn to assimilate the tear back into him. His touch was gentle to avoid piercing my skin. That would either mean death or desire, and neither was acceptable among friends.

"Your king calls to you," Marius said, the horn disappearing completely. He would have found me here anyway, but it gave him an excuse I couldn't argue against. He returned to his unicorn form, and I much preferred him in his natural embodiment. Marius and Cyrus were twins, but Cyrus's coat was white with a black mane and tail. They both were blessed with golden horns and the powers that entitled them to.

"I've been ignoring him." I gazed up at the stone wall as if it was the boundary between me and my future.

"You are the heir to the throne," Marius said. "You cannot ignore your duty."

"Duty," I huffed. "Marrying me off to some random

guy isn't exactly what I consider duty. Besides, the heir is my sister." Father would be leaving for the front soon, and I was going to have to choose one of the men—if I could find one I at least liked. Despite being capable of leading the kingdom on my own, I needed someone who could travel as a representative outside the court while I maintained the seat of the empire. Father's logic was sound, but it didn't change my mind on not wanting marriage.

"She left." Marius reminded me of something I didn't need reminding of. Marius and I had a unique bond, even looking back through history. There were no others with lives synced like ours. We'd been born on the same day at the same time exactly three hundred years apart, but that wasn't what bound us. We both nearly died making our entrance into the world and carried a mark on our shoulders from our births that was considered a sign of greatness to some. The mark on my shoulder blade resembled a crescent moon with stars. Marius's was on the front of his shoulder, but it was quite similar to mine. Some believed it meant we had been touched by Nyx herself. Others believed it was good luck, but it hadn't proven as such for me.

"I'll escort you to the throne room," Marius said.

I sighed. If I waited, it was just prolonging the torture for the crown seeker. "I guess I can no longer avoid it. Where is Leana today?"

"She is with your little brother trying to teach him to talk."

I laughed. "She has so much more patience than the rest of us." Leana was Cyrus's unicorn partner, not that different from the marriage pairing of some fae. They had been arranged, but they had fallen in love. Marius had looked after her since Cyrus and Gemma left, but it had been hard on them both. They were constant reminders to each other of the half of them that was missing.

Marius opened the small door to the side of the gates with his magic for me to enter first. From the sounds of hooves behind me, he remained in his unicorn form. People milled around in the open space between the wall and the castle, mostly those who worked here but also other citizens who had business with Father or another member of court. They curtsied and bowed to me, and I inclined my head as expected. A guard stood beside my family's private entrance, the one closest to our destination, and opened the door. Marius appeared in human form again. He preferred his true form, so he did this for me, but it was unnecessary. He stopped at the gilded door that held my potential prospect.

"You're not coming in?" I asked, ready to get this introduction over.

"Not today," he said. "This is between you and your father."

"I thought you were my friend, Marius." A grin crossed my face.

"I've never proclaimed to be anything other than your bonded guard," he said, the light thinning around him in a veil of magic. The ability to move back and forth between the forms came easier for him than others of his kind. He was once again the black unicorn feared by most.

It hurt, but he hadn't ever officially said he was my

friend. We'd become closer when Gemma and Cyrus left, but maybe not as close as I'd thought. Our bond was strong, which made us something more than friends, but friendship wasn't a requirement. I'd considered him my closest companion regardless.

"Traitor," I said under my breath.

"I heard that." Marius walked away.

"Stupid unicorn hearing." I kept my voice low.

"Still can hear you."

I smirked. The grand doors opened to the throne room. I straightened my face and my spine and entered the space as I'd been prepared to do. The vastness of the room echoed my steps even with the tapestries in our imperial colors. My eyes were trained forward, but my periphery was on alert for a strange face or voice.

"Princess Arianna Alena Christella," the herald announced. Goddess and gods, I hated hearing that long-ass name. Even if he just announced me as Princess Arianna, it would be less pretentious.

I greeted Father with a warm smile. His straight, blond hair had been pulled back on the sides so that his crown sat flush against his head. It wasn't unusual for him to wear a crown, as well as one of his formal tunics, for court business. The black and silver garment he wore was a bit more fashionable than most of his court attire.

Father seemed relieved. Had he thought I wouldn't show? I'd never embarrass my father in such a cowardly way. He'd poured his love into me and Gemma when our mother died. I didn't remember much about her, but

Gemma, being older, had. Her stories played through my mind as if they were my memories.

Since being named crown princess, I no longer had to curtsy when I saw my father for the first time each day. The bended knee was considered a sign of respect, but it annoyed me, even as I watched others do it before him. Father held his arms out for me. There were only a handful of guards in the room, but he was flanked by his two favorites--Marius's friend, Barrett, and Marius's uncle, Claudius. "Arianna, you look beautiful."

"Thank you, Father." I embraced him. He hugged me tight to him—his only acknowledgment of the day. Speaking of Mother's death and Gemma's disappearance proved too painful for him, so he stayed silent each year.

"You might not thank me in a moment." His smile turned down a smidge as if he expected me to be angry. I appreciated he recognized the situation was difficult for me.

"I know you have another suitor you want me to meet." I braced myself for the details, followed by the meeting, as it had happened more than a dozen times. Father would never force me to marry, but he would strongly encourage me to take one of the princes he had paraded in front of me. My safety was his biggest concern if something were to happen to him. The worst-case scenario he'd shared with me was many of the elders wouldn't support a woman on the throne, which might plunge the kingdom into a civil war. His best case was I'd have to rule during a time of war and would need a repre-sentative to send to the front in my place. If I were to choose someone for anything other than love, it would be a partner who could be a loyal representative of this kingdom.

"Marius has been talking I see," he said.

"He is my guard."

"He is, and I'm glad you have him to look out for you," Father said. "Now, the prince you will meet—"

I sighed. "Please tell me he's not old like Duke Langford."

"Well, I hope I don't disappoint you in that I am older than you but not as old as the Duke." The voice from behind me was velvet against my skin. Goose bumps raised on my arms.

I locked my features into a neutral court expression and turned to see dark blue eyes homed in on me from a tall, dark-haired man. A lazy smile appeared on his full lips. He bent at the waist in a show of respect for my father. "My king, I was told to enter through the side door."

"Yes, you are right on time, Rainier." Father dismissed the formalities with the swipe of a hand. He never dispensed with formalities except with me. *How well did he know this Rainier?* "Arianna, meet Prince Rainier of Agonburg."

Agonburg was at the far north side of the kingdom, sitting at the base of the Erebian Mountains. The land was lush and green, and the flowers bloomed while we were there in the springtime. "Ah," I said. "I haven't been to Agonburg since I was a teen. I recall the beauty of the land, but I don't remember meeting you."

"Yes." He held out his hand, taking mine in his. His skin was smooth save the callouses one got from sword handling. The touch was warm. A little current passed between us, caressing my fingers. "But not as beautiful as you." His jaw tightened, then relaxed as he pressed his lips to my knuckles.

Liquid heat like a bolt of lightning shot through me. I jerked my hand away, unable to take the intensity of the connection. "Where were you when we called upon Agonburg?"

He tilted his head to the side. "How long ago was this visit?"

"Do you always answer a question with a question?" My irritation grew at his casual manner. He was so at ease here with me, and that was a first.

"No, but I have traveled much for diplomacy and war. I need a timeframe in which to tell you my exact where-abouts." His eyes twinkled like he was proud of his answer.

I cleared my throat. "It was my fifteenth summer, so ten years ago."

He nodded. "I would have been twenty-two, so I was at the southern border leading a defense." We didn't really have enemies other than those across the forest, so that must be what he meant by defense. He tucked his dark hair behind his ear, and I noticed the scar running from his ear down over his jaw. It seemed to enhance his good looks as if it defined his already chiseled jawline even more.

Father touched my elbow. "I'd like for you both to dine with me at dinner."

"Yes, Father." I tore my gaze away from Rainier to regard my father, who looked far too pleased with himself.

Rainier bowed. "As you wish, my king."

"See you this evening," Father replied.

Barrett and Claudius stepped forward, quietly and carefully. I followed Barrett's line of sight and watched Rainier leave. He was as pleasing to see go as he was on arrival.

"What do you think?" After the door shut, Father gestured to the smaller table in the alcove where he often took tea with guests.

I took a seat. Rainier might be excellent for something, but he was far too handsome to keep around. Those good looks meant trouble, but I couldn't say any of that to Father. Last time I mentioned I found one of the suitors had potential, he practically had the announcement written. "He's not lacking in the appearance department. But do you trust him?"

Rainier seemed too good to be true—attractive, funny, quick on his feet—and he wanted a crown.

"Prince Rainier is the son of one of my oldest friends."

Father had never mentioned being close with anyone in Agonburg. Barrett pawed a hoof on the ground. He and Claudius both lowered their heads. The doors swung open, and Marius entered, glamoured to his humanlike form. He came to stand directly behind me. I didn't think I'd given off any more than my usual irritation at these meetings, which made me consider Marius had another reason for being here.

"Marius." Father extended his hand to an open seat.

"Albert." Marius remained standing behind me. The unicorn chose us as their charges, but they had their own hierarchy. They weren't fae and never our subjects. They were our equals if not our betters. "Are you okay, Arianna?"

"I'm fine." Maybe I had been more annoyed than usual. He must have sensed my discomfort over the topic through our bond.

"I was just wondering what Arianna thought of Prince Rainier." Father inclined his head toward my bonded. "Perhaps you can enlighten me."

"She's not completely unpleased with him like the others," Marius said.

"Get out of my head." I glared at Marius, wishing my fire magic would manifest and singe the whiskers on his traitorous face. My magic was too unpredictable though. I never knew whether to expect a spark or an inferno when I played with fire. The guards who had to run from their card game after I accidentally threw a fireball at the storage room hadn't forgotten either. They gave me a wide berth every time I saw them.

"That's better than the others," Father said.

"It is," Marius agreed. "Maybe this will be the one."

"You are such a traitor," I whispered to Marius. *And you can keep some things to yourself while still telling the truth.* I shot the words down the bond with my irritation and waited for him to wince.

He didn't flinch, and I contemplated kicking him.

Don't. You need to consider the options in front of you.

You marry Prince Rainier then.

Father laughed. "A father can dream. My daughter is difficult though."

I sighed and closed Marius out of my head as best I could. "Your daughter is sitting right here."

He stood and held his arm out. "Come. Leana has sworn Andrews will speak today."

CHAPTER 2

ARIANNA

"Andrews, for me," Leana said in her most soothing voice as we walked in. She was by far the most striking unicorn, in my opinion. Her mane glimmered with vibrant, exquisite colors in the same order of a rainbow—red, orange, yellow, green, blue, indigo, and violet or ROYGBIV as she had taught me as a child to remember them. Other unicorns had tried to get closer to her, but her heart was solely for Cyrus. Marius said she might never take another as hers. Most unicorns didn't after a loss. Fae rarely had that kind of mate. While I respected how the unicorns could love on that level of commitment, I was sad for Leana to mourn for so long.

Drew's mother, Sion, had taken her own life not long after his birth. The doctors said she had the deep sadness so many of the women seemed to have after the birth of a child and tried to hide it. She hadn't been able to even hold Drew without crying. My heart ached for her and the desperation she must have suffered to feel that was the only way to be better. I prayed the goddesses and gods wrapped their arms around her and helped her find happiness again.

Gemma had mothered Drew as best she could, and when she left just before his first birthday, he stopped speaking the few words he had learned. Leana stepped in then because I was too broken from losing my sister.

"Ari," Andrews screamed and ran across the room.

Tears pooled in my eyes. "Did you just say my name, Drew?"

"Ari," he said again as I picked him up. He hugged my neck. His hugs were the best. My little brother made all the bad days better when he looked up at me with those bright eyes.

"I'm taking credit for his words," Leana said, a smile on her face. She glanced at my father, and magic rippled around her. She shifted into a beautiful woman with white-blonde hair that glittered with colors of the rainbow. Leana bowed to Marius and no one else, but she inclined her head with respect to my father.

"As you should," I said, hugging Drew to me. I was so proud of him.

Father reached for Drew, but my brother snuggled against my neck. I should feel guilty, but I loved my little brother like he was my own. "I don't think you're his favorite today."

"I'm never his favorite." Father chuckled. He brushed Drew's golden-brown hair from his face. "But I love you."

Drew held his hand out to keep Father from getting closer. I smashed my lips together to keep from laughing.

Leana had told me not to encourage that kind of behavior, but it was hard when my little brother was so adorable.

"If you took him to the kitchen for snacks like some do, you would be his favorite." Leana laughed. She hadn't proclaimed it, but I expected anytime Leana would declare Drew her charge. Marius told me she hadn't declared in two hundred years since her first and last charge died in the war. He hadn't mentioned her decision specifically, but any fool could see they had already bonded. I'd guessed their bond would be strong like mine and Marius's, and I was thankful he would have someone to protect him.

"I can do that," Father said, holding his hands out to Drew. "I believe there are some sweets in the kitchen."

Drew dove from me to Father. They needed to bond, but my arms felt empty without him. "Guess that proves Leana's theory."

Leana flicked her gaze my way and smiled. "It was no theory. I've seen the way he looks at those little chocolates when you take him in there."

I laughed. "You're right. He looks at them the way some people admire emeralds or rubies."

"I'll see you at dinner," Father said. "Marius. Leana." Father ducked out the door with a laughing Drew.

He's speaking. Thank you, Goddesses and Gods. It's so good to hear his little voice.

"What's up with you two?" Leana asked. "You feel... off."

"One of us is a traitor." I crossed my arms. "And it's not me."

"What was I to warn you of, Arianna? How good-looking you would think Rainier is?" Marius smirked.

My cheeks warmed. "That would have been some help."

"You are my charge, not my child. I have no say in the choices your father makes for you." He seemed unconcerned with this suitor, and that was different from the other times.

"Well, I'm sorry I asked," Leana said. "I can—"

"No, you stay with traitor-ass. I'll leave." I wasn't angry with her, but I was annoyed with her leader.

"Don't forget we have training this afternoon," Marius called after me.

I held my middle finger up in a very unprincesslike gesture. There wasn't any way I'd miss training, and he knew it.

I walked down into the garden, pissed and not even knowing why. The fresh air hit me, and I took several deep breaths and looked over my shoulder to make sure Marius wasn't following. I slammed into something hard and bounced backward. Strong arms caught me.

"Goddesses."

"No, but I have been called a god a time or two."

I blinked a few times to get my bearings back and gazed up into Prince Rainier's dark blue eyes—like looking into an abyss. Was he flirting with me? *Now?* With no one around to witness it?

"Are you okay, Princess Arianna?"

Warmth spread over me. I stepped back putting some

space between us. His hand stilled on my elbow to steady me. "I..." *Words Arianna. Words. Those things that seem to have floated right out of your brain. Remember those?* I forced a smile in practiced composure. "I'm fine. I was just out for a walk."

He cocked his head to the side. "What a coincidence. I was doing the same. If you would, I'd be pleased if you would show me around."

Goddesses and gods, he was so good-looking it almost hurt to look at him. Too good-looking. He had the kind of appeal that got a man whatever he wanted, and that was trouble. Duty and etiquette dictated I should oblige him, not that there would be any punishment if I didn't other than Father's disappointment and a few whispers at court. For Father and diplomacy, I would give Rainier a brief tour. I plastered my best fake smile on my face. "Sure. I'd be delighted to."

He held his arm out to me, and I slipped mine through. It wasn't as unpleasant as I expected. His skin was warm and his muscles firm under my touch. We walked in silence for a few moments.

"Are you not fond of me or just this arrangement?" His voice was quiet like I had wounded him, and it disarmed me.

My heart pounded. None of the other suitors bothered to even ask the question. "Neither. I mean I don't even know you, but I've known for a couple of years my father wishes for me to marry."

"And that doesn't bother you? The marrying part?" He studied me. The intensity was unnerving, but it was the distance behind his stare that intrigued me. He dropped his gaze to my mouth.

I swallowed hard. The vulnerability of what the answer would mean petrified me. "No, I know I will eventually have to make the decision, but he is in good health. It will be a long time before I will have to take the throne." I hoped I was right, and his upcoming trip to the front was routine and nothing else.

Rainier looked out over the open space in front of us. "But you know war is coming. Do you not wish to ensure the stability of our empire?"

Father had portrayed the issues as small groups of dissenters, not full war, at least not in the sense of the war from two centuries ago, but that wasn't what Rainier was asking. The thought he conveyed was one Father's advisors shared. Everyone agreed that an alliance would not only ensure the success of the empire but safeguard the future of the throne. Everyone but me. A sour taste formed in my mouth. "Me choosing a husband shouldn't have a bearing on that. I'm the one who will rule."

"But you can't be everywhere in the empire at once, and your spouse would be your proxy representing your wishes." His point was valid and the only reason I entertained these meetings.

"There are some in the kingdom who want me to marry so that my husband will be the one making decisions. Father doesn't feel that way, but there are those who do." I gauged his reaction.

"So, you do see them," Rainier said, sounding as if he

offered his approval. "I wasn't sure what you would be like, Princess Arianna, but I'm pleasantly surprised."

The center of my chest heated. I'd been flattered many times and was no fool to it, but it was what he said and how he said it. Like he saw me for more than a commodity or tool, whereas the other suitors were seeking status. "Please, call me Arianna."

One side of his mouth quirked up. "Very well, but only if you call me Rainier."

"I agree to these terms." I smiled, and it was genuine.

His eyes went distant again. He seemed lost for a moment, but he recovered quickly and moved us forward.

I heard Marius's hooves clicking against the stone as he lurked nearby, obviously walking in his natural form. He wanted me to hear him, otherwise he would have been silent. My bonded was coming to interrupt and was giving me notice.

"Tell me, Rainier, do you not have a guard?"

He stopped and faced me. The far-off look returned. Where did he go in those moments? Was he speaking to his guard?

"I do. She's a bit temperamental, so I asked her to remain near the gate. Her name is Casimir, and our bond is strong like yours."

"How do you ..." I looked over my shoulder to see Marius coming closer and flashed him my best look of annoyance.

"You need to go prepare for the banquet, Arianna" Marius said.

"Banquet? It's just ..." Realization sank in, and I bit

down on my lip. Father tricked me, and he made sure Marius didn't know until the envoys arrived. I let my anger flow down the bond with my guard, and his anger met mine with equal vigor. "How many dignitaries have arrived, Marius?"

"A dozen at least."

"And what do you know of this banquet?" I asked Rainier, letting my tone drip with incredulity.

Surprise blanketed his features. He took my hand, and I ignored the charge of energy as I yanked my hand free. "I promise, Arianna, I had no idea this was planned. I'm not a fan of formal affairs."

I couldn't tell if he was genuinely innocent or putting on a show for me.

Marius moved closer to me, clearly not believing the prince. "Let's go."

I cut my gaze to my bonded. Either he was worried my untrained power would unleash on this Prince of Agonburg, or he was worried I'd get swept up in greetings in an unprepared state. Maybe both. I couldn't tell.

"I'll see you this evening, Prince Rainier," I said, emphasizing his title. I wasn't sure if I trusted him or not, but I wasn't going to be informal with someone who might have betrayed me. No one at the banquet would see the tiny opening of friendship I'd briefly allowed. There would be no mistaking we were not a match to all the would-be onlookers.

CHAPTER 3

ARIANNA

"Do you not like the makeup?" Val asked, frowning. I sat at the dressing table as she did my hair. She was the daughter of a great nobleman and my closest confidant next to Marius. Our fathers had known each other their entire lives and Val and I had as well. As a noblewoman, she could have chosen a strong marriage for power or prestige, but she chose to be by my side until I married. She was in no bigger hurry than me until Theo returned to court. The unpopular belief that a woman could run a house or a kingdom without a man by her side was one we shared.

"I hardly recognize myself. You did wonderfully." The person in the mirror had been made to look like a future queen. Although I didn't like the position I was in, it would be my mask tonight. The face everyone else got to see.

"Do you want your hair in a full updo?" She eyed the

two dresses hanging on the screen in the corner. "If you are wearing the black one, I'd go with a partial updo. Your hair will be a beautiful contrast against the dark fabric and crystals. If you are wearing that virginal silver one, then we should go with a full updo."

I laughed. A virgin I was not, although my experiences hadn't been as noteworthy as Val had described her time with her beau. The silver was beautiful, but I wanted to look strong at this banquet. I gravitated to the black one. "You obviously prefer the black."

"You are a woman and should dress like one." She smiled.

"Partial updo it is then," I said. "And you are in your signature red." Val often wore red, which was striking on her pale skin and raven-hued hair, but it was the color of her family's house as well.

"I can't disappoint my admirers." She laughed.

"Or one in particular." I raised my eyebrows at her reflection in the mirror.

"Have you heard if Theo is coming?" The excitement in her voice was infectious.

"Of course he is. Did you see the line of dignitaries? Theo is too much of a social butterfly to miss this gathering." I understood her attraction to him. He was lively, funny, and so handsome with his fine features and dark skin. His brother had inherited the duchy their father had ruled, but Duke Theodore was already respected for his war strategies. I would likely lose Val to him before I ever considered a match of my own because there was no way I would not encourage her after seeing how they adored each other.

Val grinned at my reflection in the mirror. "I hope he'll dance with me."

"Of course he will." I shook my head at her. "He's crazy about you."

She blushed and turned my head to place a few more pins. "Done. Let's get you in this dress."

THE GILDED DOORS of the ballroom stood closed for my announcement. The wait was never long enough yet too long for me every time. It made me feel like I was being paraded in like a prize even though Father assured me many times that wasn't the case. He said it was a sign of respect for both of us.

"Deep breath," Val said, knowing how much I hated the herald portion of the entrance. All eyes would be on me for the entire length of the room until I reached the dais. For my father, I would show a unified front, because I was the next in line for the throne. He'd named me and supported me, despite how many people talked about his daughter whose magic was weak and wild.

Marius stood on my other side. "She is correct. You should calm yourself."

"Thanks for the astute observation, traitor," I said under my breath.

Val snorted next to me. "I'm so glad I'm not bonded."

"You have no idea how lucky you are."

Marius blew a huff of hot breath against my arm.

"Here the fuck we go," I mumbled.

The doors opened and the music that had drifted out stopped. The herald stepped forward, hands behind his back.

"Her Royal Highness, the Crown Princess Arianna Alena Christella." His voice reverberated off the walls with the formal introduction.

I plastered a smile on my face similar to the one I put on for Rainier earlier. I scanned the lower tables closest to the dais, but I didn't see him. A pang of disappointment stabbed into my stomach. Val tugged me forward, and I trained my gaze on the crest, deep green and black, hung high near the ceiling. The intricate swirls of the crest melded into a griffin-like creature.

"And Lady Valentina." Once I was several steps in, the herald added my confidante. The companion of an HRH, a royal highness, was never announced at the same time. It was archaic in my opinion, but Father believed we couldn't do away with all the old traditions. "Choose your battles, Arianna," he'd told me.

I kept my gaze forward and high as was expected when we crossed the room to the dais, where Father, dressed in his finery the colors of the empire, took my hand while I climbed the steps. It was only then I lowered my chin. Marius went to his guard position on my side of the table behind my chair. Val curtsied to Father and moved to stand behind her seat, a plush one next to my designated spot. She received preferential treatment as my royal companion, but the formalities of the court remained. I'd pleaded for Father to relax them, not just for Val but other court attendees too, since being named heir. He said they were necessary to maintain civility. Yet, I didn't find them to be essential for the respect of our people.

Father turned to the audience assembled. My gaze landed on the person sitting in the guest of honor seat at the end of the table closest to Father's side. Rainier. My heart sped up at the sight of him. He looked even better wearing his blue dress attire.

"My daughter and I are pleased to host all of you as our esteemed guests and would like to welcome Prince Rainier of Agonburg as our guest of honor tonight," Father said, his voice warm.

My grip tightened on his hand. The room erupted in applause, and I forced my smile into the one Gemma taught me that looked happy even when I wasn't. She'd told me it was the way we could fake it until we felt it. Mine would never be as perfect as my sister's, but she never struggled with the formalities of her role like I did. What Father did tonight was a setup. He knew everyone would see an action like this as a precursor to an announcement. He meant it to put pressure on me to marry without actually announcing an engagement, and I saw it for what it was. Anger shot up my spine, and I ground my teeth together to keep my magic from erupting. Sweat beaded on my brow, and I couldn't wipe it with everyone staring at us for fear they would realize Father and I weren't aligned.

"Let the banquet begin," he said, releasing my hand and clapping twice.

I retreated to my chair, leaning close to Val's ear as I took my seat. "That was bullshit. Did you catch what he was doing?"

She leaned back so she could whisper to me and pretended to fix my hair while wiping the sweat away. "I did, and I'm certain I wasn't the only one."

"Most certainly not. That applause said an expectation had been set." Father had backed me into a corner, and I wasn't sure how to gracefully exit this situation. I was fucked.

"That's not all." She clasped her hands together so her lips could not be read. "A certain prince hasn't taken his eyes off of you since you entered the room."

"Maybe I should ask Marius to gouge those beautiful eyes of his out with his horn." I didn't mean it. What a waste to destroy those gorgeous orbs. Plus, with my luck, Rainier would probably grow back better ones. A tingle shimmied through me to know he'd been staring at me.

Val's eyebrow quirked up. "He seems quite nice, Ari. Maybe give him a chance."

"I might if I trusted him," I said, wishing I had certitude with his actions. I wanted to believe he meant well, but I couldn't afford that kind of blind faith. Not after tonight.

"What could he have possibly done to extinguish your

trust already? The prince just arrived today." She poured wine into each of our glasses.

"He knew about this setup," I said. If he'd told me upfront, I might have given him a chance. "Or at least I think he did."

Val reached for the small olive and parmesan rolls, placing one on my bread plate and then hers. "If he did, could you blame him? Many would love the chance of an introduction to the beautiful crown princess."

I blew out a breath. "I'd just like to meet someone who doesn't see me as a title but for me." I'd thought that was the way Rainier had seen me, but he had an ulterior motive.

Val pressed her lips together like she was trying not to laugh. "Really? That's so cliche of you."

I smiled then. She had no fear of calling me out. "Okay. I want them to see me as the warrior I'm capable of being. If we are facing dissenters, I want to lead my people and not hide behind the castle walls."

"And how do you know they will or won't see you that way if you don't give anyone a chance?"

Val had a point. I hadn't given many of the previous suitors much of an opportunity. In my defense, most of them had been throne seekers or title hunters. Marius had made sure I knew exactly what they were—not that I couldn't tell by their actions with over-the-top plans, gestures, and ideas. None of the others took time with me. I glanced over at Rainier, and he indeed was staring at me. He lifted his glass and inclined his head to me. I raised mine to him in acknowledgment.

"Will you dance with him after dinner?" Val asked, picking at the food in front of her.

"Undecided." Even though I'd resolved to play my father's game that didn't mean I had to make it easy for Rainier. However, getting to know him and making him an ally was advantageous. Besides, he was smart, handsome, and had a nice physique, which made him a better option than my previous suitors.

CHAPTER 4

ARIANNA

The dishes were cleared from the tables, and the dessert buffet had been set up on one wall of the ballroom. A small band entered and went to where their instruments had been set up. Theo stopped to visit with Val before heading to the buffet to get me and Val a lemon tart. Father stood and paused as all the attention in the room came to him. "I know you are used to me opening the dances at our gatherings, but I would like Princess Arianna to do so this time."

Fuck me. I whispered quickly to Val, "I suppose dragging you out there with me is out of the question."

"Unfortunately, I promised my first dance to Theo." She smiled.

I forced my expression into the pristine, perfect look a princess should have, but inside I was pissed I hadn't anticipated the move. Prince Rainier approached my side of the dais as I made my way to the steps. He held out his hand, and I slipped mine into it. A quick charge radiated from our touch. It must have been from the anger festering in me. Had he conspired with Father for the opportunity? The possibility intensified my rage.

The music was soft, an intermediate filler to give us time to get to the center. Prince Rainier pulled me close as the music ramped up to a waltz. No one else approached, so I had to dance with him. "Presumptuous much?"

"Is it not customary for the honored guest to take part in the opening of the dance?" he whispered in my ear. I ignored the tickle of his breath.

It was tradition that the honored guest opened the dance, but it was usually not with me. And just because it was the normal expectation, it didn't mean I had to acknowledge his rightness. I ground the toe of my shoe on his. His wince gave me a little satisfaction.

"Oops. Pardon my clumsiness, Prince Rainier." I smiled sweetly and batted my eyelashes.

"I promise you I did not know of these plans," he said, his tone almost pleading if not a little pained. "You are angry with me for something that was not my doing, Princess Arianna."

And we were back to the title. Ugh. But that was my fault. I'd called him Prince Rainier when last we parted and again moments ago. I couldn't expect anyone to be informal with me, especially a visiting prince, when I was formal with them. "That may be true, but how would I ever know?"

"What if we just spend a few days as friends... as Rainier and Arianna?"

I studied him and found sincerity in his blue eyes, dark like the depths of the ocean. A few days would satisfy Father, and then my focus could go back to my training with Marius. "Do you have a nickname?"

He smirked. "I do. Why do you ask?"

"If we're going to spend a few days as friends, I'd like you to call me Ari." Making a temporary friend of him didn't mean I had to bring him into my inner circle, but it had to be good enough to convince my father. It might not be a permanent solution, but maybe Father would stop looking for a while.

He leaned in close, and his breath brushed my cheek in a caress. I resisted the urge to shiver. "Most of my friends call me Rain, and I would very much like to hear you say it."

"Rain?" He was taller than me, and I had to look up to see his face. The thin scar on his otherwise perfect profile was visible from this angle, and I wanted to ask him about it. Instead, I arched a brow at him.

"There's more to it than just a shorter version of my given name, but that's a story for another day."

He likely had an obnoxious list of names like mine. I wasn't even named after anyone. Father and Mother wanted to avoid saddling me with the expectations of the past, so instead they saddled me with a long name that might as well rhyme. "What did my father promise you to entice you here?"

His face contorted into a mix of surprise and offense. "He offered me nothing beyond the chance to meet you, Princess Arianna Alena Christella." My name sounded like a sweet song the way it rolled from his lips. The music for a second dance started. "And that was all I needed."

"Ari. Call me Ari." I should move on to another to dance, but my anger subsided at least for this Prince of Agonburg. There was a connection to Rainier I wanted to ignore because giving into it could mean losing my independence. Since some of the king's advisors didn't want a woman on the throne, they would be thrilled for me to be engaged. But I enjoyed how Rainier and I fit together as we swayed across the floor. Warmth hummed in my chest, catching me off guard.

I suddenly felt overheated and the last thing that needed to happen was me embarrassing Father by starting a fire in the middle of the party. My untapped magic could be unpredictable if I wasn't in control, and I'd let a tiny bit of protection slip here with Rainier. That coupled with my erratic motions today and how Rainier made me nervous was a volatile mix. "Excuse me."

My eyes flicked to Marius, but he was already on the move—no doubt sensing the surge in me. My gaze turned to where Val and Theo danced. He smiled at her, and it was easy to see how smitten he was. Concern etched Val's face, and I gave her a single shake of my head to convey I didn't need help.

I navigated through the crowd, not even looking to see if Father saw me, to the door where the guards opened both for me. I hurried down the hall. Being outside, when the weather was cold, helped me control it. Breaking into a run for the door to my private garden, I heard Marius beside me at every step. I couldn't calm the inferno growing in me. The heat grew, hot like I burned from the inside out. My mind numbed with panic, and I waved Marius away. He ignored my gesture. I burst through the door and into the cool night air. The damp chill kissed my skin, and I stretched out my arms, letting it cover me like a cold shower. I closed my eyes and relished the relief as the heat simmered down.

"I would ask what sparked this surge, but I believe I know," Marius said.

"Not helping." I glared at him. Eyeing a pitcher of water and several glasses, left here should I entertain, I ignored the pitcher and grabbed one of the glasses, thrusting it into the running water of the spring-fed fountain. The water was frigid as it slid down my throat and calmed my internal heat storm.

"He comes," Marius said.

"Who? Father?"

"Not the king."

My cheeks burned, and a flush crept down my neck. I looked past Marius to see Rainier in the doorway. He stared at me with concern etched on his features. His gaze traveled over me and probably saw the massive goose bumps on my exposed skin.

"I wanted to be sure you were all right." His voice was soft like velvet brushing my skin. I inhaled a deep breath of the cold air and let it out slowly.

"It's cold out here." He stepped forward, but Marius took a protective stance next to me. Rainier positioned himself in front of me on the other side of the waist-high stand the pitcher sat on.

"I'm fine," I said, my voice shaky. I forced calm into it, putting my practiced everything-is-fine look in place. "I appreciate you checking on me, but I just needed some air."

"Are you sure?" He said, and that silky swath from his voice hit me again. Was he seriously trying to use persuasion on me? To seduce me in my own garden? And with Marius here to witness it? Stupid move.

Anger seeped in around me. He thought I was so malleable he could use such low-level magic on me. Wicked thoughts went through my head, but I had the perfect answer to his attempt.

"Arianna," Marius warned.

"I've got this," I said. "I'm good."

"Perhaps I should escort you back to the banquet," Rainier said, that smooth tone working on my skin.

I smiled, letting him think his weak magic could control me.

"Um... your dick is on fire." I wiggled a finger toward his crotch. It was low magic, too, but I didn't care. He wouldn't be harmed. There were no scorch marks since I'd only used illusion and not fire magic. This was purely for my pleasure.

"Wh... shit." He grabbed the water pitcher and poured it on his pants.

I stifled a laugh, knowing he would have to walk out of here looking like he'd urinated on himself.

"See you back at the banquet." I waved to him. Pleased with myself, a genuine smile spread across my face.

"You are perfectly capable of fending off persuasion. Was that necessary?" Marius chastised when we were out of earshot.

"Absolutely," I said, walking through the double doors to the banquet with Marius at my side.

CHAPTER 5
RAINIER

After I used my magic to pull the water out of my pants, I went to find my traveling companion. I brushed Casimir's coat in the stable area she'd chosen outside the walls of the castle. There was no animosity for her choice. I understood her reasons for not wanting to enter the confines of the court. She'd been worried that the other unicorns, especially one in particular, would invade her thoughts if she stepped hoof into the castle. I said she wasn't friendly, and that wasn't completely untrue. I always referred to her as antisocial, but she'd protected me during the coup. My mind drifted to Arianna, but my thoughts hadn't strayed far from her since our introduction. She was not the delicate princess I expected. She was strong, and my cock hardened thinking about how she tricked me with the illusion magic. The princess was much much more than I'd planned for, and I delighted in the challenge.

"If brushing my coat has that effect on you, perhaps

someone else should perform the task," Casimir chided, her white coat shining even in the dim light.

I looked down at the bulge in my pants. "Sorry. I was thinking of—"

"The princess. I suggest you not think of her while standing so close to me."

"Noted," I said. "Gemma was right. There is power in her sister, Casimir. I felt it radiating off of her. She is incredible. Has no one ever noticed it before?" She was special, power or not. Before her, no woman had ever stood so strong in my presence. I had to learn what she was capable of, but I wanted to know more about her.

"Power does run in her from the great general and her ancestry, but I've never heard them speak of Arianna in such a way. The references were always that the power in her couldn't be harnessed or focused. Are you sure it was coming from her?" She averted her gaze, and that was normal. Perhaps, Casamir wasn't telling me the whole truth... not that she ever did.

"I'm positive. The force was... intoxicating. I've never felt anything so intense before. It was almost like I could taste the strength if I just tasted her." My dick bit against my leathers, and I tried to think of anything but Arianna.

"Go find a young woman and bed her. Not this princess. Anything with her beyond your duty will be messy. Some random, willing woman is what you need. It's been too long, and you are confusing lust for power. Not to mention her sister will rip you to shreds." Casimir's judgmental attitude mixed with practicality in her thinking. I didn't agree with her.

"Lust." I chuckled. "I haven't fallen victim to lust in decades." I'd felt it certainly, but I hadn't let it control me. What came from Arianna was not lust. There was desire. She was beautiful and that dress tonight... fuck. I wanted to rip it off of her, but that was desire. Desire was wanting, and lust was power. There was a difference. I couldn't let either one get in the way of the mission, but I wanted inside her head to know what made her happy, what she desired, and what she truly thought of me.

CHAPTER 6
ARIANNA

I rose from my bed and drew my bath. The ladies hated when I did it myself, but I didn't like waiting for them to get my day started. There was a knock at the door, and per the usual, they would come in and take over. Today was a training day with Marius, though, so no beautiful gowns. I'd wear my training leathers. I turned to the door to tell them to enter, but something on the floor caught my eye.

An envelope. I padded across the floor to pick it up. "Ari" was scrawled across it. The penmanship was unfamiliar to me. Everyone I knew who would write if they were away was here for court. I opened it and walked back toward the bed. A second knock came as I sunk onto the plush mattress.

"Come in," I called while opening the note.

Ari,

My apologies if I crossed a line last night. That was not my intention. I only meant to calm you as you seemed upset. Please forgive my idiocy and join me for dinner in your garden tonight. Just the two of us.

Rain

Had he really written me a letter? Rainier?

I read it again, unsure if this was sincere or another way to get close to me. He'd used the nicknames we'd shared, and warmth stirred in my chest. He had apologized in writing. I could learn more about him and what he had seen on the front. One dinner would be fine.

"Ari?" Val called from the doorway. "May I?"

"You never have to ask, Val." I slipped the note back into the envelope. "You know that."

Val's cheeks were rosy and her eyes bright as she entered with the other ladies behind her. "I have something to tell you."

I glanced at the ladies. "Today is training. I can take it from here."

They curtsied and left the room.

I patted the bed next to me, and Val took the spot. She grabbed my hands in hers.

"Theo asked me to marry him."

Happiness blossomed in my chest for her. She'd forgone several suitors to stay with me. I couldn't be angry, especially not with the way I'd seen Theo look at her. "Oh, Val. I'm so happy for you." I hugged her neck.

She studied my face, and I saw relief in hers. "I was afraid you might be vexed I would be leaving."

"Never, my friend," I said. "Because first and foremost you are my best friend, and I consider you a sister. I only want you to have all the happiness of the world."

"Then, you will come to the wedding?"

"Of course," I said. "I wouldn't miss it. Will it be soon? Shall I ask Father if we can have it here?"

She hugged me. "Theo wants us to marry near his family. His grandmother is unable to travel due to her chronic illness."

"I will be there." I squeezed her hand. "Even if I have to travel like a princess." Since Gemma's disappearance, I wasn't allowed to travel without a procession, and I avoided formal events away from the royal grounds because of it. Not that I was given many opportunities to travel. I'd snuck out plenty, though, and it was one of the rules Marius supported me breaking, as long as he was around to protect me.

"Would you consider standing up with me? I know it's unusual for your status, but there is no one I'm closer to and would want by my side." She fidgeted. It broke protocol, but I'd bent protocol before I was named the crown princess and continued to bend it frequently. Val and I had been close before Gemma left. She had once told me she never sought to replace Gemma, but she did consider me her family. I felt the same way about her.

"Of course I will. I'd be hurt if you asked someone else."

Her smile stretched across her face. "Now the day will be perfect."

"All you need is you and Theo to make it idyllic, but I'm honored to be part of the day."

"Now that is settled, let me draw your bath." She stood to head toward the bathing chamber and paused. "Why do I hear running water?"

"You know I can't sit around."

She just shook her head and proceeded to get the other items ready.

I was going to be alone in this castle without my best friend. Marius didn't count because he was my guardian, not my friend. We couldn't have the conversations Val and I did. The castle suddenly felt cold and lonely. I loved Father and Drew, but it wasn't the same kind of relationship as I had with Gemma and Val. *Who would I tell my secrets to now?*

I swung my practice sword at the cloud of dust Marius had formed into my opponent. I sliced through the conjured creature. No magic came, and the sword was so heavy. I flipped the metal over in my hand, looking to make sure it was mine.

"You're slow today," Marius said, his tone accusatory. "Why are you so sluggish?"

Why was I sluggish? "Maybe I drank too much wine last night."

"You barely consumed any."

"Then you didn't see the two shots of vodka I, Val, and Theo took." Val had read my state as soon as I walked into the party and sent Theo for my liquor of choice. She knew me so well. Maybe better than Marius in some ways.

"Still not enough," he said. "You are high-born fae and have a much larger tolerance with such pure blood."

I knew what he was doing. He was making arrogant statements to coax me to talk about the surge of power I nearly had last night, but he wanted me to want to talk about it. And I didn't. Each time my power manifested without me summoning it was a reminder of what a failure I was, whether I was able to stop it like last night or not. It had come so easy to Gemma, and my power was wild.

"Maybe there was more. I just can't recall," I said, pretending to gag.

Marius shook his head. "What about the boy?"

"Boy?" I asked, intentionally looking at him like he had two heads. If he meant Rainier, that man was far from a boy by decades.

"I guess 'man' is technically more appropriate." Marius let his glamour go and took his natural form.

"Oh, Prince Rainier?" I shut him out of the bond as much as possible and acted like I didn't know who he meant. It served no point to evade his question other than to annoy him, and I needed someone to be as irritated as I was over last night.

"Yes, he seems quite taken with you."

"So taken he tried to use persuasion on me." I rolled my eyes. Rainier had used low magic on me to try to control me. If that was the kind of friend or partner he planned to be, there was no future for us.

"But your reaction to him started before that." Marius stomped his hoof, creating another shadow creature for me to fight.

"I was attracted to him. Something about him feels different from the other suitors, but the persuasion was a low blow I can't let go." Even if I wanted to get to know him better. My anger shifted in me, and I sliced the shadow figure straight up the middle from crotch to head. Dust scattered everywhere.

"That was better," he said. "You're fastest with your daggers, but you are getting stronger with the sword."

I watched the remnants fall to the ground like dirty rain. "He did send a letter of apology, and I am to dine with him this evening." I couldn't keep the little bit of hope for tonight out of my voice, and I wasn't sure if Marius would approve or not.

"Not like you to give a second chance," Marius said.

"Well, I didn't exactly give him a first chance either," I said, facing him. "What do you know of him from Agonburg?"

"He grew up fighting on the front. His father had discouraged him, but he insisted." Marius's tone carried a hint of respect. That was hard-earned. I wasn't convinced I even had his respect.

"Interesting. He's braver than I gave him credit for."

Rainier might not be as much of an asshole as I thought. I could give him some time for friendship if he was that courageous. Father would be pleased if I showed more interest in the prince too.

"There were rumors he had died on the battlefield, but they were wrong. He was severely injured."

No one had mentioned it, but if I'd nearly died, I wouldn't want to talk about it either. The battles hadn't been more than skirmishes from what Father had said, but the front lines of even a skirmish weren't kind to the soldiers. "I saw a scar along his jawline."

"Yes, evidently that was the least of his injuries," Marius continued. "He lost a lot of blood, and it was a couple of months before he could speak enough to tell them who he was."

I imagined what kind of injuries he must have had, and my stomach soured. Minus the compulsion, he seemed kind...maybe a little too charismatic but caring of others. He had come and found me when he thought I was sick. Maybe I'd been a little too harsh making him think his dick was on fire. No, he still deserved that for his persuasion attempt. I could call our deeds even if he was a good person, and I wanted to find out if he was at dinner.

Smack.

"Oof." The shadowy dust creature knocked me to the ground. I spit dirt out. "Was that necessary?"

Marius leaned down over me. The sun dipped low in the sky behind him. "Your enemies will strike when you are vulnerable and when you least expect it so always expect it."

"Noted." I got to my feet and dusted myself, knowing I'd made a foolish mistake. A mouth full of dirt was what I deserved for losing focus. "What's next?"

"That's enough for today. We'll work on magic next lesson."

CHAPTER 7

ARIANNA

Val pinned one side of my hair back, letting the waves cascade down. "Tiara or no tiara?"

I admired the diamond and light blue star sapphires on the hinged comb that had been Gemma's, gifted to her by Mother. My sister passed it along to me on my sixteenth birthday and told me how much it had meant to Mother. I rarely wore it, but Val had chosen it as soon as I chose the dress from the three she had pulled for me. The timing made me wonder if my sister or my mother or both were sending a blessing on tonight.

"No tiara." I touched the comb. "This is too beautiful to have anything distract from it."

"I agree. You look so stunning. Prince Rainier will be speechless." She helped me into my shoes. "Shall I wait for you here?"

"No, go enjoy the rest of your night with Theo." I found myself looking forward to the dinner tonight with Rainier.

He seemed to be different than what I assumed about him, and I was curious to see more of him.

Val opened the door to my chamber, and Marius was waiting in his two-legged form. Usually, Val or one of the other ladies would walk me through the castle for interactions, but I'd never accepted a private dinner invitation from a suitor either. "Come to escort me to the garden?"

Marius cocked his head to the side, taking in my blue velvet dress. "That looks more than friendly."

"We'll see," I said. "If he's really apologetic, I might not need an escort home."

Marius scrunched his face up, and I laughed, patting his arm.

"It's a joke, Marius." Maybe not totally a joke, but Rainier's looks had my attention. If he was sincere about the apology and the connection I'd felt between us, I'd consider giving in to the attraction.

Marius would smell it on me even if he didn't feel it through the bond. I'd taken a few of the suitors to bed over the last few years, and the realization after the first one was mortifying. The magic in my high-born blood, like those with the same, prevented me from getting sexual diseases, but it wouldn't prevent pregnancy. I'd taken a pill every month since Gemma started me on them and never stopped. My dose this month was right on time. While most of my previous suitors were easy to look at, they were disappointing in bed, unlike the man I'd met on one of my unapproved outings. I'd visited him several times and only broke it off after he started professing feelings for me. Hopefully, Rainier would break the trend of terrible lovers since he was older…if we made it that far. He had to get through his apology first.

"I'll be sure to be occupied tonight," he said, a hint of disgust in his voice.

I smirked. "I didn't realize you felt so strongly about my love life."

"It's not your love life I'm concerned with. It's my sanity." He mimicked the gagging face I'd made during training.

I laughed. "You chose me. Remember? I was all of four."

"Your energy sought me out." Marius paused near the door to the garden. "He waits for you here."

My stomach flipped in a way that could only be excitement and anticipation. I wanted to see the jerk. What Marius had said about him and what I'd observed so far, minus the persuasion thing, didn't paint him as an asshole. He was cocky, but maybe he'd earned that much.

"Night, Daddy Marius." I chuckled.

He let out a heavy sigh. "Be safe."

I could see light through the frosted glass, but I wasn't prepared for what waited on the other side of the door. My breath froze in my chest. Little twinkle lights glinted everywhere like were used on Yule for the ball and festivals. This time of year, there were often too many clouds to see the stars in the stratosphere, but the little lights looked like the most beautiful night sky.

"Do you like it?" Rainier smiled, taking my hand and leading me deeper into the garden. He wore casual leathers and a tunic of the same green as the empire colors. His hair, slicked back, made his striking features stand out even more. My hand warmed in his, and it was like a gentle fire warming the chill off a room.

"You did this, Rainier?"

"Rain." His mouth twisted in a bashful smile. "We're just Ari and Rain tonight."

I cleared my throat and reminded myself this was pretend. Nothing serious could happen between us. But this felt and looked like more than make-believe. "Rain, you did this?"

"I did." His grin widened. "Do you like it?"

"It's beautiful," I said, hearing the breathlessness of my own voice and cursing how vulnerable I sounded.

He led me to the wrought iron table with the mosaic depicting Nyx on it. The aroma of spices drifted up from under the cloche-covered plates. A carafe of red wine sat next to a bouquet of wildflowers from the fields. Had he picked them? He must have. Rain pulled the chair out for me, but I didn't sit. I should have a grand appetite after the sessions Marius put me through this afternoon, but the hunger eating at my belly earlier evaporated.

"Maybe we could talk a bit before dinner?" I glanced toward the path through the garden. Lights hung as far as I could see down the way, and I wanted to explore what Rain had done.

Rain inclined his head. "Whatever you wish. This is my apology to you, so you can have it any way you want it."

Heat crept into my cheeks. I wanted it. A lot. But more than words. I swallowed. "A walk is a good start."

He held his elbow out, and I slipped my arm through it. "You look even lovelier in this dress than the one last night. The pale blue suits you." His fingers brushed against the comb in my hair. "This is perfect for you."

"Thank you." My eyes roamed over his attire. He wore no royal sash tonight or pins and neither did I. "You look good in your leathers."

"So I've been told." His lips quirked up in a half grin.

My cheeks burned. Smug bastard. "You had an apology for me?"

The pretense left his gaze as he stopped and faced me. "I do. I am sorry for using persuasion on you. I don't normally draw upon that kind of magic and did not have nefarious intent. I know what it feels like to have unspent power inside that is fighting to get loose. My goal was to help you calm down, but I do understand how it seemed, especially given our situation."

How did he glean that from last night? I studied him. His face softened as if relaxed, and sincerity filled his dark eyes. His gaze locked on mine, and that warmth built in my chest again. "I've never received an apology from a man that was so wordy. I accept your insanely long amends."

He laughed, and the sound was light and genuine. "Thank you."

Despite his embedded arrogance, which was common among the nobles, he seemed to have good traits I almost missed by shutting him out. "And Rain...I'm sorry for making you think your dick was on fire."

"I don't know if I deserve a pardon for that considering how much I like hearing you say dick," he said.

The muscles low in my belly tightened, and heat spread through intimate parts of my body. Not to the explosive point like last night but the desire was still intense. I smoothed my hand over my hair. "Maybe we should have dinner now."

His heated gaze was on me, threatening to set me on fire. "I'm ready to eat."

"Shall we?" I walked forward, praying there was some ice water on the table I had missed, otherwise I would be diving into the fountain.

Rain placed his hand on my back. Warmth spread out over my body like fire through dry brush. I almost let out a gasp but stifled it before the sound loosed itself. I'd never had want like this, especially just meeting someone. I swallowed hard.

He held out the chair for me, cushier ones had replaced the metal ones normally in the garden and made sure I was settled. Then, he took his own seat. The table had been covered with a lace cloth. I wondered how much of this he had chosen himself. If what I'd heard was to be believed, not even the nobles ate like this on the front. Did he have private dinners when he was home?

"When do you return to Agonburg?"

"So eager to see me leave?" He sounded hurt, and his brows scrunched together.

"No... I mean..." Goddesses and gods, I sounded like an idiot and took a long sip of wine. "Obviously, you have duties in your province."

He smirked. "I do. I head back to the front at the end of the week."

"You still fight?" My stomach, aching at the thought, revolted as much as my brain did against the idea of him being near the skirmishes. I made a mental note to ask Father if the dissenters had grown. I'd noticed he'd sent more troops recently, but he was still calling it a small group...unless that was purely for my benefit.

His face dropped, and I regretted asking the question. "You mean after my near-death experience. I'd prefer to, but my father has me stuck on strategy duty." His voice carried agitation.

I understood that desire to be useful. It's why I trained with Marius despite Father's objections and attempts to make me a proper lady. I wanted to matter to my people. Not be a trophy to sit on a throne, which was what the advisors assumed I would be if I didn't get control of my power. "What magic do you wield besides persuasion?"

"Light magic." He smirked and gestured to the twinkling lights around us.

"And?" Most highborns who touched magic and were chosen as charges by the unicorns wielded multiple types. I'd been working for months on my wall of protection using wind. Earth teased me that I might be able to use it one day, and water was a sore subject I didn't want to revisit anytime soon.

"That's it," he said. "I'd started to learn some different ones, but after my experiences on the battlefield, I've been unable to manifest others."

I nodded, not quite believing his answer. His power

was strong, and it thrummed off him, vibrating against me. Not unusual for some highborns to deny it when they possessed a rare gift—until it became impossible to hide. The rarest powers caused jealousy and bids for marriage. Father had settled some of the matters when petitioned. The nobles didn't usually deny the question from the royal family. Well, they didn't deny my father, and I wasn't the king.

If I divulged my gifts, maybe he'd be inclined to follow my lead. "I yield fire the strongest, but I haven't been able to channel the power for the others yet. Father's experts believe I will manifest water eventually because of my affinity for it." That wasn't entirely true. I had been able to work with water, and it was easy as long as there was a large spring or similar origin. Where I struggled with water was when I lacked an obvious source, and to truly have a relationship with the element, that would have to happen at some point.

"Interesting. Both fire and water? They don't usually appear in one…" His voice trailed off.

"I know. It's unusual to wield both, but it looks like I will. My mother had a very strong affinity for water too." According to Gemma, Mother had deep, strong magic, and very few knew she controlled many different types besides water. Water was the one on display during festivals and royal events. I tucked away the sadness that crept in when thinking about Mother and wondered if she would like Rain.

"Hmm." He stared down at his plate as if the roasted

meat was the most fascinating thing in the room. "I could help you with your magic."

"That's very kind of you. I'll need to discuss it with Marius," I said, not wanting to sound too eager.

"I would like to spend the time with you." He forked a piece of meat. I watched him as he ate it. His shoulders relaxed. With so much time away from home, he'd probably had more dinners with other fae than family.

On the frontlines, he must have seen the others that were like us but not. "What do they look like?"

"Who?" Rain raised his head.

"The other elves. Our enemy. The historians said they are dark creatures, but they never described them to me..."

"They look like you and me. How are you so sure you have never seen one?" He held his fingers up next to his ears. "Maybe their ears are a little more exaggerated than ours."

I laughed at how he looked like a rabbit doing that. "No, I've never been allowed to go to the front, and none of the prisoners have been brought here."

"That's because there are no prisoners," Rain said, trepidation in his tone.

"What do you mean? I've heard there were."

"No, none. No one captured leaves the battlefield. That's the rule," he said.

I grabbed my throat as I swallowed. Sadness ached in my chest for the loss of life, ours and theirs. I'd never been told that prisoners were executed, and I couldn't reconcile that Father would agree to that practice. "That's terrible. And they keep coming at us knowing they will die?"

"Some things are worth fighting for." Rain's tone mirrored my sadness. He shook his head. "They seem to think their cause is, and your father's army is strong. His men will not let it reach you here."

"I'm not afraid," I said. His confidence was inspiring, but he proffered a guarantee he couldn't give...unless his power was foresight. He was much too sane, though, to have the gift to see that far in the future.

He leaned forward. "I wish I could say you shouldn't be, Ari, but there are other things to fear outside the walls of this castle that aren't other elves."

"I'm aware of the dangers of the forest. Marius has prepared me well to defend myself, and I'm prepared to die if that is my destiny," I said, assuming he meant the spirits in the forest.

He took my hands in his. "Promise me you will not enter the fight if it comes to you."

I stared into his gaze. I'd only known him a couple of days. Why would he ask such a request of me? The warmth in my chest returned, and my head was light. I closed my eyes against the dizziness. "I need to go lie down. I think I've drunk too much wine."

He rose from his chair and helped me to my feet. "Of course, I'll escort you to your room."

"Thank you." Nausea swirled in my stomach. Bile churned up my throat. I took a few steps and bent at the waist to wretch. What in the goddesses and gods? I never got sick.

Rain reached down and lifted my hair away from my face. Goddess, this was awful. He put an arm around my waist and guided me to the fountain. I splashed some cool water on my face and rinsed my mouth. The nausea passed, and I moved to stand. Rain steadied me.

"Can you walk?"

"Yes," I said, even though I stumbled.

We moved together slowly into the corridor, but darkness encroached on my vision like a fine mist.

"Ari?" Rain's voice was so distant.

I was floating in nothingness. The darkness overtook me.

CHAPTER 8
ARIANNA

My head ached similar to the night I snuck out and only found my way home with Marius's help. The soft scent was that of my bedroom. I squinted one eye open. Light seeped in around the curtains. The events at the end of the evening came back like a lightning strike.

"Ugh." I puked in front of Rain. I groaned and pulled a pillow over my face.

"Ari?" Val's muffled voice came through the pillow. "I have some water, juice, and the powder to settle stomachs."

"I don't need the powder. Whatever it was has passed." My throat was dry and rough. I tossed the pillow across the room and sat up. "I'll take the water though."

Val handed the glass to me. "When Prince Rainier came to get me, I was worried about you. Do you want to talk about it?"

"I don't even know what happened. It just hit me."

"Probably some kind of stomach sickness going around," she said. "Prince Rainier was really worried about you too."

"I didn't puke on him, did I?" I sipped the entire glass of water and handed it back to Val.

Her forehead creased in concern as she studied me. "No, not that I noticed, but I was focused on you."

"Thank the goddesses and gods for that." I swiped my hands over my face. The water helped my headache but not my embarrassment. Hiding out in my room for the next year seemed reasonable to deal with it. Except I'd miss out on actual life. I pulled the covers up over my head at the idea of facing Rainier.

Val tugged the covers down enough I could see her. "He wanted to stay here until you woke, but Marius suggested that wasn't the best idea."

"Marius threatened him." I barked out a laugh. "The night just keeps giving."

"He asked that I let him know when you were awake," Val said.

"Marius? He should feel it."

"No, Prince Rainier."

"I don't think I can face him, Val." I tried to pull the covers back up, but Val held them tight with one hand.

She patted my knee. "You don't have to. I can just say you are recovering in your chamber today."

"It's not very princess of me to hide." I stared up at the ceiling as if the answer to not be embarrassed was written there. Training with Marius was an option to avoid Rain, but then I'd be subject to a lecture from my bonded.

"No, but you deserve to have privacy if you wish." She studied me. I'd scared her last night by the way she looked at me like a fragile piece of glass.

I sighed. The noble thing to do was to face this, so I'd do it. "I'm up. Help me get ready? I don't feel like having the entourage in here."

"I anticipated that and told them they would not be needed this morning."

I hugged her. "That's why you are my best friend. Well, more than that, but one of the reasons."

She smiled. "Let's prepare you to face … life."

I'D TAKEN my time grooming as a guise for psyching myself up. Two hours later, by the chime of the clock in the hallway, Val and I emerged from my room to find Marius. I hadn't expected him to be there…hadn't even sensed him through our bond, but I wasn't trying to either.

"Your father has asked that you join him in the situation room," he said. "He apologized that he could not be here himself to ask you."

"The situation room? He doesn't usually invite me to those sessions." He'd only requested my attendance twice, and both times it was when he thought he might have to go address dissenters himself. Both times ended up being nonevents. Marius's tone made my stomach twist as if there was more to the request than the two times before. Could it be news of Gemma? That was a stupid thought.

"Then it must be important," Marius said. "Valentina, if you'll excuse us."

Val hugged me. "You've got this day. It's yours."

"That means a lot to me, Val." My head had stopped pounding so that annoyance was gone even as the embarrassment clung to me like the scent of the barn before the stalls were mucked. I could hide the humiliation behind my practiced court features.

Marius motioned for me, and I fell into step beside him. His morose attitude ratcheted up my anxiety. "What is going on that Father would include me?"

"Something big." Marius gave me some side eye. "What happened to you last night?"

"What do you mean?"

"I felt power from you but in the most nauseating way," Marius said, agitation laced his voice.

Was it power? There had been no fire or water or wind or earth magic...maybe a little fire, but I was certain that had been desire, not power.

"I was just sick. Val said one of those short stomach sicknesses is going around."

"Hmmm.... I was certain it was power manifesting in you. Perhaps a new one. At least I didn't have to feel the young human hormones."

"Whatever," I said. It was probably best the weirdness interrupted the night. I was starting to like Rain more than I should. He'd gotten under my skin and that was new. "Glad your concern was in the right place."

"Had I sensed danger, I would have been there, Arianna. I didn't choose you to sit by the side as you die."

"I know," I said. "I care about you too, even when you're a jerk."

Marius huffed hot air and stopped at the door. "I cannot enter this room. Only your father's guards are allowed in."

"I remember." I opened the door and glanced over my shoulder. Marius's sullen mood hadn't changed, and I was concerned about what I was walking into with Father. "See you soon."

"Arianna." Father waved me over to his side. He looked far less surly than Marius had. In fact, he appeared excited. My magic flared in my chest as if something in the room tugged on it, and I smiled at Father to hide my reaction.

The advisors leaned over the table so far that I couldn't see faces. Even Father had his hands pressed against the edge to support his incline. I stood beside him studying the map. The various markers for the armies, us and our allies, were positioned on the map, and across the Forgotten Forest was our enemy. A gasp threatened to escape when I saw the places on the southern border where the enemy had penetrated our line so far into our lands. Was this accurate? It hasn't happened in my life-time...at least that I knew.

I glanced up at the faces of Father's trusted advisor. Many weren't here the day before, so they must have returned for this meeting. They were having conversations amongst themselves. Calm conversations. As if the enemy wasn't on our doorstep. My entire being was drawn to a handsome face. Rain. I hadn't noticed him at first because he stood on the far side of Lord DeBorn who was a rather rugged, burly man. The warmth in my chest returned. Rain's dark hair was brushed back away from his face. His father, the Duke of Agonburg, stood next to him, which was likely how he gained access to the meeting, and I noticed how light his hair was compared to Rain's. Rain must look like his mother. He met my gaze, and my cheeks burned as the memory of last night flitted through my mind. I turned my attention back to the map.

"Arianna," Father said my name.

I looked up. His face became somber.

"Nearly everyone in this room will be going to the front, including myself. In my absence, you will be regent for the first time and without most of the council. Should we fail, you and Marius will evacuate to our allies in the east."

Panic sliced through me like a blade of ice, jagged and painful. Father was going to the front. I glanced at Rain. He would go too. My gaze turned back to Father. Last time he had planned to go the line was years ago, when Gemma disappeared, and he stayed for me. This time he had to go. I looked back at the map, at how far into the Forgotten Forest the enemy had moved. How had the forest not claimed them like they had Gemma? Were Father and the others going into the forest to meet them? They had to be.

I couldn't beg him not to go in front of his advisors. He would see that as weakness. And worse, his supporters would see me as a vulnerability. I had to rally with him and give support. "You will not fail, Father. You will succeed, and I will keep the throne warm for you."

The offer of encouragement bolstered my own conviction.

He patted my shoulder with confidence, but his eyes betrayed him. He was worried, but whether that was for me or what they would find on the front, I couldn't tell.

My gaze was drawn to Rain again. His eyes did not hold worry but pure sadness. His downheartedness was so intense, emotion welled in my throat forming a knot. I might not ever see him again, and an unexpected ache formed in my chest.

"Arianna, I will be here." Father pointed to a spot in the front. There was no way that position wouldn't see fighting if the placement was correct on the map. My hands shook, and I pressed them against the table to stop them. I smashed my lips together to keep from vocalizing fear in front of the advisors. "Should you need to get a message to me, this is where you send it. Do not use a royal seal. We will send out false communications that I will be in other places."

"I understand." I stared at the pieces on the map table like they were pawns. This couldn't be happening, but it was. My father was going to war, and I'd been in the dark about how serious the dissenters' attacks had been. Father had been so very protective of me since Gemma left, and that was the only reason I wasn't angry with him for not telling me how dire things were sooner.

"Where is Marius?" Father asked.

"He's waiting outside as is customary." I glanced toward the door. My guard had to be feeling my panic, but he held steady and honored the agreement between unicorns and elves.

"You can brief him on the specifics when you are in private but no one else. Not even Valentina. She can know I have left for an appearance but nothing else."

I flicked my gaze to where Theo stood. He averted his eyes. Is that what he would say to Val as well? It must be, and I hated the lie we both must tell her.

"When do you leave?"

"In a few days," he said. "You will increase your training with Marius and attend all of the council meetings until we do so. I'm sorry to drop this burden on you, but the urgency dictates it."

I always wanted to train and wanted to attend more meetings than I'd been invited to. I'd asked for more responsibility, but not because of a crisis and not because Father would be going to fight. My heart was pledged to my kingdom from the day I was born, and I committed my heart to this duty. "I will serve to the best of my ability."

He patted my back and dove into the strategy session. My gaze drifted across the map and up to the dark eyes of Rain again. The sadness I'd seen earlier took up residence in his face, and dread was palpable between us.

I wondered what would have happened if he wasn't leaving. His hard lines were appealing. While many of the previous suitors wanted a title, they were actually afraid of ruling beside me. Rain wasn't intimidated in the slightest. Would we have married in time? I'd been interested in taking him to bed. I still could. He'd be here for a few days, and I wondered if he would be a gentle lover or if he moved like a bunny fucking as was my last lover. The way Rain had been graceful but firm as he caught me last night told me he'd be gentle but powerful. The warmth in my chest rose. I blinked my eyes a few times and refocused on the map.

Any assistance I could bring to the front wouldn't be much help. I was trained to defend myself, but I'd never been near any real fights unless I counted the tavern brawl Marius pulled me out of not long after Gemma left. All I could give of myself was to be here at the seat of the empire, and I would make sure we were ready should anything change. I listened with intent as Father and his council discussed their plan of attack. When had things taken such a turn for the worse at the front? Had it happened quickly? And the most burning question in my mind was why Father hadn't told me before today. The possible answers flitted around in my head, but I settled on that he wanted to protect me from the fear—keep me safe. I was the last remaining link to my mother, who, from the stories, he'd loved fiercely.

"They do not have the numbers," Theo's father said.

Father's advisors nodded and vocalized their agreement. Even Rain's father concurred, but not Rain. He studied the map with a grim look on his face—the kind only a soldier who had seen battle would know. An over-confident attack would mean a loss, and I didn't need to be a battle strategist to know that. Marius had taught me through hours upon hours of training what it meant to underestimate the enemy and overestimate my own abilities.

I stayed engaged in the conversation and managed to not look at Rain too much to be considered indecent. I knew every time he looked in my direction as the steady heat in my chest would flare in response.

The long day ended as Father dismissed everyone but me.

"What do you think?" he asked. The weariness in his eyes begged for sleep, but I knew he'd work several more hours before he did. That was what he always did in a crisis. He'd done it when Mother died, although I remembered little more than his absence during that time, and again when Gemma disappeared. I fidgeted with the seam of my dress instead. Fear he might not come back overwhelmed my thoughts, but that wasn't what he was asking.

"The plan is solid," I said. "But how did the numbers grow so fast and infiltrate this quickly into the Forgotten Forest?"

"That is a mystery to everyone but the traitor who led them there." He ran his hand over the map where the enemy was concentrated. "They must have some magic that affords them protection in the forest."

"Traitor? Have you caught this traitor?" That wasn't a word we heard often in our empire. I called Marius one in jest on a regular basis, but no one used it in a serious capacity. Those who stood against the empire were normally referred to as dissenters. Traitor made me suspect he believed this person was from his inner circle. I hadn't noticed anyone missing, and Father told me exactly where he would be. Was this a trap to catch the traitor?

"Not yet, but I'm not sure we will," he said. "We believe it is the prince of the broken kingdom on the other side of the forest. He's known for his ability to blend in and appear as others."

My guardian had told me stories of a prince in our enemy kingdom that brought about the war. He'd aligned with those who drank the blood of fae, especially elves, for the brief use of our powers. My chest constricted in a painful convulsion at the mere thought that treacherous fae was among us. "Yes, Marius and I have discussed him at length. I'd thrust my broadsword through his heart if I came upon him."

"As would everyone who was in this room." Father gazed up at the glass ceiling of the rotunda. The natural light from earlier had given way to a dark night sky. "I'm afraid for you, Arianna. I'm afraid you will be left alone to run this kingdom."

My heart sped up. He didn't think he was coming back. I had to assure him. "Only for a little while. Then you'll return, and the throne will be waiting on you."

"I hope that is true." He looked down at his hands and then at me. "I'd feel better if you had a husband and additional protection, but I know marriage isn't necessary in your eyes."

Father wanted safety for me. I understood his wish. Rain had been the only one I'd even thought about accepting, and I wasn't sure of that match. He was going to the front with Father, so that wasn't happening anyway. "I have Val and Marius and Leana and a dozen others."

"And you will be responsible for Andrews," he said. "You are too young to be saddled with that responsibility."

While I'd never considered myself the mothering type, I would do for Drew what was done for me—make him feel safe and loved and wanted and know he had a family. "A responsibility I am happy to take on just as Gemma did for me."

He sighed. "I'm sorry."

"For what?"

"For this war... for Gemma leaving... for your mother..."

Goddesses and gods, my father had never apologized to anyone, and he never spoke of Mother. I'd turned to Marius and Leana with my grief because mine exacerbated his. I thought I was the only one who got so inside my head when everything was heavy, but Father did too. His pain trapped him like mine did me, but he didn't have anyone to turn to as I did.

"You have done nothing but protect your family and your empire." I wrapped my arms around him.

"Your mother would be proud of you," he said and pulled back. "Though I wish the announcement were for you, I heard there is to be a wedding soon. Maybe you will see married life isn't so bad once Val has taken the step."

Theo must have asked for the crown's permission. "About that..."

CHAPTER 9
ARIANNA

Amazed we were able to pull the wedding together in a few short days, I stared out at the ballroom full of people as my best friend sat next to me on the dais a married woman. Father granted Val and Theo permission to marry in the castle before the officers were scheduled to depart. It was an honor bestowed only on the royal family of the seat, so he had made an exception for them...at my request. He might have offered without my prodding, but I wanted to make sure they weren't forgotten. One of the perks of being royal was being able to pull off magnificent stunts like this, and doing this for Val after so many years of friendship and secrets felt right.

Dark hair caught my attention below, and the warmth blooming in my chest said it was Rain. He bowed before me and held out his hand. I'd only had time to seek him out once for the magic lessons, and it was brief at best. Training with Marius, council sessions, and wedding planning had taken up all my free time. He was here though, in front of me, wanting a dance. The swelling of emotion was more than I should have for someone I'd known less than a week.

"Go," Val whispered in my ear. "You'll regret it if you don't."

I turned in her direction. She inclined her head toward Rain. I stood and kissed her forehead. "Congratulations."

"Hopefully, I'll be telling you the same thing in the morning." She raised her eyebrows.

I smiled and ignored the heat rising in my cheeks.

My steps down the stairs to Rain's waiting hand were heavy. I slipped my hand into his, and he squeezed. A jolt shot up my arm like warm lightning, but I didn't flinch. "May I have this dance, Princess Arianna?"

"You may, Prince Rainier."

He pulled me close and led me across the dance floor. Several dances later, Rain had turned away every other man who had asked to cut in, some with a glance that looked like a fierce storm and others with a "no" that sounded more like "fuck off." I bit back a laugh. None of the past suitors had been brave enough to be so bold. He saved me from having to fake my way through dances with the other men. I owed him for that, and I was enjoying my time with him. I ached for Rain's touch and how close he was. A slow song came on, and he nestled me against his chest. His lips brushed my ear. "Ari."

Chills skated over my skin and settled in my most sensitive areas. "Shall we go to my garden where there are less people? I hear the third time is the charm?"

"I was prepared to kill the next man who walked up and asked to dance with you. You are saving a life."

Why was that so alluring? "Is that a yes?"

"It's whatever is next level after yes," he said.

Marius trailed behind us at a distance, still presenting as human and being stealthy, but our bond told me he was there. His presence comforted me as much as it annoyed me. My garden wasn't far from the ballroom, but the span tonight made it seem remote. I resisted the urge to run. These moments should be savored because they might be our last ever. He would leave in the morning with my father, and based on what I'd heard in the strategy session today, there was a real chance one or both might not come back. It made me desperate for time together.

I led him into the interior of the garden where the fountain concealed us from anyone who might glance inside, not that Marius would let them close enough. The night-blooming moonflowers opened all around us as if offering their blessing, but this was their routine. They would stay open until the dew hit their petals in the morning. The blooms delighted the night air with the scent that was a soft, sweet mix of jasmine and vanilla. The aroma of the flowers mixed with Rain's minty scent intoxicated me more than any wine.

"Show me what we worked on yesterday." He smiled and it was full of dare like the barn cat right before it knocked every item off a shelf in the tack room when I told him to get down. The mischievousness on Rain's face, also, reminded me of Drew grabbing extra sweets from the kitchen and running off laughing. "Throw a fireball at me and protect yourself from retaliation."

When Rain was spirited, I felt lighter as if the burden and pressure of the expectations on me had been lifted. I'd been surprised yesterday with how easily the magic had responded to him, and I hoped it would do the same now. I held up my hand, and a flame formed into a sphere the size of his head. Rain's eyes glittered like he was a kid ready to play. Excitement flipped around in my belly. He'd told me not to make my movements obvious when I threw, so I concentrated on the path I wanted flare to travel. I flung my arm and called my shield of wind. Air whooshed around me. Rain drew water in and snuffed out my fireball in a steamy mist. Then, he sent water at me. I held my shield in place.

His smile broadened into a toothy grin. I dropped the wind and ran toward him.

"It worked even better than yesterday." I threw my arms around his neck.

"I told you practice was all you needed, and that was just two sessions. Think what you will be able to do when I return."

My cheeks hurt from grinning, and I looked up into his gaze. My heart hammered against my chest. His face had turned solemn, and the reality of our situation came back to me. "I..."

Rain brushed a strand of my hair, one that had come loose from my updo, behind my ear. He picked one of the flowers and placed it there. "Perfect." His knuckles brushed against my cheek. "So soft. You are truly the most beautiful woman I've laid eyes on."

Oh, he is definitely good with flattery. My pulse pounded faster, like a rapid drum in my ears. He was almost too handsome. I ran my finger over the scar along his chin that somehow enhanced his good looks instead of detracting from them.

His lips brushed mine, and I slipped my hand around the back of his head to pull him closer, parting my lips to grant him entry. Rain slid his tongue in to meet mine, and currents shot out through my arms, legs, and straight to my lower belly. The sensations were new and over-whelming—unlike my experiences with other men. He pressed his body against mine, and the bulge in his pants said he wanted me the same way I did him. I slid my hand down his chest. He captured my hand and broke the kiss. I met his gaze, and the heat there matched my own.

"I'm not a good man, Ari, but I'm trying to do the right thing here," he said, resting his forehead against mine. I respected his attempt to safeguard me and worried this might not end in the night I thought it would.

"And this isn't my first time, so what are you protecting here?" I pressed my lips to the scar on his chin.

"You," he said. "Goddesses and gods, help me. You."

I brushed my mouth against his throat in a trail. "Not only do I not need your protection, I don't want your protection. I want you."

He moved so fast I barely comprehended him lifting me and pressing me against the stone wall of the garden. His mouth was on mine devouring me exactly like I wished him to. My tongue tangled with his in raw need. The nerves in my core danced to life in a series of tingles.

His grip loosened, letting me go so that I slid down his body feeling every hard inch of him. I moaned, and his hands sunk into my hair. He eased back and kissed my forehead. "I can't do this with you tonight."

I bit back the rejection threatening to shatter the desire in me. I sidestepped to get distance from him.

His fingers circled my wrist and held me in place. I stared at the moonflowers, wishing I could crawl in the flowerbed with them to get away.

Rain hooked a finger under my chin and turned my head toward him. His face had softened, but his eyes still burned. "I crave you, Ari, more than I've ever wanted anyone. But I'd be a bastard to give into that need tonight."

I didn't understand. We were both adults. If we had an attraction to each other, what was stopping him? "Then be a bastard, because I'm ready for some debauchery tonight."

He inhaled and shoved me against the wall. His hardness pressed against me even through my skirts. A sizzle spread out from the contact. "It's taking everything I have not to fuck you, especially when you say that."

I pressed my thighs together against the need growing between them, not that helped so whatever. If anything, it intensified the friction where his hardness pinned me to the stone. "Then what is stopping you?"

He inhaled again, his nose in my hair. "You smell so fucking good."

Rain took my hand, and, for a brief moment, I thought he was leading me to a bed, his or mine, but he turned toward the ballroom. I dropped his hand and opened the door to the closest sitting room. Still hopeful he would follow me, I paused. He looked into my eyes, and the same sadness that had been there in the strategy session filled them.

The hopelessness on his face penetrated me like a spear to the gut. "Good night, Prince Rainier."

He bent his head to mine and pressed a kiss to my cheek. "Forgive me, Ari."

I closed the door in his face. I was a fucking fool, but goddess be damned if I didn't want him even more now.

CHAPTER 10
RAIN

I lay in my bed, thinking about how long I stared at that closed door, and chuckled before walking toward my room. She was as worked up as I was, and I wondered if she'd find relief for herself like I had done upon returning to my chamber. I ran my hand over my cock, hardening again thinking about her in the dress fitted to her curves. Ari was my match. No other woman had stood up to me like she had...or walked away from me in that infuriating and sexy way. If she still liked me when this was all over, I wanted to explore what we could be together.

Satisfying myself had been for nothing since I'd met her because jerking off only soothed the ache until I saw her or thought of her. Did she know what a hold she had on me already? She deserved more than this kingdom, and I could give her that if she'd let me.

My stomach growled. I found it hard to eat around her, and it was catching up to me. She was all I wanted to think about and the only person I wanted to be around, which helped considering my task in this court. My belly rumbled louder, so I scrambled out of bed to look for some clothes.

I found my pants on the chair, but my shirt had wine on it from a glass I'd knocked over while taking care of myself earlier. Fuck it. No one else should be up at this hour. I'd go straight to the kitchen and back and no one would know. I made my way down the hall toward the back stairway I'd found, thinking about the chocolate cake I'd seen but didn't get to try.

CHAPTER II
ARIANNA

I squirmed and wiggled in my bed. My need for Rain's cock inside me had abated, but it left me wondering if I'd acted too desperate. I wanted him, but I wanted to know him too. So, why wouldn't he sleep with me? Not that my list was long, but the other men I'd slept with had been more than willing. Maybe he had someone else. Although it hadn't been the case for my parents, it wasn't unusual for nobles, men and women, to have lovers outside their primary relationship.

The covers were heavy like I was in a cell. I tossed them off and put my slippers on, grabbed my robe, and headed to the kitchen. No one would be up at this time, and I was hopeful the cooks had saved a piece of the chocolate cake I hadn't had a chance to sample during Val and Theo's reception.

"Thank the Fates," I said, when I lifted the opaque cloche to find the remains of the cake. I cut a hefty piece from it and stabbed a fork into the layers. The chocolate was sweet on my lips, and the cake was moist. That warm heat in my chest I thought was from Rain spurred to life. Apparently, it liked chocolate cake too. "Mmhmm."

"What I would give to be that chocolate cake right now." A deep baritone voice drawled from the shadows.

I jerked, nearly dropping the plate, and scrambled to keep the cake from hitting the floor. "You scared me, Prince Rainier."

"I can see that. Am I no longer Rain?" His voice was a mix of amusement laced with sadness.

I shot him an irritated look but doubted he could see it in the dim light.

"Are you not going to speak to me?"

I shoved another bite in my mouth, fully aware of how immature an action that was. My agitation and lack of relief earlier had my mind in all the wrong places, and seeing him here in the kitchen with his...

Oh goddess and gods, his chest is bare. Who walks around the castle without a shirt on?

The moonlight from the window formed shadows over his perfect abs. There were scars, too, showing just how severe his injuries had been that almost took his life. One just under his pec was in a position that it must have been near-fatal at the time, but he'd survived. Yet, he went willingly to potentially face a similar fate. I swallowed against a knot in my throat. My lower half urged me to move forward and rub my hands over his bare skin, but I took another bite of cake to satisfy the craving instead. Rain stood there, his eyes catching on the movement of my throat as I swallowed.

"What do you want?" My voice was flat, but my traitorous body was alert. I speared the cake with my fork.

"I couldn't sleep." His tone hummed a bit like a purr.

"Hmm. Maybe if you..." I looked up from another forkful and saw he'd moved closer, his eyes smoldering.

He took the small plate and fork from me. His mouth closed around the utensil and pulled until the metal was clean. "Mmm. This does taste good, but I bet there is something in this room that tastes better."

I took a step back. "I'm not interested in being rejected by you again. I'm here for cake and nothing else." My body heated at my apex at the lie, and I pressed my thighs together, wanting some relief.

Rain smiled, looking like one of the giant predators in the forest. "Believe me when I say I didn't reject you. Not even close. Did you know chocolate is considered an aphrodisiac in some cultures?" He took another bite of my cake. His lips wrapped around the fork, and I hungered for his mouth to touch my body the same way.

"Are you going to eat all of my cake?" I asked, aware of how breathless my voice was.

A husky chuckle came from him, and he forked another piece, holding it out for me. I reached for it, but he drew back. "Let me feed you, Ari."

The fork slid into my mouth, and he pulled out slowly like a stroke. My breath quickened slightly. Rain set the plate on the counter with a clatter, and his hands were in my hair. The edge of the counter dug into my back. Rain's mouth devoured mine, and he tasted of chocolate and mint. He lifted me onto the counter. His hardness ground against my center, and I moaned. The friction was powerful through my thin nightgown. The kitchen was far enough away from any bedrooms, and it was late enough that someone would have to be near the kitchen to hear anything.

"What are you doing to me?" he whispered against my lips.

"You lifted me up here." *So help me if he walks away, I'll probably burn down the castle before I can take care of this need myself…*

"I did, and goddesses and gods, I want to taste you, Ari." He licked his lips, and I yearned for his mouth on my body.

"If you pull away from me again, I'll have you castrated," I said, my lips brushing his.

His rough laugh shook his chest against mine. "Why does it sound like a delicious invitation when you threaten me?"

My robe slipped open revealing my nipples pebbled under the sheer material beneath. I watched him drink my breasts in as his hand caressed the peaks.

"Because you want me."

He nibbled on my ear, his breath tickling me. "I do want you. Every piece of you. I want to see you riding my cock like the queen you are."

The ache and need were fire in my veins. "Then take me."

"Promise me you'll forgive me, Ari."

"For what?"

"Promise." It was a growl and a demand.

"I promise," I said, but there would be no need to apologize for pleasure between two consenting adults.

He dropped to his knees and yanked my lacy underwear until it ripped free. My dampness was exposed to him at eye level. His face, his mouth so close to my sex, created a vulnerability in me that caught me off guard, and I pushed the weakness away quickly.

A deep, carnal sound rumbled from him. "Beautiful. As I expected." He spread my legs and bit down on my thigh, not hard enough to draw blood but the pleasure...

I cried out. My desire ratcheted up to new heights and left me panting. Getting caught here wouldn't be the best position for a future queen, but I didn't care as long as Rain kept going.

Rain ran a finger through the icing of the cake and drew a line up my thigh. He lapped up the icing all the way to my center.

I moaned. The pleasure lashed through me.

He licked over my slick core. "So wet." His tongue plunged inside me.

I wanted to watch him, but my eyelids fluttered with ecstasy.

"You taste better than the chocolate cake."

I shuddered. His mouth. His words. It was almost too much. His tongue swirled the sensitive bundle of nerves, and I bucked against him. I felt his smile against my flesh. He sucked down on my clit, flicking his tongue over it. My body tightened as I thrust my hips forward against him. He hummed against me. The world fell away, and I shattered into a thousand pieces on his tongue. My body jerked with a powerful release and tiny spots clouded my vision like the light decorating the garden for our dinner. "Rain."

His motions slowed, and he rose between my legs. I met his gaze, and I connected with him on a different level. He wasn't what I'd anticipated, and there was more here than just attraction. Desire ramped up in me for a different reason even though he'd just satisfied it. I wanted to be closer to him. His mouth was on mine, devouring me, and I tasted myself on his lips. Aftershocks trembled through my body, and I'd never experienced anything like it. This kind of pleasure must be due to Rain's skills. There was a growing attachment between us. The warmth in my chest every time he came near me was proof, and it was going to make it that much harder to say goodbye to him.

"That will give you something to think about while I'm gone," he said, holding me to his chest. I listened to his heart beat, memorizing the rhythm to replay as I lay in bed after he left. "There is something about you, Ari. I need to be close to you even when I shouldn't be."

"Why shouldn't you be?" I tilted my head up to meet his gaze. The sadness I'd seen in those advisor meetings was there again. I wanted to chase it away for him.

"I told you before. I'm an unworthy bastard."

"You are worthy," I said, sliding my hand down toward the hard bulge in his pants.

He grabbed my hand and kissed the tips. "Tonight is about you. It seems I owe you a thousand apologies, and there is not enough time to share them all." He gazed into my eyes as if he was memorizing me. "Let me walk you to your room."

None of my other lovers had stopped at my pleasure or even made sure I enjoyed it. Rain was attentive, and I appreciated that he wanted to escort me back to my quarters. My legs were still a little unsteady, but I composed myself and looked for what was left of my lacy undergarments. Didn't want the kitchen staff finding those in the morning. "Where's my..."

Rain held them up and smirked. He stuffed the shredded lace into his pocket.

"Please tell me you're not going to hold those up as a trophy for all your friends on the frontline." I cringed, but not because he might show my undergarments to someone else. Because he might get hurt or not come back at all.

"No, just for me on the nights until I see you again."

My insides went...gooey. It had been years since I'd let a man get in my head like he was so easily doing. He was going to hurt me as men like him did to women. I'd been hurt once about a year after Gemma left, and Marius had to enlist Leana's help to pull me out of my despair. I swore never to let a man get so deep into my heart again even as I hoped I wouldn't have to marry without love. If I never fell in love, then I wouldn't have to marry anyone. Still, I wanted more of Rain than I should, craved every inch of him and more than just his body.

Rain opened the door for me, and Marius waited on the other side. I jerked back. How long had he been there, and what had he heard? Had he felt it down the bond? I hadn't cared much with the others, but with Rain, it was different. I didn't want to share that piece with anyone else. It was meant for just the two of us.

"The king as well as the council have requested your presence in the throne room," Marius said, holding his human form.

"Now? At this hour?" I asked.

"Yes." Marius glared at Rain.

I tugged my robe tighter around me. "I need to change."

"I'll escort you," Marius said. He cocked his head at Rain. "You should find appropriate attire as well and head to the throne room. It would be unwise for you to show up at this hour with Arianna." Marius worried about my reputation, and appearance was everything at court. If the court was to respect me, I didn't need to show up in the early morning hours with a half-dressed man, even if he could be my future husband.

Rain squeezed my hand. "I'll see you there."

I nodded. Marius fell in step with me.

"We both just happen—"

"I do not need to know details," Marius said. "It is your business."

He had known of my other encounters, but this one felt different to me, so Marius likely sensed it in our bond too. Rain had only been interested in my pleasure tonight. That wasn't how my other experiences had been. Tonight was something else, and my belly clenched at the memory.

I hurried to dress on my own, pausing only to clean up

the icing left behind. My cheeks heated from the memory. Rain gave me the most intense orgasm I'd ever had, but I didn't have time to bask in it. My decision was torn between training leathers and a dress for the hasty gathering. *What happened to warrant calling everyone together in the middle of the night?* I opted for the A-line dress because it was quicker, and I wasn't sure why or who we were meeting in the throne room.

Marius paced in the hall. "We need to hurry."

"What's happening?"

"Your father will fill you in."

"Marius, you never keep things from me, and this is twice in a week," I said, a little out of breath from the rushed steps.

The doors were open to the throne room, and all the council and other trusted advisors had gathered. Father stood on the dais the thrones sat on, a gilded box in his hand. He was dressed in his finery as if he hadn't been to bed. His face was tight and his shoulders stiff.

"Close the doors," Father said, his voice commanding the room.

No announcement of my long-ass title. Thank the goddesses and gods.

"Father?"

"Come forward, Arianna," he said, summoning me.

I moved toward him, the only sound the heels of my shoes clicking on the marble floor, and stopped at the steps.

"Beside me, my dear daughter. This will be your moment." A small smile, proud but regretful, greeted me.

My moment? What the fuck was he talking about?

"Our long-standing enemy is now our ally because a new enemy has emerged."

I locked my face down as I had been taught. No one would know I was clueless as to what my father meant. But inside, I was a mental wreck of fear and what-the-fuck. What new enemy?

"Most of us are leaving today and will not return. We leave behind those we love to carry on and to welcome those of us home who survive." He turned to me and opened the box. His face softened with an expression of pride. A crown sat inside, hugged by velvet molded for it. It wasn't his crown. His was on his head. It wasn't my mother's crown nor my stepmother's. Those were behind glass in his office.

The crown he held out in front of me was encrusted with diamonds, and the metal had been dipped in an alloy that turned it near black. It looked like... a night sky, dark but beautiful with twinkling lights. It reminded me of the magic Rain had used to simulate starlight. I glanced out at the group gathered. Most faces seemed agreeable until I found his. Immediately. Rain. That sadness was still visible in his dark blue eyes, but he inclined his head toward me with the approval I wanted more than my father's and hadn't even realized it until I had it.

"A crown fit for my daughter born on the brightest night our empire has ever seen," Father whispered so only I would hear.

Tears filled my eyes, and I blinked the dampness away. "Father... it's stunning."

"And it will only ever be yours. I'm sorry these are the circumstances I must present it to you under and that I wasn't able to prepare you more," he said.

"It will be okay. You will come home." A heaviness settled in my bones, conflicted over the pride Father's confidence gave me and the dread over his impending departure.

"Kneel," he commanded.

It was only then I noticed the green and black velvet pillow between us. I lowered myself down onto the cushion. I gazed down at Father's shoes in reverence for the honor he bestowed upon me. He placed the starlight crown on my head. The metal and stones were light but of enough weight it was noticeable. The heaviness of the meaning was greater. No longer was I only a princess of the empire. I was the ruler until he returned, and the responsibility sat on me. Father would return to a kingdom well cared for in his absence.

"Rise, my daughter." He grasped my hand as I stood.

He smiled, but it didn't reach his eyes. His hand touched my elbow as he positioned us to face the crowd. "Princess Arianna Alena Christella entered this room, but she exits as Her Majesty, Queen Regent Arianna. Long may she reign."

"Long may she reign," the crowd chanted.

A knot closed off my throat, and I hoped they didn't expect me to speak. Tears brimmed my eyes. I wasn't born to the position and never desired it, but I would make them all proud to have me as the heir.

This brief ceremony was likely the quickest transition

of power the empire had seen. I was swept away with Father and his two most trusted advisors to Father's office. He motioned for me to sit across the desk from him, and the two advisors stood on either side of me. Information was flung at me at a rate I had no chance of remembering. A trade agreement had been negotiated, but I would have to sign it. A few dignitaries' visits were planned who I would need to meet with. The words bled into each other.

"Father?"

"Yes, Arianna." His gaze, full of kindness and understanding, met mine.

"Who is this new enemy?"

Father's gaze grew unfocused and distant. "We thought they were dark magic elves, but they are something else. A predator of true horror. They are fast and powerful and drink blood—ours, the unicorns. It doesn't matter to them."

Vampires? From the stories they liked to tell at the theater? That was what he spoke of. Terror burrowed into my gut, but I would not cower. The empire would prevail over this enemy it seemed even the forest wouldn't claim.

CHAPTER 12
RAIN

I leaned against the stone wall, and Casimir looked me dead in the eyes. "You are getting too close," she said. "Your feelings are getting involved as they so often do with your kind."

"And they don't with unicorns?" She wasn't wrong. I'd sensed something different between me and Ari from the first meeting, and last night changed things. I didn't want to leave, but others were depending on me—plans in motion before I knew how I'd come to care about Ari. She was meant to sit on a throne, and seeing her accept the power of that position with grace and courage after watching her gain control of her magic convinced me she would be a great leader. Gemma might be the sister who was born into that role, but Ari was a queen in every way. I wanted her at my side.

Casimir huffed at me. "We have much more control. I can feel the warmness in you when you are with her." Casimir shook as if she could shake the thought off.

"We're leaving soon. It doesn't matter," I said, a tightness balling up in my chest. Leaving meant the end, and I didn't want to say goodbye.

"But we will be back, and she will know then."

I sighed, rubbing my hand over my gurgling stomach. I'd been sick several times while imagining what the look on Ari's face would be when she found out the truth. "She's going to hate me, and I will deserve her anger."

"I told you this was a bad idea. You should not have come here. It was an unnecessary risk."

"You know I had to. We're running out of time," I said, looking at the grove of trees. Last night had been everything I wanted by pleasing Ari. And the chocolate cake...I'd never done anything like that before. I committed every lick to memory because she probably wouldn't let me touch her again when she learned the truth. The way she looked in that crown was stunning. She was born to be a queen with her strength of mind and magic.

"What will the others say when the unlovable prince has fallen in love?"

I jerked my gaze back to Casimir. "We both know I'm not capable of love. That piece of me is long dead."

"Hmmm." Casimir moved closer as if she could inspect my soul or whatever remained of it. "I'm not so sure that is true."

"I am," I said, pushing off the wall. "Be ready to go this afternoon. The king wants to leave as soon as he has completed the transfer to Arianna."

"And will you say goodbye to the princess?" Casimir asked to my back.

I didn't turn around. Ari's father had no idea how to truly protect her. The urge to say "fuck my duty and the front" to stay with her was so powerful a part of me almost entertained Casimir's idea, but one thing I knew for sure. I would never feel love again.

"She's the queen regent now," I said over my shoulder. And I was going to tell her goodbye because I'd be someone different the next time she saw me.

CHAPTER 13
ARI

Warmth bloomed in my chest, and I knew Rain was close. I didn't understand how, but I'd realized it happened when he was near almost as if we were connected.

Which is impossible, Ari.

There was a knock on my bedroom door. Val stayed with Theo to help him prepare as planned, and no world existed where I would have denied that request because I'd been named regent. I dismissed the rest of the ladies to say their goodbyes as well. That left me alone in my chamber, and I was about to invite him inside. I glanced at the bed and back to the entrance.

"Come in," I said, standing in the center of the sitting area.

The door opened, and in walked the tall man with all his hard lines who had my sole attention. I smiled despite the way my heart ached knowing this was a goodbye. "Hi."

"Hi," he said, closing the door behind him. "Should I bow?"

"Don't you dare unless you want your dick set on fire for real."

He crossed the room, standing so close he seemed to fill the entire space. "That mouth of yours does all the things to me." He slid his hands into my hair, and his mouth swept across mine in a gentle caress. "I will miss this. I will miss you."

I believed he would miss me because I would miss him too.

"Then you should hurry back to me," I whispered.

He paused, and I opened my eyes to meet his gaze. The sadness I'd seen settled there the last few days returned.

"You don't think you will come back." I studied him, seeing a silent resolution in his eyes. "Do you?"

He let out a long breath. "I've known this was coming, but I hadn't planned on you. Saying goodbye to you isn't easy."

"So don't say it. Promise to come back," I said around the sob I choked back. I hadn't known him long enough to care this much, but I did. I shouldn't feel this way so soon, but the tightness in the center of my chest confirmed it. My heart ripped in two—a piece to stay with me and the other half to go with him.

"Even if I promise, you will not like who comes back," he said, his voice low as if it hurt him to say the words. I'd heard stories of how the great war had changed some elves. Marriages broke because those who survived were no longer the same. Others refused to be near anyone like forming an attachment was painful.

"I want you to return, Rain." I paused, thinking of a way to break the intensity. "And you owe me a proper fucking."

He smiled, and it was wickedly devastating. His thumb ghosted over my lower lip. "That mouth. Are you not satisfied from this morning?"

"Oh, it was satisfying, but having you here makes me want something else." I wanted him inside me, but we didn't have time for it. The procession would be leaving with Father. Rain would be expected to be at the king's side, and I had to be there to see them off as my first official duty as queen regent. Then, they would divide and go to their designated areas of the front. I'd have gone anyway, but now, it was required.

"If you want my cock when I return, it is all yours," he said. "And I will be yours if you will have me then."

Confounded by the jumbled feelings between us, I couldn't put a name on what had developed. Not here. Not today. Whatever flame flickered in our touch would have to wait to be named until he returned. "We've only been acquainted a short time and certainly not in a way to say we belong to each other."

"Acquainted? We're a bit more than passing friends. Aren't we? I know enough to know we could be good together," he said, his tone serious. "I want you. If you find me worthy upon my return."

"I— "

He pressed a finger to my mouth. "Don't answer yet. Wait until you see me again."

Dread nestled into the deepest recesses of my chest like it foretold something terrible still to come. But our new enemy was on our doorstep, and Rain would be at the front. That had to be what sparked this dark fear... and the realization that I cared, not only for what happened to him but for him. How did this happen so quickly?

He adjusted my crown and held out his hand. "May I walk you to the end of the hall?"

I slid mine into his, letting the spark of his touch caress me. "Of course."

Rain made small circles on the back of my hand with his thumb. The touch seemed more intimate than last night...like it was an unspoken declaration. He kissed my cheek, and we joined Marius in the hall. My guardian was in his natural form, but the scowl on his face told me he was pissed.

Marius was in my head immediately. *He cannot be at your side when you step out for the first time as queen regent to the people.*

I know, Marius. He knows. He's just walking me as far as he can.

There is something about him you need--

Stop, Marius. He's leaving. Now, get out of my head.

Marius and I didn't often speak in each other's minds out of respect for each other's privacy, but it came so easily to us it was a conscious effort not to. Not many unicorns had that type of bond with their charges, and I was thankful he chose that way to communicate instead of embarrassing me in front of Rain.

We reached the end of the hall, and Rain pulled my hand to his lips and skimmed a soft kiss across my knuckles. "Until I return."

"And you will return." An ache formed between my shoulder blades and into my chest. This would not be our final goodbye.

He disappeared, and I checked my crown in the mirror of the hall as an excuse to blot the tears spilling one by one. I'd never wanted to wear a tiara, but here I was with a bespoke crown. One Father had made for me that reflected the night sky I loved so much.

"Ready?" Marius asked. His black coat shimmered in the light, and the sun glinted off his horn.

"You should be wearing a crown too," I said with a smirk, shoving my despair back for when I was alone. "You are the leader of the unicorns."

"Unicorns do not wear crowns or headdresses," he scoffed.

"What if it was butterflies?" I asked, teasing him.

"I will kick you, queen regent of your people or not." He turned his backside toward me.

"I thought unicorns were sworn to protect their chosen charges, not hurt us?"

"It depends on whether they are being insolent or not," he said.

I laughed. I had to get control of my tension before my introduction.

"Compose yourself for your people," he chastised but

not too harshly. He understood my nerves better than anyone here.

"And yours?"

"They know what is at stake."

"The empire." I smoothed out the long skirt of my dress.

"And more."

I wanted to ask what he meant, but Father's voice boomed out, "I leave you all in the hands of your new queen regent."

It was time to make my entrance. I stepped out into the courtyard, and it was full of citizens—families saying goodbye to their loved ones. My heart skittered to a stop.

"Breathe," Marius said.

I inhaled and let it out. Val and Theo were the first two I saw. My closest friend stood near her new husband. Her eyes were on me, and she smiled. Theo never took his eyes off of her, and I fought the urge to break protocol and smile at them. Their love gave me hope I might one day find that kind of love.

Maybe when Rain—No, Ari. Don't even think that.

Val curtsied and Theo bowed. I scanned the courtyard to see everyone was showing reverence. It wasn't what I expected. Maybe I should have, but I didn't.

Father motioned for me to step onto the platform. "Rise."

Eyes came up and were on me, but there was only one pair I sought out. Rain's. I found him near the gate with his bonded, Casimir. It was the first time I'd seen his unicorn. Casimir was an elegant example of the species.

Her coat was a white so bright it reflected the sun, but her mane and tail were both a deep steel gray. She must be an elder, and I wondered if Marius knew her. I hadn't thought to ask before. Casimir's gaze went past me to Marius. He was their leader. She lowered her head toward him.

You definitely need a crown of butterflies. I sent down the bond with my guardian.

Focus on your task, Regent.

I held my smirk back but hoped it went down the bond.

Father concluded his rousing speech to cheers, and I wished I'd listened harder. He turned to me, and I hugged him daughter to father, not queen regent to a departing king. I remembered the last time I hugged Mother, one of the few memories that was crystal clear. She was near the end, but her hug was strong and full of love. Father's was the same, and I hoped beyond all else this wasn't our final moment together.

"Don't do anything stupid and come back to rule your kingdom," I said.

"I feel like I should be giving you that talk," he said. "I love you, my sweet, strong daughter. You are the future, and I am so proud of who you have become."

I hadn't really cried since my mother died, but I'd lost count of the number of times I blinked back tears the last few days. "I love you."

CHAPTER 14

ARI

I'd been going through the queen regent duties for a week with no word from Rain or my Father. Val received a letter from Theo. She said the carnage was bad when they arrived, but Theo assured her there hadn't been any activity since the mass of our forces arrived.

So why was there a deep ache in my chest? The heart-broken pain of sorrow like when my mother had died. I'd been young, but out of everything from that time, I remembered the way my heart shattered into tiny pieces. I was certain it hadn't gone back together in the same way.

"I see you are in your training leathers," Marius said as I entered the training space. "I'm glad I didn't have to remind you today. It only took a week."

"One usually wears training attire when training. You're extra cranky today." I studied him and noted the tightness of his shoulders. "Have you heard something?"

"Whether I did or didn't does not matter. You need to

be prepared to defend your country, your brother, and yourself."

"If anyone can get close to Drew with the meltdowns he's having, I might let them have him." I wouldn't, of course. Anyone who dared to get close to him would meet my sword and my magic, if it ever worked right. The only real success I'd had was with Rain in the garden. The memories gnawed at me, and I tucked them away. "What are we working on today?"

"Your magic." He leveled his gaze on me.

Fuck me. "Why magic, Marius? I'm better with my sword."

"Your sword will not always be enough," he said. "Now create fire in your hand."

I held out my hand and created the ball of fire like I'd done with Rain. Conjuring a fireball was the easy part. It was everything that came next where it got crazy. "You do remember the last time we played with fire? I burned down a guard shack."

"And you will continue to make those errors until you trust yourself and focus."

"I do focus," I said aware of how whiny I sounded. I inhaled and loosed my breath.

You are queen regent. Act like it.

"Split the flame and bend it into an arc over your head."

He'd never asked me to do that before. It had always been target practice—throwing it was where it went badly every time except with Rain. Dread coiled in my belly. What would I set on ablaze this time? I held my other hand over the fire and pushed my hands together. My fingers warmed, and I willed the ball to expand. As I separated my hands, the sphere formed a stream, and I held my hands in the air. Bend. The blaze arced above me and illuminated the space in an orange glow. "I did it." I'd actually done it. The magic responded to my request, and I didn't burn down a room.

"Yes," Marius said. "It seems I just need to be harder on you."

I looked at him, and the flame disappeared. Goddess dammit. He was right.

He shook his head like I'd made a childish error. "How easily you lose your focus. I've been too easy on you, and I hope we have time to remedy that."

If Father were to be injured or worse...I shivered. But if Father were to be incapacitated, the expectation would be for me to lead the soldiers. "Am I going to have to go to the front, Marius? Is that what you're so worried about today?"

"No, I'm not worried about you going to the front. I'm worried the front is going to come here, and you will not be prepared."

While there had been infiltrations prior to Father and the nobles taking the bulk of our forces to the frontline, nothing had been reported since they arrived. "Theo said it had been quiet. No altercations."

"It doesn't mean the danger has abated." Marius moved closer. "Let's try water magic."

I scanned the area for a bucket or puddle. "There's no water out here."

"Water is everywhere, Arianna. You have to look beyond the obvious. Call the water to you."

Water was easier for me. It responded quickly, and I had more control over it...if there was a fountain or, better yet, a larger body of water. I didn't wait for Marius to tell me what to do. I held out my hands and pulled the water from around me and formed it into a giant ball. Surprise flickered in my bonded's gaze that mirrored my own, and I ignored it to retain concentration on the task. I flared my fingers and flicked the ball to hang over Marius.

"If you drop that on me, I will kick your ass across this courtyard."

I laughed, but it died on my lips. The power gripped me. The firm hold constricted around me, and I couldn't break it. Panic sliced through me. "Marius, it's happening again."

"Break it," Marius said.

"I can't," I yelled. The magic radiated around me. This was how I was going to die. Drowned by my own water magic. Dark mist clouded my vision. "My hands won't move."

"Do it now," Marius ordered.

I jerked my hands free, and the ball fell on Marius. His coat was slick with his mane plastered against it. He shook his head, and I turned away as droplets flew through the air.

"Did you do that on purpose?" Marius asked, his voice flat.

"No, I promise," I said, stifling a fresh laugh. "Why

does it keep happening? I feel more connected to water than fire." My frustration showed up as an aching jaw.

"Fire requires your magic to come to life. Water shares a piece of itself with you."

I groaned in the most theatrical way like in one of the plays my father hosted in court. "And you can do it all. I know."

"Unicorns are born of magic. It is our essence. You have to earn the magic in your blood as all beings like you do," Marius scolded. What had him so cranky today?

"Something is up. What are you not telling me?" Maybe it was unicorn dealings and that was why he was holding it back.

"I wasn't going to tell you until we had confirmation," he said.

"Spit it out, unicorn."

"I hate when you call me unicorn."

"That's what you are," I said.

Marius's magic drifted out until it encircled me, surrounding us both in a bubble. He was muffling us in a place where no one else was. Panic gripped my chest, and I stopped breathing. He was worried about my reaction.

"There are rumors your father is missing. Nothing has been confirmed. The guards are not certain. It is just a rumor amongst the unicorns for now."

My body felt tense and loose at the same time. I fought dizziness to stay upright. "But there's usually a grain of truth in rumors."

"Remain calm," Marius said. I think he said something else, but my mind had drifted off already.

Is he okay? Has he been taken? Oh, goddesses and gods. Is he dead? How will I tell Drew? He'll be fine. He will. But what if he's not?

I was vaguely aware of dampness at my knees. The air around me crackled with energy. I sucked in a breath, but my lungs refused to accept it. Everything was too tight. I grabbed at the collar of my leather vest and unsnapped the buttons around my neck.

"Ari," Marius commanded. He hadn't called me Ari since I was little. "Control. Focus."

I didn't know what he was talking about because all I could think about was that my father might not be coming home. Intense light filled the space around me, temporarily obscuring Marius and everything else. My skin was on fire. Something heavy slammed down on me, and everything went dark.

My head throbbed. I blinked my eyes open. Val sat on the bed beside me, a cloth in her hand. She dabbed the wet fabric along my brow. I tried to sit up, but she pressed against my shoulder.

"You have a fever. You've been out for a couple of days."

"Days?" I rasped out, my throat rough as if it was full of sand.

"Yes, two days." She dipped the cloth in water and patted my arm. "And Marius has been pacing in the hallway. I think he blames himself."

"It wasn't him," I said, shame creeping into my words. What if there had been news of Father? Days the kingdom could be without a leader. If I'd been needed, I would have been out because I didn't know how to command what came easy to the other fae. If ever there was proof every leader needed a proxy, I'd solidified it. "I lost control."

"How are you feeling?" She poured some water into a glass but didn't pass it to me. "Want to try a sip?"

I nodded.

She slipped her hand under my head and cradled it while I took a small drink. It went down like a flood over drought-ridden land, and I coughed.

"My head." I reached up with a shaky hand like my hand alone could stop the ache.

"I can get some of the powder the healers left to use for your father's headaches," she said.

"Thank you. I need it."

Val patted my hand and stood.

"Val?"

She turned around to face me once again. A frown formed on her mouth. She looked concerned.

"Can you ask Marius to come in?"

Her face relaxed. "I don't think I could stop him once he knows you're awake." She smiled and headed toward the door.

Val wasn't her usual conversational self, and I wasn't sure if that was worry for me or if there had been news. I willed myself to stay calm.

Marius entered the room, and the only sound was his

hooves clacking against the floor as he came to stand beside my bed. "You look awful, Arianna."

"I feel like shit," I said. "What happened?"

"Your power... it exploded out of you. I've never seen anything like it before."

Great. My magic was a bomb. "Did I hurt you?" I looked him over as best I could and didn't see any wounds.

"I am not so easily injured."

"Is that why my head hurts so badly?"

"Likely." Marius laid his chin on my forehead, his whiskers tickling my nose.

"Now you're scaring me. Since when do you give hugs? Especially in your natural form?"

"Since I pushed you to this point," Marius said.

"This was me. This wasn't your fault, Marius."

He raised his head and took a step back. "You've been out with a fever for two days because I pushed you. I used information as a weapon to get you to use your magic, and I was wrong for it."

Because he had asked more of me, I found a way to tap into my power. I needed to learn how to repeat it and contain it. My strength was better, and I took a sip of water without shaky hands or coughing. "One of the reasons I accepted your bond offer was because I knew you wouldn't take it easy on me."

"You couldn't have made that decision at the young human age when we paired," Marius said.

"You took me as your charge, and we had a strong connection. Stronger than most. But we did not perform the bonding ritual until I was eighteen. I was old enough for the choice, and I chose it because I wanted someone who would push me and challenge me." If he let guilt build, he wouldn't keep demanding more of me. Besides, I didn't blame him. The onus was on me for not understanding how pivotal his methods were to reaching my magic.

"I went too far," he said.

"No, you didn't." I shook my head. "The incident highlighted I needed to be pushed harder." The truth in my words hummed through my blood. My father loved me and wanted me to be strong, but he would never push me the way I needed. The one thing I knew for sure after the magic explosion was that my lack of control over my power was a bigger issue than I'd acknowledged before.

It had been three days since I'd woken up and five days since my magic eruption. Since then, my magic had taken on a new persona, like a child sulking and refusing to come out to play. When I asked Marius, he said it would return, but sometimes it took time to recover from those outbursts. I'd never seen another elf have that kind of magical mayhem. Marius, of course, assured me my mother had them although he admitted he'd never witnessed them. There was something comforting in knowing I was like her in any way.

Physically, I felt fine, and the sunshine drew me outside. No news had arrived from the front or my father, and the court duties were done for the day. I'd spent a couple of hours playing with Drew until it was time for his nap, and Leana ushered me out. My bonded hadn't reached out to train this afternoon, so I walked down to the field where the guards at the gates said I could find him. Their grins said Marius must have something hard planned for me today.

Marius looked strange as I approached the area.

Is he on his hind legs? Why is he... Oh, goddesses and gods.

He was mounted atop a white unicorn. I covered my eyes and turned away, hurrying down the way I'd come, stumbling over rocks.

Fuck. That's like seeing your parents in the act. Bile rose up my throat. I might vomit.

He must have blocked the intimate moment from our bond. I hadn't sensed it, but that would have been preferable to seeing him in that position. What in the hell was it going to take to burn that from my memories?

I hit the steps and wound around the stairs on the way to my chamber. Liquor. Strong liquor. I changed course for Father's study. The liquor options were sufficient there. They had to be.

The door groaned open as if it had been closed for months or years instead of a couple of weeks. I took in the space, allowing myself a few memories from my childhood to flow. Father would be back. His desk. The couch. The rug. The bookshelves. They all looked untouched since his departure—ready for him. The beverage cabinet in the corner was well stocked. I grabbed one of the bottles and took a swig in a most unprincess-like way. The burn shimmied down my throat and into my belly, and the images of unicorns fucking blurred.

I shuffled my feet through the thick rug as I crossed the room. My head lightened from the amber liquid, and I ran my fingers over Father's desk, taking another swig from the bottle. Papers and leather-bound journals were still stacked like Father would return for them any minute. I missed him and seeing his handwritten notes was like viewing a memorial. I dropped down into the plush chair and took another sip from the bottle, my courage growing with each drink.

Would taking a peek at his papers be so bad? I am queen regent. No one would challenge my right. I should know these things to run the empire in his absence.

The first set of papers was about the plans for next year's crops and potential irrigation needed based on the expected moderate drought. Important but not so urgent it needed me to weigh in with my liquor-fuzzed brain. I opened a journal that turned out to be a ledger of gifts bestowed on Father and the kingdom. There was an entry I didn't recognize about a box from Agonburg, but the contents weren't listed. It was at the same time as Rain's arrival, so probably an oversight that the actual items contained in the chest were not recorded. I closed it and reached for another one that looked well-used.

I scanned through it, and it was Father's personal notes from advisor meetings. He still dated using the lunar calendar even though we had adopted the solar calendar across the empire. I smiled, running my fingers across the date. He'd been so adamant, fighting to keep the lunar calendar, arguing that our kingdom had been founded and won our freedom in the moonlight. He thought our calendar should reflect respect for that part of history. The council wanted to be more in line with other empires and kingdoms we would trade with, and Father granted their request. I remembered what he told me. "Always choose your battles wisely, Arianna. If you fight for everything, you can't impact the real change that needs to happen."

3023 12 10

The Marquess of Rhone came today to inquire about my plans to marry. I let her know I was more concerned about finding a suitable husband for Ari than any match for myself. She informed me she was willing to help find suitors for Ari. My formidable daughter would not be easy to match, and I told the Marquess someone else was already working on the task for me. She didn't need to know it was me personally. I am hopeful for Prince Rainier from what I've heard of his bravery and gallantry. He might be the strong character match Ari needs. She'll require someone to stand with her in public but not be afraid to challenge her stance in private.

I laughed. I had no idea Father was fending off suitors of his own. The fact he understood more about me than I'd realized was a blessing to see in writing. It was like a weight lifted off of me. He wouldn't push me into marriage with some of the lazy aristocrats who had visited. I knew that, but seeing it in his handwriting told me he understood me more than I realized. It would be my choice, and he was right. I wanted someone who wouldn't seek to dominate me in public, but who would spar with me physically and verbally in private. Rain might be that person.

The next few entries were all business as usual with topics on trade and such. Another note was made of Rain's pending arrival because he'd been delayed by an attack. Rain hadn't mentioned that, but we hadn't talked all that much about his life before his visit except for the awkward moment about his experience on the front. I should have asked more questions about his life before he came to meet me. There were no details of the attack itself either.

I flipped the pages and found an entry the day before Rain arrived, and my mouth fell open.

> 3023 12 19
>
> The new enemy has invaded the space between kingdoms, and we find ourselves in a potential alliance with the other court. I'm torn between my duty to our empire and my personal feelings over Gemma. They refused to let me speak with her but assured me she was still well.

What the actual fuck. He'd just let me think there was no word, but Father had known she was there ... and alive. My heart sped up in my chest. My sister was alive. I continued to read, my booze-induced haze clearing.

> Gemma went willingly and was allowed her

unicorn, but what chance had they stood against elves possessing dark magic? Her ability to sneak off and sacrifice herself was something I'd have expected from Arianna. I'd have anticipated it with her, but not Gemma. She was the one who played by the rules while Arianna made her own. How did I not know both of my daughters were so fierce?

Tears burned the back of my eyes. I blinked back the blurriness and pushed the bottle of liquor away. I didn't need it messing with the emotions I had after reading Father's words. His entry rocked me. He'd never called me or Gemma fierce to our faces that I recalled. I read on, looking for more information on my sister.

Even if I align with the other court, they have refused Gemma's return. Her marriage will stand, and we gain nothing in terms of her freedom. If I don't agree to the alliance, both our kingdoms will likely perish to the new enemy. The thought of both my daughters dying from the latter is not an option to me. Even as I negotiated with the evil court's proxy, I knew this would be where we landed. My daughters will live, even if they are on opposing sides after we defeat the new enemy and the alliance with the remnants of the kingdom on the other side of the forest ends.

I reread the paragraph. I ran my hands over my face. Gemma was alive and married. My sister was married to one of our enemies. Was she safe? Was she happy? What was her life like? Did she have children? Was I an aunt to a niece or nephew? Questions flowed through my mind at a dizzying pace. The taste of betrayal danced over my tongue that Father kept this from me, but I understood why. He was afraid I'd go after Gemma, and he was right to draw that conclusion. I hated he carried this burden alone.

A knock at the door made me jerk. I slammed the journal shut and shoved it under a couple of others on the desk. I was queen regent. I could look at any documentation in this empire if I wanted to. This was sensitive, though, and not everyone needed to be in the loop. I was a bit shocked Father had even written it down or that he left it behind. That was telling too. The move to the front had been rushed, or he would have made sure something like this was on his person. The knock came again, and I inhaled a breath, letting it out slowly.

"Enter," I called and flung my hand toward the door to swing it open. Surprise flickered through me that the magic had answered. Maybe booze was the key to conquering my magic.

Marius walked in on two human feet, looking more relaxed than usual, and I grabbed the liquor bottle again to blur the memories from earlier. *Barf.*

"How did you know to look for me here?" I asked, taking a large sip.

"Your scent. It's stronger when you are mens—"

I held up my hand. "Stop. It's disturbing that you used that to find me, and we agreed to not talk about bodily functions, especially my female reproductive cycle."

"We should always use all our senses to determine a situation."

"Not when it comes to my menstrual activity." I frowned at him.

"Then maybe we can talk about what you saw." Marius lowered his head. "I sensed when you panicked and ran."

"I didn't run." My voice sounded a little funny, unnatural and high. I reached for the bottle again. Those images of Marius were going to have to be removed by a kinetic.

"No, put the bottle down. You've had enough."

"Trust me," I said, my voice definitely weird. "I've not had nearly enough."

"Why does it bother you so much to have seen me and Amelia?"

Oh, goddesses and gods, now I wouldn't be able to look Amelia in the eye. "If you have to ask, I'm more concerned for your mental state than mine."

I tilted the bottle to my lips again. A wave of dizziness passed over me. The room blurred. The bottle slipped from my fingers. My vision narrowed as I heard the crystal shatter against the floor.

ARI

"Arianna?" Marius's voice drifted in the haze around me.

My vision didn't clear, and it wasn't the fact I was inebriated—a real mist or fog of some sort settled upon us. Darkness in little droplets veiled the room. "What is this, Marius?"

"I believe this is you," Marius said, awe filling his voice.

"Me?" I squeaked out. "I've never been able to use air magic other than a wind shield."

"No, but this is as much water magic as air and...something else," Marius said, his voice full of wonder. "You have come into your power."

He had to be mistaken. "By creating fog?"

"It's cloudy because your mind is cloudy," Marius said. "Let's go outside."

I wasn't positive I could stand. What if others realized this was my magic being wild again? "For what?"

"To see how far your reach is." Marius had excitement in his voice, and he never showed enthusiasm.

My fear of what I'd find outside matched his eagerness. I took my time walking down the stairs, letting Marius have a healthy lead.

"If you walk any slower, I'll age another century waiting," he said.

"I was hoping you'd forget before we made it outside since you're so fucking old," I said.

Marius chuckled. "Well played."

"What are we doing out here, Marius?" I didn't need to see another failed example of my lack of management over my magic.

He stopped in our normal courtyard, the one where we had full privacy to practice. He faced me and his eyes were black but shiny like polished obsidian. "Touch the ground, Arianna. Connect with it."

"You know I can't command the earth." I knelt down and splayed my hands wide against the damp soil. A buzz tickled my palm, but nothing happened. "Now what?"

"Dig your fingers into the earth. Feel the energy there."

I shoved each of my digits at once into the ground. They sunk in like finely fitted gloves. Power coursed through me. The soil vibrated, and pieces lifted off the ground. Elation feathered over me. I'd connected to core elements. "You are seeing this, right? I'm doing this?"

"Yes, you are." The amazement returned to Marius's voice. "Try to form something out of it."

I focused on a familiar shape. A unicorn made out of the soil particles appeared and galloped across the space between me and Marius. My cheeks ached from smiling. I'd really done it. My magic hadn't conked out.

"Beautiful," Marius said. "Daphina was very gifted in all elements, but her greatest affinity was with the earth, and it was, also, a long-kept secret. I wondered if you would inherit that too."

I remembered how she used her gift to grow some of the most beautiful flowers in the garden. It was one of a handful of memories I had of her. She planted and nurtured the moonflowers in the garden for me, because I always loved the night sky. It was strange hearing someone use my mother's real name. Most people referred to her as the late queen. Gemma looked like her, and I wondered if any part of her survived in me. I had my answer now. Her power lived on in me. An overwhelmingly heavy feeling landed on my chest. It went hollow, and I choked back a sob that tried to escape.

Grief is a sneaky bitch. I hadn't cried in years, but it broke me. I crumpled. The tears fell as if a dam had broken, and it felt like I'd fill the courtyard. Marius stood close in front of me but didn't say a word. The dark mist clung close to me.

"She would be so proud of you, Arianna." His voice was soft and consoling. "Your gift will be so important." When I blinked away my tears, a large, black butterfly with bright-colored wings flew in front of me. There were shades of purples, blues, greens, yellows, oranges, and reds. "It looks like a rainbow."

It fluttered around me but lit on the end of Marius's muzzle.

"Get off me, cretin," Marius said with a huff.

I held out my finger. "You'll be safer with me."

As if it understood, the butterfly took flight straight to my finger where it flexed its wings back and forth. My heart gave a stuttered thud.

"We have company," Marius said, his voice tense.

I glanced over my shoulder. It must be the liquor I consumed or my blurred vision from crying because the person standing there looked like Rain. My heart sped up, and I spun the rest of the way around. The butterfly startled from my finger and flew straight to Rain. It fluttered around his face and landed on his shoulder as if greeting an old friend. "Is it really you?"

"It's really me," Rain said with a slow smile. He held his arms out for me.

My excitement to see him ran so deep I could hardly catch my breath. He wasn't mine, not really, but in that moment, it felt like he'd come here just for me. I closed the distance between us. He enveloped me in his arms, and the warmth between us was like … home. The butterfly claimed one shoulder, so I laid my head on the other.

"I missed you," he whispered against my ear.

"It's only been a couple of weeks." I missed him like a piece of my soul had left with him. Thank Nyx's realm he was safe. *Had he come to give me news of the front? Of Father?* A dozen questions raced through my head, but my mind was still fuzzy from the booze. The murkiness made it difficult to make sense of my thoughts other than the one obvious one. Rain was here.

"So, you didn't miss me?" he asked, kissing my cheek.

"I didn't say that," I said. "Your absence was annoying."

He chuckled, and it rumbled against my chest. "I missed your mouth."

"Then show me." I ran my hand up his arm and around the back of his neck.

He leaned down and pressed his lips to mine. I tasted mint and chocolate like the day we ate chocolate cake in the kitchen—when he made me come on the counter. A need built in my body.

"You taste like an entire cart of liquor. I'm sure there is a story there, but you'll have to tell me later." He kissed my cheek. "When we're alone."

"Marius doesn't care," I said. "If you saw what I did today..." I froze. There were at least a dozen men behind him I didn't recognize.

"Later," he whispered.

"Who are all these people?" Their uniforms weren't any from our empire. The people, soldiers, weren't from our kingdom. I glanced back at Marius, and he closed the space between us.

"I'll explain everything after we get the alcohol out of your system." Rain rested a hand at my waist and guided me toward the door of the castle.

Ari was drunk and the whiskey tasted strong on her, but she was the most beautiful thing I'd seen, not just in the days at the front but ever. Her power was manifesting, and she commanded earth with a connection bordering on symbiotic. If I wasn't mistaken, dark mist even embraced her. She could touch all the elements. Damn. My cock hardened at the sight of her. I wanted her, but I couldn't fuck her until she fell in love with me. The real me. And I had to make her fall in love with me before I told her everything.

She might forgive me if she loved me, but I doubted she would if she just cared about me. It was much easier, in my experience, to cut someone out of your life if you had mild affection for them versus love. There was so much she didn't know about what was happening outside the palace walls. The great cities. Deals her father struck. Her sister's role. I wanted a future with Ari by my side, and I didn't give a fuck what anyone else thought. I could have sent someone else for her when the king renewed his alliances, but I came back for her.

"Let's go get some food in you, and you can ask me all the questions burning in that incredible mind of yours. I'm sure you have many inquiries about what is happening on the front."

"I do," Ari said, scanning my men. Marius scrutinized me but didn't interfere. "So many."

I slipped my hand in hers, holding the gift I made for her under my other arm. "My crew is hungry and tired. They will want to eat in the dining hall, but I'd rather we have a smaller audience."

"I'd prefer that too," she said, her words a little slurred. She was an agreeable drunk, but I wouldn't take advantage of that. Despite our opposing positions, I respected her more than my advisors liked but fuck them. They didn't know Ari the way I did. If they wanted to push it, I'd replace them.

CHAPTER 18
ARI

I gave the kitchen instructions to see to Rain's men. The alcohol blur started to clear, but I'd drank a lot. Why was he with members of a kingdom's colors I didn't recognize? The alliance Father struck. That was it. Rain and I settled in Father's private dining area with the plates and drinks we absconded with from the chef's items. I wanted to ask about my father, but the words wouldn't come. My fear tempered because if something had happened, Rain would have told me. They might not have even been in the same place from what Father had said about keeping their location hidden.

Rain reached across the table and took my hand. "I did miss you, Ari."

I studied him and the softness of his face melted me. The familiar sadness I'd noticed multiple times still lingered, but there was a warmth there too. "I wondered if you did when I didn't receive letters like some of the others."

He squeezed my hand. "If I'd known it was letters you wanted, I'd have written you letters every day in our enemies' blood."

"That might be an extreme for when you return, but a couple of lines to know you are alive would be appreciated," I said, not wanting to pressure him. He'd been battling our enemy, and I was jealous of others receiving correspondence. I'd been selfish, but I was relieved he was in front of me even if it was for a short time.

"I did bring you something I made while there."

"You made?" I tilted my head to assess him unsure if he was joking. He looked completely serious.

He gestured toward the linen-covered item leaning against the wall he'd had tucked under his arm earlier. I'd assumed it was something related to war since he'd been so protective of it and thought I'd ask about it later. Excitement quick-stepped up my back and tingled at my neck.

Rain lifted the rectangular item, holding the cloth in place over it. He looked around and then walked over to the bookcase, placing the object on the middle shelf that had a larger ledge capable of holding the piece.

He studied me with a nervous expression but smiled. "Ready?"

I clasped my hands together in front of my chest. "Yes."

He tugged the linen until it fell to reveal a painting. I gasped. It was my garden. Beautiful and vibrant and full of moonflowers...only they were purple, not white. He'd painted me lying in the middle of them with my head turned to the side as if I were looking at something or someone.

"It's beautiful." I wiped at the tears forming in the corners of my eyes. "I love it. You had time to do this on the front?"

He'd thought of me while he was facing the enemy. Really thought of me.

"This was how I spent the little free time I had. One of the officers is a painter, and I asked to borrow some. I've never painted before, so I wasn't sure if it was good enough to give to you, but I wanted you to know I was thinking about you every day—every hour, every minute, and every second. I'd imagine myself in front of you with you looking at me the way you are in the painting—the way you are looking at me now."

"You've never painted before this?" I was in awe. The strokes were like that of some of the most talented artists I'd seen in the kingdom.

"Not once. I did draw some when I was a child, but this was the first time I picked up a paintbrush. I hope it's not so ugly you won't want to display it."

My heart thrummed as I reached out to embrace him. I was sure he would feel the pounding, and I was fine with it. I wanted him to know how he affected me. "It's more than good enough. I have painted before, and you did a thousand times better than I would have. I'll hang it in my bedroom, so it's the first thing I see in the morning and the last thing I see at night to remind of you."

"I had the perfect inspiration guiding me with every stroke." He kissed my temple.

Warmth spread throughout my body as if a fire had been lit from within me.

"Thank you for this gift." I pressed my lips to his cheek.

Rain leaned back, brushing the loose hair from my face. He looked worried, and I assumed it had something to do with what waited for him at the front.

"How long before you have to return?"

"It depends, but I don't have new orders yet," he said, drawing my fingers to his lips. "Do you have any idea how exquisite you are?"

My cheeks heated. "Why are you flattering me? I'm already alone with you."

"I'm not flattering you. I'm speaking the truth, and you should not be afraid to own how striking your beauty is."

I hadn't felt beautiful much, despite compliments. My mother was a beauty, and Gemma looked like her. I favored my father more, and while I never felt unfortunate in the looks area, I never considered myself exquisite, as he said, either. To hear Rain say it would never be unwelcome.

The weight of my father's whereabouts was a heaviness in the room. For some reason, I couldn't bring myself to ask him about Father and if the strange men were part of Father's alliance. It was like something in the back of my mind prevented me from doing it. Like a unicorn. A large menacing unicorn with a golden horn. *Marius, get the fuck out of my head.* The weight lifted like a curtain. Why wouldn't Marius want me to get any information I could on Father? I paused against asking the question for a whole different reason. If a unicorn wanted a secret kept, there was a reason. He respected me enough to not push me when I wanted him out, but his intention was clear. *Don't talk about your father here and don't ask about the strangers.* I filed it back to ask Marius about his reasoning after dinner.

I took a bite of the root vegetables on my plate and put my fork down. I wasn't hungry. "I don't feel like eating. I'd rather go for a walk with you."

"I'd like that too." He rose from the table.

I linked my arm through his. "My garden?"

"Lead the way."

The walk to the garden was silent. I soaked up our closeness and leaned my head against his shoulder. He let out a big sigh.

When I turned the corner through the gate of my garden, I gasped. The entire garden was blooming except my moonflowers. They wilted as if they were in mourning. I released Rain's arm and ran to them. "What could have done this?"

"I don't know," Rain said, his voice soft.

"I need to tend to them." I knelt in front of the first flowerbed.

"Of course." He squeezed my shoulder. "Can I help?"

One of the flowers perked up as I ran my fingers over the soft petals. "No, I think it's me they need."

He kissed the top of my head. "Very well. I'll make sure

the troops are settled. They get a little rowdy without direction." Rain ran the back of his knuckles over my cheek, sending a shiver down my spine. "May I come see you afterward?"

"I'd like that." I paused. If this flower's response was an indication, it wouldn't take long here, and I wanted to read more of my father's journals. "I'll probably be in my father's office. It's in the—"

"Monarch's wing." He smiled. "I know, my queen."

"Regent," I corrected. "Queen regent."

He stood and bowed in a grand gesture. "I must ask for forgiveness."

I tossed some dirt at him. "Stop. Go take care of your men. There is much for us to discuss when you're done."

His face turned somber. "There is." He kissed the top of my head again. "I'll find you as soon as I can."

I held his hand lightly until he walked too far, and my hand fell away. He stopped at the gate and turned. "I really did miss you."

Then, he was gone. My heart pumped in an erratic rhythm because those words, his words, did something to me. And goddesses and gods, I'd missed his presence, and I shouldn't have. We had only met a few short weeks ago, and he'd been gone most of those. *Call it what it is, Arianna. Lust. Infatuation. Nothing more. Just enjoy it.*

I rose and ran my hand over the tops of the flowers in the bed. They all responded as if it were a drought, and I was a soaking rain. The dark mist encroached on my vision, and I took it as a sign. I threw my hands out and the mist blanketed the garden, bathing the flowers in a sheer veil. My garden lapped the magic like the plants needed it to survive. Satisfied my garden would endure, I took a moment to bask in my power. I wasn't the weak princess after all. Worthy was the word that flittered through my mind.

I opened the gate, and Marius stood there. "Were you being a creeper again?"

He tilted his head. "You are my charge. It's part of our sworn bond to be aware of your location and safety. Besides, I told you earlier—"

"Stop." I stared at him for a second. His expression was an entire novel of worry. "And does that go for trying to control what I say too?"

"Let's go somewhere private to discuss that," Marius said, his voice lower.

"I was just headed to my father's office if you want to join me. I found some interesting reading material there." What I most wanted to discuss with him was why he would manipulate my ability to speak on certain subjects.

Marius glamoured into his human form and fell into step with me. "I suspected as much with what transpired earlier."

I cut a glance at him but didn't say anything else the rest of the walk to the other wing. He followed me into the office and closed the door. I sat behind the desk in the big leather chair and clasped my arms in front of me.

Marius stood on the other side of the desk, and we stared at each other for a long moment. He knew things. Things he hadn't told me.

"You want answers," he finally said, taking a seat in one of the big leather chairs on the other side of the desk.

"I do."

"Those aren't easy, Arianna. You know we can't break the oath of unicorns, especially me. You need to ask your questions."

"Maybe start with why you didn't want me to talk about Father with Rain... I mean Prince Rainier." I leaned back in the chair and studied him. Did he not trust me, or was there another reason he was keeping information from me?

"Your father is behind enemy lines." His tone was gentle as if he was afraid I'd break, but Marius had never been afraid of breaking me until recently. Why was he being careful with me now?

"And Rainier doesn't know this?"

Marius shifted in his seat like the question made him uncomfortable. "Not many do. Your father wanted to make it look as if he was missing, so he could move more freely."

Father wasn't missing or a prisoner. That was a relief. I glanced at the journals and the dots connected on why he would need to be in the enemies' territory incognito. "He's going after Gemma."

"Yes," Marius said, his voice a whisper.

"Why now? When we have another enemy at our door?"

"Because the other court is distracted and there is a temporary truce with them."

I wanted my sister home more than anything. I didn't

understand why he would put me in the position of regent if he thought she would come back to take her rightful place. He could have left the seat open for my sister's return. "Then why did he leave me in charge?"

"If he does manage to rescue Gemma, she will never be able to lead the empire, Arianna. The people would not fully trust her as they would you. You saw their allegiance when your father left."

"Because she was kidnapped and held in the other kingdom. That doesn't mean she's betrayed us," I said. Gemma wasn't a traitor. She did what had to be done.

"She went willingly," Marius challenged. "You are clearly aware of this fact."

"To save us. To make peace."

"But without revealing the details of her selfless act, the people will never know the truth."

"What will happen to your brother? Will Cyrus return with her?" Unicorns had that collective consciousness, but the bond Marius and Cyrus shared was one only twins would have.

"I cannot say. He's shut me out since they left." He'd never told me that before, but I realized he meant it every time he'd told me over the last five years he knew how I felt.

"Even now? Knowing Father is coming for Gemma?"

"Cyrus is very protective of your sister. Her priority to him is greater than his to me."

The crack in my chest from Gemma's absence split open further for Marius and Cyrus. If Gemma could still communicate with me, I was certain she would have. Why did it have to be one or the other, though, for Marius and his twin? Couldn't it be both? But it could have been both and his connotation became clear. "You mean Gemma asked him to shut you out and thereby shut out me, Father, and the rest of the kingdom."

Marius nodded. "She had a mission of her own design. Whether any of us agreed with it didn't matter. Her decision was made."

"She hadn't made her resolution on a whim. Gemma wouldn't have left if she didn't feel it was the only way," I said, thinking about how Father made it seem she'd been kidnapped. She wasn't though. She'd made a conscious choice for the empire, and no one would ever know her real intent. "It's not fair my sister will be refused her rightful place."

"Life is not fair, Arianna." Marius's voice softened again. "That's a lesson you learned at a young age, and a lesson that will return throughout your life." His head dipped. "It's a lesson I wish I could take for you, but that is not the way the fates work."

His tone was too kind for Marius. He never spared feelings. It was one of the things that made me trust him and endeared him to me. So why was he being so gentle right now?

There was a knock at the door, and I jumped. The door creaked open. Rain stuck his head in. Father hadn't returned but Rain had. I could trust Rain with what I'd learned.

"Sorry. I thought you would be alone." His gaze landed on Marius.

"No apologies needed. Come on in."

"Arianna," Marius said, nodding at me and leaving Rain and I alone in the room. Hooves clicked against stone. He'd returned to his normal form, and the nudge in my head told me to be careful. My guard was showing power and warning me. But from what...

Rain closed the door and walked over, sitting on the edge of the desk. He covered my hand with his. "Things seemed tense between you two."

"Being at war has us all on edge." It was the truth. Just not the truth of what created strain between Marius and me.

He lifted his hand and touched my shoulder, swirling small circles with his thumb. "It does, and I fear it will get much worse before it gets better."

A chill drifted from the base of my neck down my spine. My magic hummed under my skin, but it wasn't out of control this time. "You sound as if you know something you haven't shared yet."

"There are many things I know, but I never want to deliberately deceive you." His face shifted into a crestfallen expression, and I wondered if he thought he had to break the news of my father's absence to me.

I almost told him I already knew, but he had other things to explain. Instead, I decided to give him space, to drive the conversation. "Thank you. I need people I can trust around me. And—"

"We haven't known each other all that long." He let his hand drop. "I get it. What do you need to know about me?"

"Did you see my father?"

He pursed his lips and shook his head. "We were not in the same position."

Wouldn't he think he needed to tell me that information first if he knew it? Unless he thought Marius had. This was a game, and I decided to play to see what I could learn because quite literally my father's and my sister's lives were at stake. I thought of random questions to open discussions that might tilt him a little off guard. "What was your childhood like? When did you first go to the front line? Do you get along with your father? When was your first kiss? Who was it?"

He chuckled. "Slow down." His gaze caught on the music player in the corner. "Does that work?"

"Yes, as far as I know." Father listened to it from time to time. Although, I couldn't remember the last day he did.

Rain scanned over the round discs that played music, clearly avoiding the questions. "Hmm." He selected one and placed it on the player. Soft music drifted out over the space. Rain crossed the room and held his hand out to me.

This game was far too easy to play because of the attraction between us. I slipped my hand in his, and he pulled me up from the chair against his chest. It felt right being so close to him. The heat from our bodies entwined, and I thought it could last forever. He would have to answer a long list of questions for my trust to fully form, but I could see a life with him. That scared the hell out of me as much as it thrilled me.

"This is so much better than being shoulder to

shoulder with another officer," Rain said into the top of my hair.

I laughed against his chest, but I didn't miss how carefully he chose his words and actions.

He was guarded, and for us to have a future, those walls would need to come down.

CHAPTER 19

ARI

Rain led us in easy movements across the office floor. I lifted my head enough I could press my lips to his neck. He let out a sigh.

"That is both bliss and torture." Rain turned me around the room in time with the music. "While I was on the front, I thought of what your lips felt like against mine. Against my skin. What you tasted like arched against my tongue."

My cheeks heated as my core tightened. "Sounds like you tortured yourself."

"Thank the goddesses and gods I had my own tent." He slid his fingers into the hair at my nape and caressed the hollow of my neck with his thumb.

"Why would..." I paused realizing what he meant. "Oh."

He chuckled. "Chocolate cake played a vivid part in the memory as I took care of the need. I longed for the sweetness of it mixed with you."

"You don't need the memories now. The real thing is here in front of you."

He inclined his head and devoured my mouth. His weight pushed us across the room until my back was against the hardness of the wall and his bulge stiffened against my belly.

"My room," I said, my voice sounding rough with demand.

Rain's forehead fell against mine. "Not now. I have work to do first. But soon if you'll have me…"

Was this who he was? Duty first. Personal second. And where would that put me? Always second or lower. Maybe it could only be sex between us because his first priority would be to the army and the front despite my hopes Father's notes penned in his journal were right. I hadn't realized how much I wanted to believe Rain and I could have been a good match.

I cleared my throat and patted his chest. "I'm tired. Probably the alcohol after seeing unicorns…"

He tilted my chin up. Amusement danced through his eyes. "Unicorns what?"

"Don't make me relive it. That's why I was drinking in hopes of drowning out those memories," I said, moving around him. "I'll see you tomorrow."

Rain caught my wrist. "Don't do that."

"What?"

His head tilted. "You're shutting down. I'm still an offi-cer, and we are still at war."

"I know." I understood it, but it still tasted like rejec-tion on my tongue. Distance and time for the alcohol to clear would give me perspective and help me decipher the bigger gambit he had.

He lifted my wrist to his lips and caressed the soft skin. "Don't run from me."

"I'm not." I smiled and opened the door, waiting for him to exit. He stopped in front of me and brushed his knuckles over my cheek. Warmth spread over the skin he touched.

"I hope you forgive me one day," he said and was gone before I could respond.

He was as confusing as they came. I closed the door behind me and saw Marius leaning against the wall in his human form.

"I'm going to bed. You don't have to walk with me." I wanted to be alone with my thoughts to try to figure out what was going on in my head and my heart.

"You are queen regent."

As if I needed reminding of that. I shot through our bond and glared at him.

"Something is off with communications," Marius said.

"Get out of my head."

"No, not yours. The comms from the front." His voice was low enough I almost didn't hear.

My head jerked up to meet his solemn gaze. "What do you mean?"

"There was a flurry of unicorn communications regarding confusion of forces and then it was cut off. It's not the first time, but the only information coming in is through Rainier's men."

"Why would the unicorns cut off their thoughts from the others?"

"Battle could be one reason. We shut down our connections, so we aren't experiencing others' pain and death. It can make us vulnerable on the field."

"Reduce the distractions. That seems like a valid reason at the front."

"It does, but usually, it is planned."

Unease wound into my magic, but I maintained control. We stopped in front of my door. I opened it and motioned him inside. "And this wasn't because you think they were attacked suddenly? No time to advise they were going dark?"

If they had been overwhelmed, then we needed help, but a wise ruler didn't act on rash thoughts. I needed to weigh the risks and not rush into a battle zone. I could almost hear Father's voice in my thoughts.

"That is a possibility," Marius said, changing to his unicorn form.

"But not the one you think happened?"

"No," he said. "There were devices used during the war that can block communication."

"Like between twin unicorn brothers?" I asked, understanding registering.

"Yes."

"So, they could all be dead or prisoners by now..." *They are not dead. They are not dead. They are not dead.* "We should gather who we can and make our way there."

"You must stay in the seat of the empire, or it will be

lost." His voice lacked the conviction I'd have expected from him for that statement.

Fuck the seat. The empire could be lost if the enemy was making their way toward the castle, but if I led the remainder of our forces there, we could at least give our kingdom a chance. "I can't stand by while they could be injured or dying. My father is there."

Marius's nostrils flared. "We don't know exactly where your father is right now, and the risk is too great to take you to the front."

Plus, my brother. "And I can't leave Drew." He'd just started talking again, and I couldn't leave him. Marius was right. I had to remain in the seat, but there had to be another option. Dark mist flitted across my vision as if my magic was trying to give me the answer, but I didn't know how to interpret it. "Do you see that?"

"See what?" Marius asked.

He didn't. "Never mind. I'll stay here...for now."

ARI

The agenda for the day was full. I prepared for my court duties with Val at my side as usual. There was a trade agreement to be signed with our most distant neighbor, and they were coming to court for it before their soldiers joined ours at the front. Father had brokered it, so all that was left was for me to sign.

I lifted my crown from the pillow it sat on in my dressing area. Silver thread embroidered the blue velvet of the cushion for the Night Sky Crown's pedestal. I ran my fingers over the lettering. AR for Arianna Regina, which was the old-world term for queen. A small silver plaque on the pedestal bore the name of the crown. Father must have been planning to bestow the crown on me for a while. It seemed strange to wear it and hold court with so many of the members away on the front. Not just court members but citizens too.

"Here." Val held out her hand. "Let me."

I smiled and handed it over to her. Val's shoulders

were tight. Even with regular letters from Theo, she'd told me she worried for his safety, yet she'd managed to remain positive despite the sparse details in the correspondence.

"Are you nervous? You so rarely get anxious."

"No." I watched in the mirror as she secured the crown. I was nervous a lot, but Marius was the only one who knew. I hid it from everyone else. Whatever metal he had chosen was surprisingly light. The majority of the weight came from the diamonds instead. "I'm just a little concerned about so little news and intelligence coming in from the front. Going about our daily business as usual feels wrong."

I wanted to know my father was safe, and I wanted to go to the front to help. Part of me considered that Father may have left me here because he didn't think I was strong enough. Order almost maintained itself at the castle.

She pinned the crown into the elaborate half-up and half-down hairdo she'd fashioned. "But it's not. We have to maintain our lives here, so they have something to come home to."

"That is true," I said.

"Plus, my husband has assured me all is well on the frontline." A bright smile spread across her face when she said "husband." It was contagious, and I couldn't help but mirror the action. The pressure in my chest eased. Val rubbed my upper arm. "Are you ready?"

"I am." Actually, no. I wasn't sure I'd ever get used to leading a formal affair, but this was my duty. I would do it for my father and my kingdom.

Val opened the door to a waiting Marius. Val took the left and Marius the right, and each remained two steps behind me as was custom for respect to the sovereign.

"You look very queenly," Marius said, a hint of humor in his voice.

"Good morning to you too," I responded.

"Have you seen your agenda?" The jocularity from moments ago was cast aside.

I'd familiarized myself with the schedule, and I hadn't been unprepared for any of the meetings. "I've reviewed it. A trade agreement for grain, concerns over a potential water shortage—"

"And a visit from a dignitary of Agonburg."

I jerked my head over my shoulder toward him. "When was that added?"

"This morning. Apparently, he arrived in the early hours."

"Does Rai...does Prince Rainier know?" Strange he wouldn't have informed me of one of his dignitaries arriving. But maybe word hadn't been able to get to him on the front, and he didn't know the representative was here.

"No, he does not to my knowledge. The request was to only let you know. Do you want him added to the court session?"

I shook my head. "Not at the moment. Let's see what this dignitary has to say."

"As you wish." His grim tone said more than any words. He shared my concern. If the Agonburg noble wanted the visit a secret, it wasn't random that this person chose while my father wasn't here.

THE TRADE AGREEMENT had been signed. With Father's expert negotiations laid out, there was little for me to do but oversee and authorize the document. The predicted water shortage plan was made and could be easily implemented if needed. The final item on the agenda that had been added earlier was the dignitary from Agonburg. The pit in my stomach made me weak, but I sat composed to the room.

"What is the representative of Agonburg's name?" I asked Phen, the council member in charge of setting the agenda.

He gulped. "Prince Felipe."

Rainier's younger brother. Marius was in my head.

Yes, I'm aware of this member of their family.

He was friends with Gemma, but he hadn't been to court since her disappearance. Since she left. Felipe was much younger than his brother, and Rainier had never attended court that I recalled. Rainier's attention was said to be solely on building our forces, and that made even more sense after meeting him.

Marius's gaze went distant, and the door opened. *I'll be back by the time this meeting is done.* He ducked out in his human form. Unusual for him to glamour to his human persona unless he wanted to blend. I trusted him, but the pit in my stomach spasmed.

Felipe entered and bowed low. He had filled out from the time he and Gemma were close. How different he was from Rainier. They were equally handsome and tall, but Felipe's hair was darker and his skin a deep olive tone.

"Rise, Prince Felipe."

He smiled. "Queen regent."

"It's good to see you well." I gestured to the open chair closest to me.

"And you." He nodded to the council members and sat, crossing his legs.

"What brings you to court?"

"I was hoping I could be of help to you with my father and brother both on the frontline." He appeared casual in his offer.

A twinge in my gut tightened. He didn't know Rain was here. Communication wasn't traveling as fast as normal. I hadn't even known Rain was able to leave or was on his way. Still, the fact tasted sour. The conversation with my father about a traitor played back in my head. Felipe was Gemma's friend, but that was five years ago. He might not be the same person he was then.

"Who is minding your lands while you are here?"

He smiled, an easy friendly gesture as if he was thankful for my question. "My sister and brother."

"The twins? Are they old enough?"

"They are twenty-one by the current calendar."

I nodded. "If you feel confident in their abilities, I welcome you to join the council in your father's absence." I paused. What better way to determine a rat was near than with a piece of cheese... "But your brother is here. He's returned for a few days."

Confusion clouded Felipe's eyes. His brows bunched together. "Rainier is here?"

His reaction appeared genuine, so I continued, "He is. Shall I send for him?"

Felipe's jaw tightened. "I'd very much like to see him if you don't mind, Your Majesty."

"Please, call me Ari, as we did when we were younger."

He smiled. "Please, Ari. I wish to see my brother if he is here."

I motioned to the non-unicorn guard at the door. "Please find Prince Rainier and ask him to join us."

Marius, you might want to get your ass in here. He didn't respond.

CHAPTER 21
ARI

The doors opened and Rain strolled in, his gaze finding mine before he saw his brother. His steps slowed with recognition. The smile he'd given me faded.

Not a happy reunion but they weren't ever close from what I remembered.

"Ah. There's the imposter," Felipe said, leaping to his feet.

I cut my gaze, expecting humor on his face, but there was none. He was serious, but what did he mean? Rain had stood by their father in the strategy sessions. What was Felipe trying to do by declaring his brother a fraud?

"I know you don't like who I have become, Felipe, but I am still your brother." Felipe advanced toward Rainier.

The guards, ready to draw swords, looked at me. I held up my hand for them to stay their positions. Secrets were about to be exposed. The magic humming under my skin promised answers.

"But you are not loyal to your empire or your queen, are you?"

Marius, where are you? Felipe and Rain...Felipe is calling Rainier a traitor.

My bonded didn't answer. I reached for my magic, but it didn't respond to my panic-laced request.

Rain's men entered the room behind him in their blue and silver uniforms. He held up his hand in the same fashion I'd done with my guards. One of the opposing kingdom's elves approached him. "It is done, my prince."

My prince? A sign of respect or was he really a traitor? My hands shook, and I twisted them into my thick skirt to hide my fear.

"Kneel to your queen," Rain said to the elf. Felipe's eyes were wide, but he didn't move.

"Queen regent and that's not necessary," I said, forcing calm into my voice.

"Yes, it is." He focused on his men. His voice menaced as he bit out each word. "Kneel to your queen."

All of his men, foreign elves, knelt in front of me and stayed there.

"It's up to you when they can get up," he said, his voice lowered and softer toward me.

"Rise," I said, not understanding this display. "Rise."

The men stood and glanced from me to Rain.

"Confine her to her quarters until we leave." He motioned to me before gesturing to Felipe. "And take him and the others somewhere they can be kept quiet and out of sight."

Shock shuddered through me as the pieces fell into

place. This was a coup, and my kingdom, the empire, had fallen. *Not fallen.* I'd practically handed it to the disgusting dark court on the other side of the forest.

"I'm not going to my room," I said, my magic vibrating at my fingertips with my nerves more like the old unpredictable version. *My brother. What will they do to him?*

Leana was out with Drew. They had to run.

Marius? Can you hear me? I hoped he wasn't shutting me out. He wasn't normally this unreachable. I begged my magic to let him hear me.

Yes. I'm coming.

Thank the goddesses and gods. My throat was thick.

They would expect the unicorns to rally in my defense. Defense of the kingdom. If I asked Marius to leave, Drew would have a chance. I couldn't risk my brother's life, and if our historians were accurate of past takeovers, the revolt would end in execution for both of us. *Rain has taken over the kingdom. Get Leana and Drew and as many of the others as far away from here as you can.*

I will not leave you behind, Ari. You are my charge and my bonded and my friend.

He'd said my nickname, the name my friends used, and I bit down on the side of my cheek to keep from letting out a sob. He'd called me a friend. My eyes burned.

You have to, Marius. Do this for me.

Silence stretched out for so long, I thought he'd shut me out.

Promise me you will get Drew somewhere safe. Please, Marius.

A sigh drifted into my head, followed by a huff.

I smashed my lips together. He was acquiescing to me.

I will promise this to you as I promise to return for my charge and revenge.

I suppressed the small sigh of relief that tried to escape. Let Rain's men see my tears and think I'm scared. *Let them report to Rain I was a weepy female and nothing more. Let them think I'm weak. It will make revenge that much sweeter when they find out I'm anything but a desperate, help-less person.*

Only if Drew is safe and only if you can sneak in here without being noticed. No risks for me. I don't think he will hurt me. He doesn't see me as a threat.

Another long pause. *I found Leana. We're headed to the mountains.*

Thank you, Marius, my friend.

Stay alive, friend.

His last words drifted through my mind. There were limits to this type of communication, and I knew he'd be out of range in minutes if not seconds as swiftly as the unicorns moved.

The room filled with more men. More foreign elves. Three encircled Felipe, and he struggled against their grasp.

"He's a prince. Put him in my room with me."

Rainier's eyes narrowed on me and darkened. Anger flashed like a streak of lightning in his gaze. "No other man will be in your room, Ari."

"Don't call me that, Prince Rainier. I am queen regent to you and your men."

One of his men shoved me in the back, and I stumbled

forward. A thud sounded behind me as I regained my footing. Rainier pinned the man who prodded me against the wall. His hand swiped at his throat, but he couldn't break Rainier's hold.

"No one touches her," Rainier said with a growl. "Do you all understand?" He released the man who tumbled to the floor, but it gave me a clue as to what Rainier's magic was. Only someone with wind at their fingertips could move like that.

His men stood on either side of me but didn't dare come too close to me.

I'd been regent for only a month, and I'd lost the empire because I believed a stupid man might like me, even when I knew he wasn't what he seemed. I saw his behavior and still allowed myself to think there was hope. My heart hardened to stone, and I used that stone to build up a wall between me and whatever Rainier planned to use me to accomplish. And if I couldn't escape and he planned to use me as a pawn against my father, I knew where the moonflowers bloomed.

RAIN

It wasn't how I'd planned the decommissioning of the kingdom to happen nor how I'd planned Ari to find out. My error in judgment couldn't be undone, and I hoped Ari would listen when I explained. Prince Felipe had to show up. His appearance was a mistake we couldn't afford. I met Casimir at the edge of the vast courtyard.

"Did you track Marius and the others?"

"I'm not a dog, Rainier," she said. "They have all shut the connection off as expected, but the actual dogs will find the scent of the child."

I nodded. The timing was fucked. I should tell Ari the truth, but it would be too much all at once. She needed to be eased into all the changes. Partly because I worried about how she would take the full truth, but more because I needed time to figure out how to explain everything. Laurel had made it look so easy with Gemma, but I wasn't my brother and Ari wasn't her sister. "How did Felipe get through unnoticed?"

"He is gifted with forward sight, albeit brief. He must have seen something to allow him the ability to sidestep our efforts."

"That can't happen again." I paced a path in front of Casimir. The timing of our activities and Ari's safety depended on no surprises.

"You have him now," she said.

"Did he see that coming? Does he have a plan?"

"He will be confined," Casimir said. "Unless you plan to execute him."

I spun to face her. "Goddesses and gods, no. The plan has always been as little bloodshed as possible."

"Then you need to move up your plans." She blew a huff of hot air my way.

I nodded. "I'm already on it. And your people are still with us?"

"You asking that question is a dishonor to my people."

The disruption and the tears on Ari's face had shaken me. I hadn't expected Ari to concede so quickly, and I was convinced she hadn't. That beautiful mind of hers was working through the problem we'd created for her. She was more intelligent and powerful than I expected, but her fear of her power lessened her threat. If she ever came into the actual level of power she was capable of... The sooner I got her out of the castle the better. She needed space from this place to see the truth.

CHAPTER 23
ARI

Val was in my room, curled up in a ball on the floor. Her red dress puddled around her like a cocoon. She lifted her face when the door opened, and tears spilled down her already-stained cheeks. The red rims of her eyes told me she'd been here most of the day. Maybe since I'd left this morning. My heart dropped at the sight. He imprisoned my friend, and he would pay for that choice first.

She pushed up off the floor and ran to me, wrapping her arms around me. "I was so worried they…"

The door closed, and no footsteps were leaving. His men remained outside the door.

"He didn't hurt me." My voice was emotionless as I awkwardly patted her back. If I let myself feel anything, I would break down, and that wasn't going to get us out of here. "Are you okay?"

"Yes," she said. "But one of his guards told me Theo would pay if I resisted. Disgusting, vile creatures."

I pulled back and nodded. "We have to get out of here."

"Can Marius help us?"

I shook my head. "I sent him..." Val was my most trusted friend, but I stumbled even telling her details. "To safety with Drew."

She let out a long sigh. "I prayed you and Drew were both free."

"Just Drew." At least if I died, Father's legacy would live on in Drew. Mother's would die with me. A tremor ran through the castle, jostling me and Val. I grasped at her to steady both of us. Magic like mine with earth was rare, and it would have to be refined and strong to create that kind of movement.

"Was that an earthquake?"

"Seems so," I said, scanning the room to see my hairbrush and other small items displaced. *Did I do that?*

"We haven't had one in years."

"Yes," I agreed, not having experienced once since the day Mother died. "What timing. A sign of displeasure from the goddesses and gods perhaps."

I'd never shown a hint of any kind of power that strong, so if it was magic, it wasn't mine. The goddesses and gods seemed like the only acceptable answer.

"Have you tried to reach Marius?"

I shook my head. "He's out of range now." I walked to the window and looked out over the courtyard. Elves, from the court of our enemy, filed into the enclosure. When did they form this alliance? I scanned the space until my gaze found him. Rainier stood near his unicorn.

He would die. It would be at my hands, and I didn't need magic to do it. As if he felt me, he turned his gaze up to my window. His expression was grim as if he understood the silent challenge I laid down. If my magic would cooperate, I'd send it all at him, but it was hiding from me. "Prince Felipe is in the castle. He arrived today."

"What? I always thought he was so nice."

"He still is. They don't appear to be working together since Rainier locked him up as well."

"What is happening, Ari?"

"I'm not sure. I thought this was a coup, but looking at the size of this force, it looks like something else. Like an invasion." There were so many of them, similar in size to the force Father traveled with, and maybe more.

"How are you so calm?"

I wasn't. I wanted to scream and cry, but I couldn't let the emotions out. One break in my facade and everything would tumble out. Control of myself was all I had left to take my empire back. "Because I have to be."

THE SUN BEGAN TO SET, and the door opened. An elf from Rainier's army, and that's what they were now in numbers —his army, entered. He sat a tray of food, more food than two people needed, on the small table in my sitting area.

He turned to me, and I conjured the iciest glare I could summon. He flinched ever so slightly, but it was enough to give me some satisfaction.

The guard inched back. "Your presence is requested for dining elsewhere."

"You will address her as queen regent or Your Majesty." Val stood at my side, her voice as cold as my stare.

The guard wasn't stupid. He cleared his throat. "Your presence is requested for dining elsewhere, Your Majesty."

The audacity to think I would dine with him. Rainier had balls. I'd give him that. I sat down on the couch. "I decline that invitation."

The soldier bowed and turned on his heels to leave. He paused, his hand on the door. "Have you been beyond the borders of the empire?"

"I've been to other kingdoms."

"But outside your father's reach?"

It was information, but I didn't see what he could do with it. "No, I have not."

He nodded and shut the door.

Why would he ask that or even care? I studied Val, obviously hungry the way she was looking at the food, but she poked at it like it was poisoned. She might not be off in her skepticism. I wouldn't put anything past Rainier at this point.

"Have you been past the borders of our empire?" I asked, pushing the plate in front of me away.

Val scrunched up her nose. "No. Why would I want to? We have everything here."

"Why do you think he asked that?"

"Probably just a nosy ass," she said.

I nodded. *But why that question?*

Heavy footsteps carried through from the hall. The door flung open, banging against the wall. Rainier entered, and he looked pissed. *Fuck him.*

He glanced at Val, the untouched food, and his hard gaze settled on me. I tilted my chin up and crossed my arms over my chest. His eyes softened, and he let out a breath. "You need to eat." His gaze flicked to Val and back to me. "Both of you."

"I'm not hungry," I said. Val's stomach growled behind me, and I sent a silent command to mine to not answer.

"Then come walk with me." He held out his arm.

I'd rather go fling myself off the highest turret, but that wouldn't help Val. My training took over, and I stood, straightening my spine to my full height. Even though I was tall, I had to look up at Rainier's face. I slipped my arm through his elbow and ignored the warm jolt between us.

He relaxed. "The food is safe to eat. It is the same meal for us all. You have my word," he said to Val. I hoped Val would eat something, but I wouldn't fault her if she didn't. No, that blame went to Rainier.

Val, for her part, narrowed her eyes at him.

"If you hurt..."

He held up a hand. "I would never hurt the queen regent."

But he already had, and I shoved the rush of emotion the acknowledgment evoked deep down, locking it away.

Rainier led us through the castle to my garden in silence. I'd known before we got to the gate. The path was one I'd taken so many times—on my own, with Marius, as an escape. Instead of straight through the palace, he guided me along the alternate way that skirted the perimeter, still inside the stone walls. He'd been through this path enough it was familiar to him. The closer we got, the slower my steps came as if I moved through thick mud. I wondered, not for the first time, how Gemma had navigated the river of quicksand said to mar the space between the empires on the opposite side of the forest I'd never seen. Never been that deep into the Forgotten Forest before Marius would yank me back. The stories told how the quicksand formed from a river of blood during the war that split the empire in two. As children, we were told the quicksand would swallow us whole, body and soul. I'd never once believed that Gemma had died like that, and thanks to Father's journals, I knew she hadn't.

Rainier paused in front of the gate. My safe haven would be tainted by this visit. But this garden, my garden, held the largest concentration of moonflowers, and that was useful. Rainier looked at me expectantly. I twisted my hand in front of me, and the blood magic on the lock gave. The gate hadn't been secured in years, but once I became queen regent, Marius insisted on the garden being locked. Once I engaged the lock, the gate swung open as it would only do so at my will.

A smile, not evil but it didn't reach his eyes either, crept up Rainier's face. He led me into my garden. I tried not to recoil, but I wanted to grab all the moonflowers in reach and shove them down his throat. The flowers weren't blooming yet and wouldn't for hours, but every part of the flower could be poisonous if enough was consumed.

Rainier stopped and faced me with a sympathetic gaze. His expression was softer than with his men. "I know you are angry with me."

I snorted and looked out over the garden. Angry didn't begin to cover the rage I dreamed of inflicting on him.

He hooked his fingers around my chin and urged me to look back. When I did turn, I let all the fury inside heat my eyes like fairy fire. I would not cower before him.

"Ari," he said, his voice gentle as if he tried to caress me with it. Not compulsion magic. He apparently wasn't stupid enough to try that. Again. Here.

"You've lost that right. I'm Prin..." I stumbled over my

own title. "I'm Queen Regent Arianna. You may address me as such."

"If I were to offer you your freedom, what would I call you then?"

I scoffed. "At what cost? What of my people? What of my kingdom? And why would I trust you?"

"You're right to question, and it is right to ask for answers." He ran his fingers along a rose. Harmless flower, save the thorns of its defenses. I was more like the rose than the moonflower, but that would change from today. "Marry me, Ari. We can unite our empires into one again. Unite our people again under one rule."

His eyes met mine, and my magic crackled around me with my defiance. I considered letting it go in all its glorious chaos, but my fear of hurting someone innocent stopped me. Rain was delusional at best and insane at worst. I didn't deign to respond to his statement with an answer.

"We can do this together."

"The dark of our kind, those from across the Forgotten Forest, would let you rule them?"

Glamour shimmered and his features, still his, refined to a look chiseled out of stone. Somehow, he was more handsome, but he also looked harder, colder, than he had before. He hadn't aligned with our enemy. He was the enemy. Nausea curdled in my empty stomach.

"No," I said. "I reject your proposal."

"Even to save your father's life."

I went still, my breath hanging in my chest.

"What about to save your sister's?" He studied me,

and a chuckle rumbled in his chest. I despised everything about him. His shoulders relaxed. "She is safe."

"But what about your people? They would never accept the queen of a rival kingdom as their own."

My arguments were a delay tactic. I knew it. He knew it. The refusal was a dance in the game I was forced into by his actions. Yes, moonflower would be a wonderfully brutal death for him. I would stand over his body as he hallucinated, watching as the poison took over and evolved into the stage of seizures before he died. He had no idea what I had in store for him. Regardless of whether I got the kingdom back, he wouldn't be ruling anything except a dishonorable death.

"I'd like to return to my room now." I leaned against the flowerbed. Slipping my hand behind me, I grasped a handful of the plant and concealed my prize in the pockets of my skirt.

He raised a hand to touch my face. My body betrayed me and craved the connection, but if there was one thing a lady of the court understood how to do, it was to school her features into neutral. And that was what I did—forced my face into the silent protest of a lady and stepped out of his reach. His hand dropped to his side. Pain flashed across his face, and that almost made me reach for him.

He'd asked for my forgiveness once, and I understood exactly why now. And I would never give it to him.

CHAPTER 25
ARI

Several days passed. I tried to reach Marius multiple times a day through our bond with no response, which meant one of three things. They never made it to the Erebian mountains. They made it, and he hadn't been able to return close enough to be in range. Or something blocked the ability. The first and last weren't options I would entertain. I believed in the middle that he hadn't been able to get close enough to reach me.

A sad routine had settled into the days. Val and I remained locked in my room with our meals delivered. Each evening, Rainier would show up without additional guards to take me to my garden, and every time we were there, I'd grab more moonflowers while rejecting his proposal of marriage. I didn't tell Val about the proposals, but she saw the moonflower I stashed in a box on my vanity table. Tonight, I'd worn a dress with pockets deep enough I'd be able to carry more.

When Rainier knocked and opened the door, I was on my feet and ready for our stroll. Not to spend time with him, of course, but to gather more moonflowers. After tonight's trip, I would have enough to make the poison strong enough to kill him. Behind Rainier, the two enemy guards at the door eyed me with clear disdain. I returned the sentiment to them.

"My garden awaits," I said, slipping my arm around Rainier's elbow. But as I stepped into the corridor, I found more guards waiting. I studied their fine light blue and silver garments. These were royal guards from the dark kingdom. I glanced at Rainier.

He only smiled. "I thought we would do something different today."

And I guessed it was nowhere near moonflowers.

I nodded and moved forward as he led us through the castle and out of one of the side gates. My heart pounded in my chest, and I willed it to slow. This was it. He was bringing me here to execute me.

"Are you chilled?" He slipped his jacket off and placed it around my shoulders, mistaking the reason for my trembling body as cold night air. His mint scent all over it, I inhaled against my better judgment. I blinked away the memory of the night in the kitchen...with the chocolate cake.

We reached a clearing, and there was a blanket spread along the ground with food. This was a glen I knew well. I'd often snuck out here on my own to look at the moon and stars, especially after my mother died and when

Gemma left. It was a refuge for me in my darkest times, and here was where he'd chosen to set up this...this intimate meeting. I wanted to kick the food across the field, especially the chocolate cake propped up on a stand. My body reacted the opposite of my mind, heating and tightening at the sight.

The guards spread out in directions along the perimeter leaving us alone. They were not missed.

"What is this, Rainier?" I gestured out over the intimate display he'd set up.

"An apology," he softly said. He reached for me, his fingers barely touching mine as he led me closer to the blanket. "I'm sorry everything went down the way it did. That I couldn't warn you."

I narrowed my eyes at him. What game was he playing? He could just force me to marry him, so why try to have the appearance of amends? "If you hadn't done unforgivable things, there would be no need to apologize."

"Come. Sit." He dropped onto the blanket and tugged on my hand.

My body desperately wanted to be near him, but my heart and head urged me to turn and run. I knew the landscape better, but there were more of them and no guarantee of safety for Val or anyone else if I escaped. I lowered myself down next to him.

"You made yourself my enemy and an enemy of this empire, so why try to court me now? Why go to all this trouble? Why do any of this at all?" My frustration rolled out in my tone, but I brought it back in and buried it.

"As I said, I wanted to show you I was sorry for how I had to mislead you." His tone was sincere—believable—but I didn't trust him.

Oh, he misled me alright. I had started to fall for him, and worse than that, I still cared about him while simultaneously hating him. My body still wanted him, but I'd never let him touch me in that way again.

"I didn't know I would have feelings for you, Arianna." He met my gaze. The sincerity in his expression surprised me. "It wasn't my plan."

"Clearly." I huffed.

He stretched out on the blanket and gazed up at the night sky. I leaned back, supporting my weight on my hands. The stars twinkled so much like the crown I'd only worn a short time. I blinked the dampness in my eyes away. There would be time for that later...after I killed Rainier.

"I want to take you to the other side of the forest," he said.

I keyed in on that piece of information. Gemma was there and my father, presumably, was still there. "My sister and father." I swallowed against the knot lodged in my throat. "Are you sure they are okay?"

"They are," he said. "But we're running out of time."

"For what?"

"For you to marry me and unite the power of the empires."

I stiffened. "You have the seat of my kingdom. Why do you need me?"

"Because both our people will be lost if you don't." There was no pretense in how he said it. Just facts.

Even though he had concealed and lied, I could sense that was the most honest thing he'd probably said up to this point. The people of my father's empire were proud and loyal. They had prospered under the rule of my family. No one starved like in the stories from before the war.

"Marrying me is the only way to ensure the survival of your family and prevent bloodshed on your land. More importantly, it's the only way our people survive."

I looked back to the stars. *Goddesses and gods, I can't believe I'm considering this.* "What assurance do I have my family will not be harmed?"

"My word," he said in a hopeful tone.

I snorted and didn't look back at him. "That is worth nothing. I'm going to need more than something you toss around so trivially."

Arianna? Marius's voice whispered into my mind like an easy breeze on a summer day. I bit down on my lips and closed my eyes for the briefest second.

Marius? Are you and Drew safe?

Yes, but we can't get back to you. There are too many of them.

So, it wasn't enough to take the castle and the seat of the empire. Rainier and his dark army had instigated a full-on invasion as I suspected. There wasn't a way to fight back without loss of life, but with the unicorns on our side, that might give us a chance. I noticed the lack of unicorns for his army. Surely that was a sign from the goddesses and gods.

Your father has been captured on the other side along with the officers. The unicorns have retreated to determine if we will intervene.

Marius, you are the leader. A king in your own right. Please tell me you're not abandoning me and my father. My family.

Never, but we will avoid bloodshed where possible.

My mind quieted, and I knew Marius was gone. I'd never felt more alone in my entire life, and I hadn't thought that was possible from the time after I lost my mother.

Goddesses and gods, help me. Is this my only choice? No, there are the moonflowers.

If I used the poison on Rainier, then his men might kill my family. If I used it on myself, there would be no reason to keep them alive. I rubbed my hands over my eyes.

"Arianna?"

I realized Rainier had been talking, but I had no reference to what he had said.

"What were you saying?"

"I'd hoped to give you more space to adjust to the idea, but there is no time left for consideration or acclimation," he said. "The enemy has infiltrated deeper into the forest and is on your borders and ours."

"And a united army is the only chance at defeating these bloodthirsty creatures?" I asked quietly, already feeling the truth of the words along with the curses I wanted to spew at him.

"I'll ask you one last time." He met my gaze, and there was a fire lit deep in the dark blue. "Marry me, Arianna."

What choice did I really have? I'd always thought if I ever did marry it would be for love, like my parents had, but I should have known from the tragedy around me that was never meant to be. My fate was to be married to my enemy.

"For my kingdom, for my people, and for my family, my answer is yes."

ARI

I gathered the things that would travel with me through the Forgotten Forest. So many times, I'd wondered what it would be like to enter only to be stopped by Marius. The stories in our kingdom said that no one who ventured into the dark woods returned, and maybe this was how I would die. There was a path though. Elves from a different kingdom had made it here and Gemma and Father there. The stories could have been in place to protect us, but I'd heard the howls from the forest too. They were not fae or unicorn. I placed my crown in the box Father had used to present it to me. It was a somber moment, but the crown would be on my head again.

"You cannot do this, Ari." Val paced the entire length of my room. "There has to be another way."

"There's not." Goddesses and gods, I wish there was. "The unicorns are scattered, and it would take a blood-bath to get them here for support." Marius had connected with me in the early morning hours and told me there were simply too many of the enemy. He promised to keep Drew hidden and safe until I found a way to get a message to him. I didn't intend to tell him of my plans. Once I crossed the Forgotten Forest, there would be too much physical separation for our bond to span the distance. Once I got free, I'd travel far enough to reach Marius.

"Then I'm going with you." I turned from the window to face her. Val had her hands on her hips. She looked so determined, but her life was here with Theo when he returned.

"You're safer here. You should stay." I knew no one in the court of the other empire, except my sister I hadn't seen in years. She might not even want to see me.

Val packed one of my favorite dresses in tissue. "I probably won't get to wear any of those. He's likely going to lock me in my quarters there too."

"I don't think so, Ari." Val shook her head.

I didn't believe it either. He was going to parade me around like a prize, and I had to obey so both kingdoms wouldn't be lost. I'd make sure every moment I was with him was his own personal hell. I handed her the hair comb Gemma had given me to add to the items in the trunk.

Val leaned the painting Rain had given me against the trunk.

"I'm not taking that. We should burn it."

"No, I think you should keep it. If you want to burn it, do so on his lands."

I sighed. I didn't want to light it on fire. The painting was lovely, but I'd never look at it without thinking of him.

Val was right in that it belonged on his lands. When I escaped him, that would be all he'd get to keep of me.

There was a knock at the door. I waved Val off and opened it myself.

The man there was an enemy to be sure, but his features were striking. He was one of the most handsome of their kind I had seen. Not that I'd been looking, but he was the first one who held a candle to Rain's exquisite face. The elf bowed before me. Why bother bowing before a kingdomless queen? I nodded to him.

"The prince has asked if there are any texts from the office or jewels you would like to take with you for the journey. I'm to help you gather and pack them." He smiled, and it was blindingly bright as if the sun lit him from within.

My mind was saying no, but my gut was saying yes. "There are a few meaningful things I would like to take with me."

He held out his arm. I hesitated. Rainier had told others not to touch me, but this elf was different from most of the guards in the way he acted and the way Rainier treated him.

"Can Val join us as well?" Her mouth gaped open as I looked over my shoulder at her. She'd noticed him too.

"Of course," he said, his arm still extended for me. I slipped my hand through, hooking my elbow around his. Val nearly tripped over her own feet as she trailed behind us.

"My father's study is the first place I'd like to gather some things."

"Rain thought that might be the case. There's a trunk waiting for us there." His voice was so gentle, almost soothing. I enjoyed the deep melody of it.

He must be close to Rainier if he called him Rain. "What is your name?"

"Laurel." He studied me as if he expected me to introduce myself. His eyes glittered like... like the starlight...like my crown. They turned hazel, not the greenish-hazel my sister had, but more amber. It happened so quickly I thought I imagined the ethereal glow. The color complimented his dark blond hair.

"I'm Ari," I said, giving him my nickname. First rule of court is that you build familiarity to make others comfortable confiding in you, and I was aware that his friendly demeanor could be a similar facade to disarm me.

He smiled again as we entered Father's office, the same place I'd gotten drunk to erase the image of unicorns fucking. Although that was more than a week ago, it felt like a century had passed. I ran my fingers over Father's journals.

"Do you want to take these?" Val asked, looking at the stack of about a dozen.

"Yes, and this one." I pulled out the leather-bound book I'd shoved under a few papers last week and handed it to her. She added them to the trunk.

Laurel watched my every move with keen eyes. "Why have you not tried to use your magic?"

Val and I both straightened and looked at each other before my gaze traveled to his. *Does he not know the answer?*

"Are you teasing me?" I asked, forcing a smile.

He pushed off the wall and came to stand in front of me. "I would never tease about magic." Amusement danced across his face. "Such a serious subject."

He was half teasing then. Rather than tell him how chaotic my magic was, I told the other side of the truth. "There are too many lives at risk."

"But you could save yourself."

He tested me, but I wasn't sure what he was assessing. "My life alone is not worth that of all the people in my empire. Not worth the lives of my family in exchange." And that was the truth. I'd rather sacrifice myself for them than live knowing they were the price.

"Your power could surely wipe our army out though." His voice was lower and warm.

Did he know? Was this an attempt to get me to say it aloud? "I do not seek death for anyone. Even my enemy."

"You will." He winked at me. "When you see the real enemy."

There was no malice in his tone, but his eyes were distant like that of someone in grief. The twinkle left his gaze. Grief. I knew it well.

"You've lost someone to this enemy," I said softly.

He inhaled and turned away. "Like so many others, I have lost several."

I don't know what came over me, but I wanted to comfort him and touched his arm. His skin was warm. "I'm sorry, Laurel."

He patted my hand. "Perhaps when you are settled in your new home, we can share our losses over a drink."

"Perhaps." I eyed the decanter of amber liquid I'd left

on the desk. No one had moved it, but someone had been in here without me. Rainier. It had to have been him. I just knew without knowing how. "That's all I need from this room. There are no jewels I wish to take other than my personal mementos. I've never been much of a jewelry person."

Laurel cast an approving glance. "Very well." He extended an arm out to me, and I took it without hesitation.

PART TWO
COURT OF STORMS

The End of the Great War
From the diary of King Veran's court secretary archived at the
War Museum.

King Veran paced the expanse of the sitting area. "There has to be another way. Daphina must come home."

"I'm sorry, Your Majesty," the nobleman said. "When she leaves, the field of glamour begins to breakdown. Perhaps if we located others in the general's bloodline with the same type of magic, we could rotate them."

The king slammed his hand on the cart of liquor and knocked all the crystal airborne. The tinkle of broken glass followed by the pungent smell of the mixed alcohol tainted the air. "There are no others. Her magic is goddess-given and only to her heirs will it pass."

"I'm sorry, my king." The nobleman bowed. "Is there anything else I can do?"

"Send for the bloodline specialist. I want to speak with him."

The king had yet to take a wife in hopes of Daphina's return, but the council had paraded an endless number of women in front of him—some were strong bloodlines and others were incredible magic wielders. None of them were his beautiful and brave Daphina, though, and she was the only one he wanted.

One visited more often than others. Her interest in him was purely for status and power, and he wouldn't be expected to share a bed often with her or shower her with the attention he reserved for Daphina. If he were forced to marry before he found a way to bring Daphina home, then the status-seeker would be the one he chose. He would never love her. That part of him was for Daphina alone.

CHAPTER 27

ARI

My things, the ones most important to me, were packed for the trip to the other empire. I brought my crown, not sure any longer that it would ever sit on my head again, but the metal and diamonds were the last thing my father had given me. The crown represented the night sky I loved. I tucked other mementos safely in the trunks as well, like a tattered doll of Gemma's that I'd refused to let anyone throw away when she left and the smaller portrait of my mother that hung in Father's office. The box with the moonflower plants I'd stashed was buried deep in the trunk with my training leathers. Val piled pretty dresses on top to hide both.

A knock sounded at the door. Val and I met each other's gaze. The fear in her eyes matched the sickening twist in the pit of my stomach. She crossed the room and opened the door.

"Laurel," she said.

"Val." He inclined his head toward her.

His pale green eyes landed on mine. He bowed toward me. "Are you ready, my queen?"

"I'm not your queen, Laurel." He was easier to be around, but I wondered why Rain wasn't here and what treachery he was doing to my kingdom...my people.

"You are the queen," he said. "Better to embrace it and carry yourself as such than let anyone have doubts."

He made it sound like advice from a friend, and maybe he could be. I pushed the thought away. I would have no friends in the Court of Storms and Trickery. I sighed and turned to Val, wrapping my arms around her like a lifeline.

"I can come with you, Ari," she whispered. "Let me come with you."

"No," I said, my voice firmer than the breaking in my heart.

"She is welcome—"

"No," I said again. "She will stay."

I wasn't sure where she would be safer, but anywhere seemed safer than the enemy empire. I blinked back my tears and lowered my voice to an almost nonexistent level. "Find Drew and Marius. Stick with them."

She pulled back and gave me one small nod to confirm she understood.

"I'm ready."

Laurel opened the door and motioned for a couple of guards to come in and gather my last trunk. He held out his arm for me, but his demeanor was different. An awkward moment passed. I glanced at his arm but walked out without taking it. He placed featherlight fingers on my elbow and steered me down the hall ahead of them to my fate.

Coaches awaited in the courtyard, and Laurel opened the door to the one with the royal crest on it.

I raised an eyebrow. "That may get a little awkward."

He held out his hand, and I accepted it as I stepped into the carriage. He seated himself across from me.

I wanted to ask where Rainier was, but I didn't want to see him either.

"I'm riding with you."

"Clearly."

"Rainier will meet us later."

I nodded. He couldn't even be bothered to ride with me as his future wife. If I was lucky, maybe there would be a deep ravine I could throw myself into along the way. I didn't mean it. I wouldn't end myself if it meant my people would suffer, but the thought of living the rest of my life with the enemy was nothing short of hell.

The forest wasn't more than a hundred yards past the outer wall, the tallest wall in our kingdom that ran along the entire length of the border with the forest. I'd ventured on the edges many times, but Marius had stopped me each attempt. The first few efforts were out of curiosity, but the later ones were my tries to find Gemma. Marius never chastised me or told me I shouldn't be there, only that it would be safer on the other side of the wall as these lands belonged to no empire.

"What are you thinking?" Laurel's smooth voice jarred me from my memories.

"Just remembering," I said.

He nodded, looking lost in his own thoughts. "The forest does that."

"Is my father safe? My sister?"

His face went neutral. "Yes, they are both unharmed."

"Will I see them when I arrive?" What a reunion to have my sister and my father together.

"That will be a question for Rain."

"Where is he?"

"Taking care of our arrival." He stared out the window.

My questions seemed to make him uncomfortable, and for some reason, I wanted to keep going. "Do you have family there?"

"Some." His answers weren't as warm as yesterday. He'd seemed genuine then, and I wondered if it had been an act. His demeanor seemed awkward compared to our other encounters. "Were you and your sister close?"

I wasn't prepared for that question and stared at him for a moment. The memories flooded back from happier times. "Gemma..." My voice came out soft. I cleared my throat and tried again. "Yes, Gemma and I were very close until our stepmother died."

"Why did it change then?"

"She took on the role of mothering Andrews, and that was a full-time job," I said, remembering how exhausted she was at times. "I tried to help, but she refused. She said it was good training for the patience it takes to rule a kingdom."

"I lost my parents during the war, and my sister raised me," he said, confirming my thought he was older than I'd initially thought. Laurel and I slipped into silence for a moment.

"Will it take long to reach the other side of the forest?"

"By coach?" He chewed on the words. "A couple of hours."

I supposed he was a soldier used to traveling on foot.

"Are you not bonded to a unicorn?" I asked, realizing I'd only seen horses for some of the officers. It was their horses that pulled the carriages and not the ones from our stables.

His eyes widened a little and then went back to neutral. "We do not encourage the bond and not many have it."

Once in our lands, the unicorns chose more citizens, but the war had reduced their numbers as it had ours. The unicorns became more selective and only agreed to bond when it was strong. Marius had prepared me that Drew might not be bonded, but then Leana connected to him. I wished she'd bonded him already so that his protection would be secured.

We rode in silence for what seemed like a long time when Laurel reached out of the carriage window and tapped on the side. The carriage slowed and came to a stop.

"We'll wait here, on the edge, for Rainier."

I nodded, dread filling my gut, bile churning there. My new miserable life awaited.

"If you want to stretch your legs, I can walk with you."

"In the forest?" A stroll through these lands had been

forbidden to me my whole life, and the opportunity might not come again.

Amusement flitted across his face. "I assure you it is safe." His hand rested over his heart. "I swear to you on my life."

Why does he seem so kind and trustworthy when I know damn well I shouldn't? What the hell is wrong with me?

As if he knew I would cave, he slid over and opened the door, making his way out. He held out his hand, and I took it. *Ari...* Gemma's voice was a whisper on the wind. I jerked my head around.

"Are you okay?" he asked.

"I thought I heard my name, but it was just the wind."

His smile faded. "It's not the wind. It's the ghosts in the forest. Many who died on these grounds are trapped here."

My brows scrunched together as I processed what he said. "I've never heard that before. You're making up stories like I'm a gullible child."

His eyes cooled and his mouth turned down. "I'm not. While it is possible to shield your mind from them, they are here. Thousands of people died on these lands and were never allowed to move on."

My stomach roiled. He wasn't teasing me. He was serious. Gemma's voice couldn't be her trapped spirit. I wouldn't accept that outcome. "What trapped them here?"

"The magic used to end the war."

"Magic didn't end the war. It was a treaty between the empires."

He smirked, raising a single brow. "Was it? Were you there?"

"Were you?"

"Yes," he replied, his head cocking to the side. "Your husband approaches."

"He's not my husband," I said. Hopefully, I'd find myself clever enough to devise a way to save everyone and stab Rainier in the heart for breaking mine. My foolish, foolish heart. My trepidation at marriage played a part in my situation, too, because if I had married anyone, even the old-ass duke, I wouldn't be standing in a forest full of spirits.

Ari... Gemma's voice floated on the air around me. *Ari...*

"Oh, shut the fuck up."

Both of Laurel's brows shot up then, and he glanced over his shoulder.

"Is that any way to speak to your betrothed?" Rainier said, humor lacing his words. His velvety tone slid over me like a caress, and I wished for my body to have any reaction other than the tightening in my belly.

Heat burned my cheeks. "I wasn't ..." I looked to Laurel for help, but he backed away with his hands up. "Never mind. Can we just go?"

Rainier stopped in front of me. A hint of amusement danced in his eyes. "Ready to go so soon?"

Ari... A shiver ran down my spine. "Yes." I turned for the carriage.

Rainier grabbed my hand and pulled me back. I stumbled against his chest. I looked up into his dark blue eyes and a connection sizzled between us. His lips hovered close to mine. "You're going to ride with me." His voice deepened. "The carriage will return."

He tucked loose hair behind my ear, and his fingers lingered there, brushing along the skin of my neck and under my chin. My eyes fluttered in anticipation of our lips meeting, but I placed my hands on his chest and pushed back.

"Where is your carriage?" I stalked toward the way he'd come.

"We're not going by carriage. Have you never traveled by vanyshen?"

"What is that?" I'd never heard of anything called vanyshen.

"Hold on." A mischievous grin built on his face.

The world spun around us, and his grip tightened around my back, crushing me against his chest. I locked my arms behind his neck as the ground fell away from us. My hair whipped against my cheeks, but my terror slid away when the colors, all of them, danced in front of me. A veil of grey blanketed us, and the colors twinkled above like a night sky only in shades of blue, green, yellow, pink, red, orange, violet, and more. It was the most beautiful thing I'd ever seen.

I caught glimpses of the forest, but they were gone in moments, replaced by strange images I didn't recognize in a foreign city. I buried my head against his chest as I looked down at the bustling streets. Then a courtyard came into view with white rock and marble walking stones, and Rainier managed a soft landing despite my trembling body. The ride had been exhilarating, and if I'd been with anyone other than the enemy, I would have asked to do it again.

He held me close as if he knew exactly how weak my legs were from that trip. "How do you feel?" His voice was soft, full of concern.

I backed out of his arms, determined to put distance between us. "Where are we?"

He waved guards off from a door, and I managed a glance up at the massive façade before he ushered me inside. We were surrounded by guards in blue and silver uniforms, and I couldn't see much of the hallway other than the pristine marble floors, delicate sconces, and occasional light from a window. After a long walk, the guards parted, and a door was in front of us. Rainier opened it and held out his arm.

The room was larger than mine at the castle, and the colors of the space were masculine from a light dove grey for the curtains to a large, dark midnight-colored couch that could seat about ten people. Coordinated throw pillows in a range of harmonizing colors were arranged around it. There were matching upholstered chairs. A massive coffee table sat in the middle of the sitting area with a crescent-shaped moon carved in the center. My gaze drifted to an enormous fireplace, but the size wasn't the most impressive part. The material twinkled as if made of pure starlight. I moved towards the hearth and ran my fingers across it, the surface smooth but cool to the touch. Stones glinted as if they were winking at me.

"My family harvested the ore from our sacred mountain. Only those who can commune with the stone can fabricate the material."

"Your family?" I continued to study the fireplace.

"I do have parents and a sibling."

I shook the awe from my head. "I meant here." But the truth of what he was saying hit me. "Of course, you're not from Agonburg."

"I will explain it to you. I promise."

He held back information from me again. The rage in me erupted, and it screamed at me to come out. I didn't have it in me to hold it inside any longer. *What is the point? So, I'll let it go.* "Fuck. You. Rainier. And your explanations. And your promises. And your sweet words that were lies. And your family. Fuck your invasion of my garden and my kingdom." He moved closer to me, and I backed away. "Fuck you for ruining chocolate cake for me. And fuck wherever this is."

I didn't move when he came closer, partially because my back was against the fireplace and partially because I didn't know where to go. My magic had wound its way from its usual hiding place and was ready to dance. I narrowed my eyes at him daring him to come closer.

He speared my hair with his fingers and claimed my lips with a kiss. His mouth devoured my gasp and swallowed it whole. My core tightened, and I cursed my wretched, traitorous body as I relaxed into his touch. When he pulled back, I couldn't form a thought much less utter a word. He stared into my eyes. A wicked grin crept up on his face. "We'll have to rectify that chocolate cake memory. It would be a shame to ruin something so tasty."

His gaze dropped to my lips and then my throat as I swallowed. I slammed my hands into his chest, summoning wind, and blew him back where I was out of his reach. "If you didn't understand my message before, let me clearly articulate it. Fuck you."

But that kiss had been everything, and it couldn't happen again.

CHAPTER 28

RAIN

There was so much to tell Ari, but I was concerned about overwhelming her. Her world was still living as if nothing changed after the war, but life had moved on everywhere except for the empire she inherited. She was far from weak, but her kingdom didn't even have words for some of the things in my world. Besides, Gemma had agreed when I suggested we ease Ari into all that she would see here.

"Why don't we start with something you have wanted for years—seeing your sister?"

Her eyes widened. "You'll let me see Gemma?"

"Of course," I said. "You are a queen, not a prisoner, Arianna."

"It certainly feels like the latter." Her voice was hard. She was stronger in spirit than anyone I'd known, even Laurel, but everything she'd known was a lie. That kind of news would break lesser people. I didn't think it would break her, but it was going to hurt her. My chest constricted at the thought of anything hurting her when all I wanted to do was protect Ari.

"Have a seat. Gemma should be here any moment."

She opened her mouth and closed it again. A reunion with her sister wouldn't lessen the blow of catching her up on what she'd missed being isolated. I had to deliver or explain things that were no doubt strange to her here. I'd planned to do it at a slower pace, but we were out of time with the real enemy at our door. She and Gemma could have today, and tomorrow she would be introduced to my advisors and maybe to the city if she wasn't overburdened with what she learned within the palace walls.

"Why did you bring me here..." her voice trailed off in confusion. "I don't even know your real name."

"It is Rainier," I said. "That wasn't a lie, and my friends do call me Rain."

"So, one truth in a mountain of lies is supposed to make me trust you?" She quirked up an eyebrow.

I smiled, knowing it would probably piss her off, but I liked how she challenged me...hell, everything. She made me want to grin like an idiot all the time, especially when it wasn't appropriate. "No, I hope the trust comes with time as you see more and more truth."

A knock sounded. Gemma didn't usually knock on any doors here, so she must be as nervous as Arianna. Or my brother was with her.

The door opened, and Laurel walked into the room. My heart deflated, but then there she was. Gemma. A missing piece of my world stood in front of me. My eyes burned as I took in her striking red hair. It was no longer to her waist but cut up to her shoulders and smooth as silk versus the wavy girls' style of our youth. Her face though. Her face was all her--green eyes filled with tears. She moved toward me, and I flung myself at her.

"You're real." I patted over her arms and face because I couldn't believe she was standing in front of me. The fineness of her soft sweater was accented by a light gold thread woven through it, and she was wearing black pants. I'd never seen her in pants other than when in training.

Her fingers swiped at the dampness on my face I hadn't even realized was there. "I'm here and so happy to see you."

I hugged her close again. "All this time. I never thought I'd see you again."

She pulled back. "Maybe you two could give us some time." She stared at Rainier and Laurel with a fierceness I didn't remember seeing before. "Alone."

Laurel turned for the door as if he wouldn't question Gemma. Rainier only nodded once, and Gemma returned it with an inclined head. They left us alone in Rainier's room.

The only word I could get out as we sat on the couch was "How?"

"There is so much to tell you," Gemma said, her tone calm and understanding.

"I want to know everything." There were so many questions I wanted to ask. "How did you get here, and where is Cyrus?"

"Cyrus is in the kingdom." The way her tone lowered, I wondered if he was a prisoner, but she smiled. I didn't miss how small it was or the sadness in her eyes. "We'll get to unicorns later."

"Why did you leave us?" I braced myself for an answer I wasn't sure I wanted to hear. She could have left because staying after Mother's death was hard on her. She parented me in our mother's place and then Drew when his mother died as well.

Gemma took my hands in hers. "I uncovered how things had been hidden from us and the citizens of the empire, and I couldn't unsee what I learned."

"Like what, Gemma?"

"Our mother was from here."

The air rushed out of my lungs, and I struggled to regain my breath. "How can that be?"

"She was born here. Raised here. Our parents' marriage was arranged as part of a...treaty."

"Our mother was dark fae? Why would Father not tell us any of this?" My sister must have been brainwashed to believe such a tale.

Gemma shook her head. "Maybe our age when she died. I think it was Mother's choice to conceal it from us, but I can assure you we are as much a part of this kingdom as we were the one where we were born."

Dark fae. From this kingdom. We were part of the dark elves. I looked at my hands as if they would answer all the questions circling in my head. No. It wasn't true. I looked back at Gemma. She gave me an empathetic look.

"I know what you're thinking, Ari," she said, her voice so soft and sincere. "We've processed things so similarly our entire lives. You don't want to believe it, but the quicker you accept it, the sooner you will be able to meet our mother's family."

I'd never met my grandparents on either of my parents' sides. Gemma and I were told they left this world before we were born. Disbelief and shock rattled me. I almost couldn't speak. "Her family?"

"Yes, and there is someone I want to introduce you to right now if you are up to it." Her smile beamed with love.

I nodded, wondering if she meant one of our long-lost relatives. "Yes, I'd like to meet anyone important to you."

She stood and waited for me. When we were in the hall, Gemma slipped her arm through mine. We strolled forward as if we were strolling through the corridors of our home in the Court of Love and Prosper. Gemma was relaxed and at ease as if this was indeed her home.

We covered quite a distance to a separate wing when she stopped in front of a door. "She can be a little shy, so give her some time."

She opened the door. A little red-haired version of her came running toward the entrance. "Mommy!"

"Hi, sweetie." Gemma scooped the little girl up in her arms and kissed her cheek. "I want you to meet someone. Is that okay?"

The little girl looked at me and back to Gemma and nodded her head enthusiastically. My sister's daughter. I'd missed years with them both. My eyes burned at the sweet face of the beautiful child.

"Daphina, this is your aunt, Ari. Can you say hi?"

Named after our mother. The girl dove at me. I reached out for her. Daphina wrapped her arms around my neck. "I knew you would come, Aunt Ari."

Knew I would come? I glanced at Gemma, and she just smiled. My niece was gifted.

"I'm so glad to meet you," I said, as I hugged Daphina to me. She wasn't much younger than Drew, but she was a lot smaller. Yet, Daphina seemed much more advanced than my little brother.

"Glad to meet you," she parroted back to me. "You're pretty."

"Thank you, so are you. You look a lot like your mommy."

She sighed. "Everyone says that, Ari. Mommy says I act like you."

I smiled and glanced at Gemma. "Does she now? I guess that means you are perfect."

"Yep," she said in her little voice. "Can I go play now?"

"Of course," I said, setting her down. She ran down the hall of their chamber and turned a corner. "She's amazing. How old is she?"

"Stop doing the math in your head. She's nearly four."

So, almost two years younger than our brother. Surely my sister wouldn't have married one of the enemy. "Her father?"

Laurel stepped out from the shadows. "That would be me."

The good-looking-nice-guy friend of Rainier's was the father of my niece. He was sleeping with my sister.

"Close your mouth, Ari." Gemma laughed. "I assume you have met my significant other."

"Ouch," Laurel said, grabbing his chest where his heart would be. "Does that mean you are mad at me for not sending word we got Arianna out of there?"

He slipped his arm around her waist in a casual gesture like he'd done it a thousand times.

Gemma focused on me. "Laurel is my mate."

It made sense. He'd seemed so familiar with me at the castle. He'd acted like he'd already known me. How had I not seen it before?

"Mate, not husband?" I glanced between them. The only time I'd heard that term used was between the goddesses and gods.

"Mate is a higher term than husband or wife," Laurel explained.

"While we do have those who marry as husband and wife, the mate connection and bonding ceremony is above all others. Only true mates can complete the joining. My bond with Cyrus changed when Laurel and I let our mental shields down and the blurred connection became clear." Gemma's voice was tinged with sadness. How long ago had it happened that she still grieved? Then I imagined my bond with Marius being severed, and I understood the sorrow. I wasn't sure it was something I would recover from.

"How?"

"I'll let you two catch up while I make sure Phina isn't using magic on something she shouldn't." Laurel moved down the hall.

"Come and sit?" She motioned for me to join her in another room. We walked forward into a light-filled family room. There were toys in the corner, some I recognized and others I didn't. There was a fireplace, not as large as the one in Rainier's room but still large, and above it was a shiny black picture. It looked out of place among the otherwise warm colors that were all Gemma.

I sat on the overstuffed couch with her. She was alive and had a family. My amazing sister was living this strange life, and my heart swelled with pride at her strength.

She patted my knee. "I've missed you so much, Ari."

I wrapped her up in another hug. "I just can't believe we are sitting here."

"There were so many times I wanted to come for you, but we were afraid of what Father's retaliation would be if we did. Then, the nosferatu came, and I knew there wasn't going to be another time we could. Plus, Father was trying to marry you off."

"Nosferatu. That's what the vampires are called?"

"Yes, and they are dangerous but not as big a threat here as they would have been." She let out a breath. "I told Rain he had to go stand in as a suitor, to court you, and get you out of there before the vampires attacked. You were no longer safe, and I couldn't be the one to get you..." She wiped away tears.

Her voice trailed away, but I knew she meant she couldn't come because she would be recognized. She sent him to court me. Everything was a lie, even the attraction I thought he had for me. It hadn't felt fake, but he must have done what he deemed necessary for me to leave. Could he be that good at pretending? No one could feign the kind of connection I thought was from him. Could they? Maybe that was part of his magic. Disappointment settled in my stomach and soured it. I wanted to talk about anything else. "Do you know where Father is?"

She nodded, her face grim. "He's sequestered in the north wing for now. We'll have to find a place to hold him, but I asked them not to move him until you were here and knew the truth."

The thought our Father was on house arrest in a foreign land because of me crushed me. "And you're okay with our father, the king, being held like this?"

Gemma sighed, and a gust of wind blew through the room.

"You have wind magic."

She smiled at that. "I do, and I am okay with him being held. I can't say more than that because Rainier has asked me not to."

Anger narrowed my vision. "He told my own sister not to explain. Unbelievable. Why would you concede to him?"

"He didn't tell me anything. He requested I not, and I'm respecting that ask for now."

Small footsteps came down the hall closer and closer. Just Daphina's presence calmed me down. I couldn't help but smile at her.

"Mommy, can I watch TV now?"

"Later, sweetheart," Gemma said. "After Aunt Ari leaves. We're going to visit for a bit longer. Where is your daddy?"

"He's napping," she said, making a pouty face.

Another strange word but Daphina wanted to do it, and I wanted to make my little niece happy. "What's TV? Is it something we could do together?"

Daphina's face lit up. "Yes, have you seen the unicorn show?"

Unicorn...show? The only unicorn show I'd seen wasn't appropriate for a little one like my niece.

"Phina," Gemma said, sounding so much like our mother I was jarred from my confusion. "Later."

"Yes, Mommy." The pout on Phina's mouth was every

bit Gemma from when we were kids. My niece turned and stomped back down the hall.

"She is just like you when you were a child." I chuckled.

Gemma turned that look on me. "Please. You're younger than me. You don't remember me at that age."

"Oh, I remember the tantrums you would throw that frustrated the hell out of our mother."

"I did no such thing." She laughed. "You are the one who was so good at sneaking around like a Cu-Sith."

I shook my head and smiled. "What's a TV and a unicorn show?"

Gemma's mouth opened, but there was a knock at the door.

CHAPTER 30

ARI

Rainier stood in the open doorway looking relaxed. He'd rescued his friend's wife's sister. He'd done his duty, so why was he even here? *Asshole.* And why was I mad? I didn't even like him.

"Perfect timing as always," Gemma said, sounding as annoyed to see him as I was. "What did you have my husband do that has him taking a nap in the middle of the day?"

Rainier's gaze flicked to me and back to Gemma. Shadows seemed to veil him and then disappear. "All he had to do today was ride with your sister, so maybe ask her."

I narrowed my eyes at him, wishing I could summon my magic to push him into the hall and slam the door in his face. "We just rode in the carriage until we met you at the edge of the forest."

"That explains it." Gemma shoved her shoulder against mine. There was no animosity between Rainier and Gemma. I had the urge to spill everything about my confusing feelings for Rain and desperately wanted time alone with her to see if she could help me make sense of it. She knew him and much better than I did.

"Is that my brother?" Laurel's groggy voice came from down the hall. "Tell him to go to..." He turned the corner, eyes widening as if he'd forgotten I was there.

Brother...my sister is married to a prince of this kingdom. It must have been love. That was the only excuse I could accept.

"Are you hungry?" Rainier focused on me. My stomach growled. I couldn't remember when the last time I ate was.

"We could take Ari to that restaurant..." Gemma paused, glancing between Rainier and Laurel. "Sorry. I'm getting ahead of myself."

"What's a restaurant?"

"It's a place where you can get food," Rainier said.

"Like a market?" I asked. "Or a tavern?"

"More like a place with some ambiance where you sit down and they serve you a meal on a plate."

I nodded, but I still didn't know what they were talking about. So many peculiar words to learn. My sister used them naturally, and I struggled to make sense of them.

"I requested dinner be sent to my private dining room for tonight." His gaze shifted to my sister. "You and Daphina are welcome and I guess my brother too." A genuine smile crossed his face, and his dark blue eyes lit up.

MORE STRANGE WORDS had popped up during dinner like "phone." I added it to the list with restaurants, TV, and unicorn shows to ask Gemma about the next time we were alone. Gemma waved as she headed down the hall. Her hand slipped around Laurel's waist, and she rested her head against his shoulder. Laurel carried Phina in his arms, and she was sound asleep. My sister was alive and had a family...a life that had nothing to do with me. As in awe as I was of it all, my heart grieved for the time I'd missed with her.

With a gentle touch, Rainier grasped my elbow. His fingertips barely touched my skin and he tugged me inside the suite. Since my sister left me alone with him, I decided to find out what some of the unfamiliar words meant and maybe more about this place if he'd tell me. He closed the door, and we stood near each other. Too near. The heat of his body penetrated my gown and licked across my skin. Wasted attraction considering I was just duty to him. I turned my head and walked toward the sitting area decorated in the colors of the night sky.

"I know you have questions. You must have so many, but I can see the dark circles under your eyes. I have a room made up for you. Would you like to retire for the evening?"

"I'm not sleepy yet, so maybe answer some questions."

He nodded and held his hand out for the couch. I took a seat.

"Can I see my father?" Gemma's opinion of our father was passionate, but I'd lived with him the last five years since she'd been gone. He wasn't what she thought he was.

"Not tonight, but tomorrow if you wish."

I rested my hands in my lap. "I'd like that, please."

He nodded. "We can go right after breakfast."

"Can Gemma go with me instead?" If she went with me, my sister could see for herself our father was the man who raised, protected, and loved us.

Something akin to pain flashed in his eyes, but it was gone quickly. "Yes, if Gemma wants to see him, she is welcome to accompany you."

I didn't miss the twinge of anger in his words, but he had no right. He'd forced me from my kingdom whether at my sister's behest or not. "Laurel is your brother, not your friend?"

"Half-brother, technically. We have different mothers, but we've never dwelled on that."

I thought of Drew. I'd never referred to him as my half-brother either. Although we had different mothers, he had always been my brother. "And who is older, you or him?"

"He's younger than me."

I hesitated to bring it up since it was on my list for Gemma, but Rainier was here, and my curiosity got the better of me. "What is a TV and a unicorn show?"

He tilted his head back and laughed. "Phina is the only source that information could have come from."

I didn't see what was so funny. "Is it a child's game?"

"Of sorts," he said, smiling. "Let me show you something. It's not something you have in your kingdom."

He picked up a rectangle thing with buttons off the table and pressed one. The floor started to rise from in front of the coffee table. A thin black painting similar to the one over Gemma's fireplace was there. Then, color erupted on it, and sounds flooded around me.

I gasped and drew my legs up under me. "What kind of magic is this?"

He punched buttons. A bar and numbers appeared on the screen and the sound lowered.

"This is a TV, but it's more technology than magic" He pushed more buttons, and images flipped past.

Unicorns appeared on the screen, but they didn't look real. They looked like dancing drawings. I glanced at him, and he was watching me. "What are they?"

"It's called animation. Think of it as an artist's take on something. A portrayal of sorts."

I studied the dancing unicorns on the screen and scoffed. "Marius would be offended to see unicorns portrayed this way. I can't believe Gemma lets Phina gaze upon such insolence."

Rain snorted. "It's a children's program, Arianna. Unicorns are rarely bonded here, and our population is a bit larger than what you are used to. This introduces unicorns to the children in a way they can consume the information."

"It's so trivial," I said. "How much time do your people spend in front of this moving painting?"

"Television viewing depends on the person, but they

aren't all animations. Some shows recap the day's news and others that are people acting out stories...like a play but a bit more realistic looking."

The thought of my kidnapping being shared with the entire court mortified me. "Show me the recap of the news. Does the courtier speak of my arrival?"

Rainier chuckled. "Let's ease into that. I brought you here under the veil of my mist. We'll introduce you after you have a chance to acclimate."

I wasn't sure if it should make me nervous he kept my arrival a secret, but it did the opposite. Knowing there weren't many who knew I was here put me at ease. I leaned back against the couch cushion. It enveloped me in its softness like a cocoon.

"How much bigger is this city than the villages of my empire?"

He stood and held a hand out. "Let me show you."

I looked at his extended palm for a moment before conceding and sliding mine into his. I ignored the warmth of the touch. He led me to a large set of curtains. He punched a button and the curtains slid away revealing a glass window from floor to ceiling. There were lights, so many lights, glittering out before us. He reached for a handle and slid the glass opening.

"A sliding door."

In my home, there were wooden ones that moved on tracks like the glass one. A balcony was beyond the door, and he helped me out onto it. We were up high, like on a mountaintop, but it was a building, and I could see for what seemed like miles upon miles of lights. I looked at him. "How many…" My voice was thick with awe. "How many people are here?"

"Brace yourself," he said.

I gripped the railing of the balcony.

He smiled. "Our last census counted over one million."

I gulped. "A million?" I gazed out again at the city in front of us. The number buzzed around my head. My kingdom had nowhere near that many citizens. "So many."

He leaned in close, his breath tickling my ear. "And you will be the queen they desperately need."

"I was never meant to be queen and definitely not here. Why would they need me?" Over my shoulder, I gazed up into his eyes. A light lit in his deep blue orbs. I studied the spark, intrigued despite my dislike for him. Maybe I didn't loathe him as much as I thought.

"I need you." He brushed his lips against my temple.

Fire ignited from the touch and blistered my insides with desire. I wanted him, and I shouldn't. I couldn't. He was my enemy, but the idea of killing him appealed much less to me.

"Come." He wrapped a hand around my waist and guided me back in, shutting the door and curtains with the wave of a hand instead of the buttons and handle. His magic came so easy to him. "I'm sure you are tired. Let me show you to your room."

He guided me down the hall and a door opened. Rain leaned against the doorframe. "I gave the staff the night off this evening, but you will have attendants in the morning. There are some sleeping clothes and undergarments in the dresser and a bathing chamber beyond that door." He gestured to the door in the corner. "There are additional clothes for day and parties in the closet, and the staff will unpack your trunks tomorrow."

I noted the trunks in the corner.

"My room is on the other end of the hall." He turned sideways and pointed in that direction. His eyes lingered on my mouth as if he waited for me to say something. "I'll see you in the morning."

I nodded, working on a swallow. I couldn't form words, but I watched him walk down the hall. His hard muscles were visible under the shirt and that ass. I shouldn't be looking at it. Goddesses and gods, what am I doing? Rain turned and entered a different room from the door he'd said was his bedroom.

As soon as the door closed, I allowed myself to explore the room. The bed was bigger than mine at home with lots of pillows and a step stool to climb into it. Two nightstands held lights, but they weren't lit by candles. Magic must be responsible for the glow. One of the black paintings...no, a TV, hung on the wall in the sitting area. A couch and end table were placed on top of a grey rug but faced the TV. I opened the closet door. There were so many dresses and footwear. Shoes with thin heels lined a shelf toward the back They looked more like weapons than to wear. I closed the door and moved to the dresser to find night clothes.

I opened the first drawer of the eight-drawer dresser to find some sheer items that I assumed were undergarments. The drawer below held gowns and a silky robe. I picked those, kicked off my shoes, and padded barefoot into the bathing room to change. My mouth fell open, and I knew it because I saw my reflection in a wall of mirrors over a marble countertop. The floor was marble and warm as if fires were lit under it. A rectangular bathtub large enough for three people sat in front of a window with coverings that were narrow strips of wood strung together. I saw a button like Rainier had used for the curtain and pushed it. The shades hummed and opened. There was another view of the city that anyone using the bathtub would have if the shades were open. I hit the button again, and the slats closed. The bathtub looked inviting, and it had been a travel day. I'd drawn my own bath many times, and I knew how to work the faucet. Or so I thought. I finally got it to turn on and hunted for towels in the cabinet.

There was a door in the corner. I would rip Rainier's eyes out if it gave him access to this room. I flung the door open, but it was just the water closet.

As the bath filled with water, little candles flickered to life, but there was no fire. Some kind of magic animated them. The overhead lights dimmed. I marveled at the sight. It was... peaceful.

I peeled off my clothes and let them fall into a pile on the floor. The water was warm against my skin as I slipped into the giant tub. My thoughts filtered in as I sat in the quiet. Guilt at leaving my people behind. Leaving Val behind. I couldn't do anything about that now, but I did wonder if Val was okay. At least with my brother in hiding, I knew the unicorns protected him. And what about

Rainier? With so much wealth at his disposal, why did he want to marry me? There had to be a nuance I'd missed with him. He could marry any woman. I imagined what a walk down the aisle to him would look like, and it wasn't unpleasant. An anxious flutter quivered through my stomach. I closed my eyes and leaned against the back of the tub.

The tub relaxed me to the point I almost fell asleep. By the time I climbed out, my skin had pruned, and I was barely able to keep my eyes open as I dressed in the night clothes. I was ready to climb into the giant bed.

CHAPTER 31
ARI

A knock jarred me from my sleep, a very sound sleep. I wasn't unaccustomed to being waited on, but it wasn't something I relished. I'd take training leathers over finery given the choice.

"Come in," I said, pulling on my robe.

Two women entered wearing elbow-length tunics in dove grey with white cuffs and collars along with darker grey pants. They curtseyed in front of me. "Your Majesty."

"Please call me Arianna. I prefer it. And you are?"

They exchanged looks of confusion and maybe some judgement. The darker-haired woman took a step forward. "I'm Bridget, and this is Melly." She gestured to the shorter woman with light brown hair. They were fae-- definitely elves, and I suspected from this kingdom, but they didn't exude the same power I'd felt from Rainier and Laurel and their men. They could be spies for Rainier. Probably were. I'd keep my court-trained persona up with them.

"Prince Rainier has requested breakfast in the dining room with Princess Gemma and Prince Laurel."

"Will you help me choose proper attire, so I don't stand out?"

"Yes, my lady," Bridget said. "Let me open the blinds for you.

Melly disappeared to the bathroom, and Bridget crossed the room, opening the slatted window coverings to let the natural light in. It cast a golden hue across the chamber, and I noticed a dressing table I hadn't seen last night.

"How do you normally like to wear your hair, my lady?" Val normally did my hair, and I wondered if she was safe.

"Arianna, please," I said. "Usually down or with the sides braided back."

She smiled.

"How do most women wear theirs here?" I asked, recalling how Gemma's was down when I saw her.

"They mostly wear it down in loose curls or straight and sometimes with a headband."

"A headband would be nice to keep it out of my face today," I said.

Bridget nodded. "We'll begin unpacking your trunks and should finish while you're at breakfast."

"Thank you," I said, taking a seat in front of the mirror for her to start my hair. Part of me worried they would find the moonflowers, but I'd hidden them well.

GEMMA AND LAUREL sat at the table with Rainier talking in hushed tones. Phina wasn't with them, and the room fell silent when I entered. Bridget had mentioned she was informed to encourage me to dress for walking today. I was in a light blue sweater and tan pants. A headband matching the sweater rested on my head, and I'd chosen the boots Bridget suggested. I thought I looked good when I left the room, but now I reconsidered, swiping my damp hands on the thick material. Dresses were my normal attire if I wasn't training, but I preferred pants.

Rainier's gaze swept over me and then dragged up the length of my body starting at my feet. When he reached my face, his eyes were warm. "How is your room?"

"Very nice," I said and looked at Gemma and Laurel. I'd wanted to see her again for so long, and even with her in front of me right now, the day still seemed like a dream. "Good morning."

Laurel inclined his head, and Gemma smiled that big smile she wore when she knew she was right about something. What she predicted correctly was a mystery, but I would ask her when I got her alone and hoped that would be sooner rather than later.

"Good morning." She took a sip of juice. "You look very nice."

Rainier gestured to the seat next to him and opposite Gemma. "Have a seat."

"Are you going with me to see Father?" I blurted out to

Gemma. My urgency to resolve what had broken between them made me a little too enthusiastic.

She reached over like she had done when we were kids, putting fresh fruit and bacon on my plate. I poured tea into my cup watching the steam.

Gemma halted her hand for a second, and when I looked up, her smile was gone. "No," she said in a cautious tone. "I have my reasons that I'll share later, but you should be prepared, Ari." She paused. "He is very angry."

"Imagine being angry when you're held prisoner in a foreign land," I said.

Rainier's fork clattered against his plate. Laurel let out a low whistle.

"You are not a prisoner," Rainier said, his voice low and eyes glittering with a challenge.

"Protect my people or come here to marry you. Sounds like kidnapping and imprisonment to me," I said, loading my voice with vitriol.

Gemma snorted and laughed. "I see your ways have not gotten any better with women, Rain."

She used the nickname his friends used. She had a casual ease with him. My sister must have spent time with the prince to have that kind of relaxed banter between them.

"Maybe we should head out to our duties," Laurel said, leaning towards Gemma.

"Not a chance. I want to see how your brother explains this. One hundred gold on my sister."

Laurel chuckled. "I'm not stupid enough to take that bet."

Rainier shot a glare at both of them. Laurel shoved a forkful of eggs in his mouth. A smirk crept across Gemma's face. My sister was never one to back down from anyone. "What's the matter, Rain? My sister was too smart to fall for your charm?"

I winced. I hadn't been. That damn chocolate cake. I'd let him between my legs. My cheeks heated at the memory.

Rainier's gaze shot to mine. I resisted the urge to give him a vulgar gesture.

Gemma's mouth formed an "O." My face grew even hotter. Goddesses and gods, why were we having this conversation at the breakfast table? Gemma cleared her throat. "After you visit dear old dad, I would like to show you the music room. I usually go while Phina is napping."

My sweet sister remembered the me from five years ago, before she disappeared, who loved music. I didn't have the heart to tell her I hadn't played since she left. We'd spent hours in our music room and even made up our own songs Father would have us perform at various events.

"I'd like that," I said, giving her a genuine smile.

"Good." She turned her focus to Rainier. "Where shall I meet you to collect my sister?"

She'd gone into her protective-sister mode, and I smiled at the memories of her doing that when I was teased about my magic. We had the freedom to move about the empire then, but when she left, things changed.

"We'll meet you there around three," Rainier said, his voice even.

She placed her napkin on the table and pushed back, coming around the table. Gemma gave me a side hug. "I'm really glad you are here, little sis."

I leaned my head against her shoulder, swallowing down all my emotions. "I'm so glad to see you. I missed you."

"Don't let this one scare you." She patted Rainier's shoulder as she passed by him. "He's an awkward ass, but he does have a heart."

Laurel stood. "I look forward to getting to know you more, Arianna."

"Ari, please," I said.

He inclined his head toward me and turned to Rainier. "Brother."

"Brother. Gemma." Rainier frowned and dismissed them both with a hand.

I pushed some food around on my plate and ate some of the berries, very aware that Rainier was watching my every move. "Do you have some comment about the way I eat?"

"No," he said, his voice so soft. "I'm glad you are eating."

I met his eyes, and there was kindness twinged with sadness.

"You look lovely today." He paused. "I mean, you look lovely every day, but this color of blue suits you. It matches your eyes."

I swallowed, and his eyes followed the bob of my throat. My cheeks heated again, and I lifted my glass, drinking down the remainder of the cold juice.

A clap of thunder rattled the room, and the whoosh of rain poured down outside, the sounds filtering in through the windows. Hairs on my arms raised. Heat rushed to my cheeks at how easily I startled.

"Ready?" His tone was kind but guarded. He stood and held out a hand.

I slid mine into his, ready to see my father and figure a way out of this court. "Yes."

ARI

Guards were posted on either side of the double doors. The North Wing, Rainier had explained on our walk over, was often used for visiting dignitaries of other empires. He called them countries but explained they were similar to our kingdoms. Not all were ruled by kings and queens, which seemed strange.

Rainier nodded his head at the guard, and he opened one door for us to enter. Another set of guards met us on the inside and walked us through a small sitting area and a suite of finely appointed rooms beyond it. Father sat alone on a couch with a tray in front of him. He wore the deep green and black of our empire, with no disrepair visible on his clothes. His jaw tightened. My heart shattered at the sad set of his face. He looked broken.

"Father?" I called out. My steps quickened toward him. His eyes widened as if he was surprised to see me. Rainier grabbed my elbow, halting me a few feet away. I jerked my arm, but his grasp was firm. "Let me go."

He held one finger out in front of him.

Zzzp.

"Oh," I said. There weren't many fae who could produce the kind of magic to create a field around someone, and even fewer who could maintain it. That meant one of the guards must be the owner of that magic.

"If Albert's anger remains in check, we can lower it," Rainier said against my ear. I pulled away from him. My father had always been kind. I didn't understand. He'd rarely ever gotten angry, but who wouldn't be pissed while locked in a cell, even with plush surroundings.

"Ari," Father said, his voice normal. "You shouldn't have come. Who is running the empire?"

I cast a glance full of my promise of death to Rainier. The asshole smiled as if he was pleased with my look. I softened my face as I turned back to my father. "We can talk about that later. Right now, I want to know if you are okay."

"I'm well, other than being a prisoner. They have not mistreated me. Have you seen Gemma? She's been kept here too."

My gut twisted. She'd chosen to be here, but he didn't seem to understand that. "I have."

"You both need to leave. This place is corrupt." He gestured as if the air itself was evil.

"Gemma seems happy here."

His eyes flared in wild rage I'd never witnessed from him. "It's a trick. They want to use you both to control our empire."

How do I tell him they already did?

Rainier stood close. I met his gaze. "What will it take to free him?"

"That's a conversation better had away from here." Marrying Rainier to unite our kingdoms, but why wouldn't he say it in front of Father? Rainier didn't seem like the type who cared what others, even the king of another empire, thought.

"Do not worry about me, Arianna," Father said. "I'll be fine. Get out. Go home. Before they turn you into a gods-damn whore for their breeding like your sister."

My mouth fell open, and I had to will myself to close it.

"Brace yourself," Rainier said, stepping closer.

Father's face contorted into pure rage as if a mask had slipped away. He grabbed a vase and chucked it toward us. I put my hands up in defense, but it shattered against the magic field. His eyes glowed a mottled red that wasn't normal. "She's just like your mother. A harlot to her core, lying with these vile creatures. You're a demimondaine too. Aren't you?" He looked me up and down with disgust that nearly dripped from his tongue. "Goddesses and gods be damned. Be gone from me with your shame, and go spread your legs for your new dark lord."

I staggered back. My heart ached as if it had been sliced from my chest with a rusty, dull blade. My father had never spoken to me or anyone in such a way.

"Enough." Rainier's voice reverberated around the room. A clap of thunder punctuated his words.

"You will not speak to Arianna in such a way, nor to any other member of this empire, but especially not to her."

My father spit at Rainier. The saliva sizzled against the magical field. "She is not and never will be a member of your court."

Father turned to me, sliding a finger across his throat. "Better you slit your own throat than lie with this depraved pretender. Another usurper attempting to steal my throne."

My blood thrummed in my ears. Coldness closed in on me. Dark mist clouded my vision. I could hear my own breathing. I looked at Rainier, my knees weakening. He slid his arm around my waist to support me and led me towards the door.

Father was still yelling at me. "You let him touch you so intimately? You are already dead to me, you wretched, worthless traitor. Finish the job for yourself before I unleash my army."

The doors closed behind us, and the air was lighter in the sitting area. I gripped the back of a couch and gulped down air. "What has driven him mad and so quickly?"

Rainier rubbed my back but didn't say anything.

"Where are his bonded? Claudius and Barrett?"

"Their bond was broken when we found him. Although, their allegiance may still be intact. They wouldn't leave his side until we collected him."

"I don't know the man in there," I said. "How do we heal him? Do you have healers?"

"They have examined him but can find nothing wrong," Rainier said, his tone apologetic. The sympathetic gaze he gave me said more. His guards would know what was going on in Father's head until the bond was broken. "He is himself."

"In the twenty-five years of my life, he has never once talked or acted like that. He is most certainly not himself. I want to talk to his sworn guards, Claudius and Barrett. Take me to them."

"That is not possible."

"Why not?"

"They left, and in keeping with the agreement under the treaty, we do not hunt or hold unicorns." His hand, still on my back, warmed.

A broken bond was a death sentence for most of our kind. Yet, Gemma was fine, and Father reacted more like madness. Not that there were many bonded and even fewer broken in my lifetime. In fact, I didn't know any except for my father and my sister. The rest were stories from when bonds were more frequent. My hatred raged out. "Let me guess. He didn't want to join you. What did you do to him? Force a bond separation?"

Hurt flashed in his eyes, a lighter blue lined them, and then his features were masked with those only a ruler wore. "Neither I nor my people have done anything to him, Ari."

Everything in my life fell apart the second Rainier stepped into my line of suitors. I didn't feel safe in his kingdom. "I want to go home."

"I'll take you back to your room."

"Your room is not my room. I want to go back to my home, and I want to take my father with me."

"Ari—"

"Do not call me Ari ever again. If you refuse to address me by my title, then call me by my given name."

He grasped my hand and ran a thumb over the back of it. Ignoring the heat, I pulled my hand free. "You are nothing but a greedy kidnapper, and I want to be as far away from you as I can."

"I'll take you to Gemma then," he said.

Gemma would try to convince me to stay, but I didn't want to spend another second with Rainier or think about my disloyal body's reaction to his every fucking touch.

CHAPTER 33

RAIN

I dropped Ari off with Gemma in the music room. Gemma's narrowed eyes told me what a mistake she thought it was to take Ari to see her Father, but I wouldn't deny her, despite the circumstances it took to bring her here.

"What is this feeling inside me when I'm near her?" I asked Laurel as we sat in my office watching the monitors for any hint of a vampire in our city. "My chest tightens just watching her glide around a room, even when I'm certain she wants to put a dagger in my eye."

Laurel smirked at me and clasped a hand on my shoulder. "You're describing more than lust, Brother. I think you are infatuated with her. Gemma sees it too."

I topped off our glasses.

Laurel raised an eyebrow and smirked. "She is lovely. It appears to run in their family."

A low growl rumbled in my chest, but I didn't know why. Gemma was the most beautiful woman I'd ever seen

... until I laid eyes on Ari. She'd taken all the air from my lungs, and for several moments, I saw only her.

Was I infatuated with her? I thought about her almost every waking moment. But she hated me for what I'd done. I was positive of it. She'd said it. Goddesses and Gods. If we'd had more time maybe it would have been different, but as it was now, she would never be mine. Not really. Not after that meeting with her father. That wasn't how I'd planned for her to be introduced to the truth, and she only saw him as a prisoner wanting to be free. She didn't see she had been a prisoner herself.

I wanted to tell her the truth about her father, but she needed to see and understand many things about the world outside her empire before I dove into Albert's role in getting us all to this point.

"Those dreams still haunt me." I swirled the amber liquid in my glass, ice clinking against the side. "Of what was to become of her if we didn't intervene."

"That's probably the only reason Gemma hasn't tried to kill you herself." He lifted a shoulder. "And why she's giving you space to tell Ari in your way. *But* her generosity and patience are only going to go so far, my brother."

"I know." I stared at the liquid and swigged the remaining contents down. "She told me I should just tell Arianna everything. That she could handle it."

"They are blood of blood and blood of old. It whispers between them even when they are unaware of it."

I let out a long breath and rubbed the tender spot between my eyes. "I'll consider it."

"Do you have another headache?" Laurel asked,

moving closer, studying me like when I was a kid and had these pains. "Have you been to the healer?"

"Yes, she said it's magic buildup, and I need to release it."

"Then, why haven't you?"

"You do see the storm outside, right?" I paused. He looked at me expectantly. "I've been releasing a little at a time. If I let it all go at once, the city will be flooded."

"We don't want any tornadoes."

"No, that last one..." I still had guilt darkening my soul from it.

"Can you funnel any through Casimir?"

"Casimir is off doing whatever Casimir does when she doesn't answer me." I suspected I didn't want to know what she was doing anyway when she left for unicorn business. She'd been one of the primary researchers for the reproduction issues they'd experienced.

"Are you still planning to break your bond with her?"

I shrugged. No one knew we weren't bonded. Not like Ari was with Marius or Gemma had been with Cyrus. Casimir had chosen me, but we'd struck a deal to not do the bonding ceremony so she could move freely. We were connected without the confines of the bond, but that meant neither of us benefited from the strength of it either. "I don't know. It's her I'm worried about if I do. Not myself. But she deserves to live out her last years without a fae in her head."

"Even if it diminishes your own power."

"Ari is here now." Her power eclipsed all of ours. With training, she'd be able to rebuild what had been lost.

"What if she doesn't stay?"

If she didn't, it would be the end to us all. I'd let the world burn to save her, but none of us would be here if I didn't help her, guide her, to the truth. Being honest with myself, Laurel had done a great job introducing Gemma to the kingdom, and I'd already fucked it all up in every way possible for Ari. I wasn't Laurel and Ari wasn't Gemma and the state of the world wasn't the same as it had been five years ago.

CHAPTER 34
ARI

Gemma sat at the piano playing a song I'd never heard. Her fingers danced over the keys in a familiar way. I smiled at the memories of us playing together as children.

"That's a beautiful melody," I said.

Gemma scooted over on the bench and inclined her head. "Follow along."

I dropped down next to her. My heart split in many directions. Leaving her to go home wouldn't be easy, but staying in a kingdom where I didn't belong seemed even harder. "I haven't played since you left."

"You did the same thing when Mom passed," she said, her voice tinged with sadness, but her fingers never missed a key.

"The grief was similar," I whispered, unable to say it too loud in case I might speak it into fruition.

She glanced at me. The woe in her eyes matched my grief. "But I'm not dead."

"No, but I thought you were, and you didn't come back." I swallowed against the knot in my throat, but it didn't budge.

"I knew you would find me, Ari. You always found me. I could never hide from you. It was one of your gifts." She never missed a note.

"And yours was making people feel better. Taking away their hurt. Making them feel whole again." Unshed tears burned the back of my eyes, blurring my vision, but I placed my hands on the keys and joined in as one half of a duet. "Did you leave because you were in love with Laurel?"

Gemma chuckled. "Goddesses and gods, no. I was in love with him, yes, but I left because I understood I could do more for the world here. Make a difference I would have never been able to do in...with the limitations of where we were raised."

"And you couldn't tell me?"

"No," she said, her voice thick. "And I'm sorry for that."

I believed she was sorry. Gemma had been the best big sister, and she comforted me when our mother died. She encouraged me to practice. "I have Mother's earth magic."

She smiled. "I knew it. I knew you would receive that gift from the time you and Mother started tending that garden."

I wasn't ready to let go of this moment between us. It reminded me what life was like for us when our family was whole, but I had to ask the question. "What's wrong with our father?"

"Nothing," she said, her voice turning cold. "Not a single thing."

She hadn't gone with me, so she hadn't seen how being here harmed him. "He wasn't himself, and his guards abandoned him."

Gemma let out a long sigh. "There is a lot to the story, Ari. What you see of him is who he was during the war."

"The war? He wasn't born when the war happened."

Gemma stopped playing and turned to me. Sympathy softened her expression. "He was. Mother used her magic on him to make him good, and as long as he stayed on the other side of the forest with her magic, the spell remained intact. When he crossed the forest, the magic she tethered to him disintegrated."

My stomach dropped, and I was sure it landed on the floor. I grabbed my head. It had to be a story. A fantasy built by our enemy. "This isn't a game, Gemma."

She took my hands in hers. Pain filled her eyes. "No, it's not. It's our lives, and it fucking sucks."

My magic vibrated like it recognized the truth in what she said. "How long have you known?"

"I understood very little until I got here. Not enough to confirm it, but enough to make me suspicious."

My sister and I were products of deceit. "Why did she do it? Why did Mom use her magic like that?"

"To end the war. She sacrificed herself to save lives."

"And we were always going to be a reminder of that sacrifice," I said, my voice barely above a whisper. "How do you know it's true?"

She started to play again, a sad lamented tune. "Don't

you feel it in your bones and blood? In your very essence? Her magic is grounded here. Her spirit is here."

I couldn't deny it. Every part of me sang with the truth. But Gemma had been here among this court for years. They could have corrupted her mind with magic and glamour. The power to do the dishonorable deed was rare, but in a city this size, there could be an elf capable of it.

Fae no longer recognized the courts of old, but remnants of them remained. As children, we were told the stories of the court that once represented these lands. The Court of Storms, and the addition to the moniker many used to refer to it. The Court of Storms and Trickery. Had they used some old dead language and spell to taint Gemma's mind?

"I know what you're thinking, and no, I'm not under their influence. Mom taught me how to protect my mind. No one is getting in there," she said and scoffed. "Except maybe Phina. She's gifted. Like you."

"I want to talk to him again—Father. I want to hear this from him."

"He'll be glad to share his disgust with you. His detest for this court both old and new. He'll spew hate as long as you want to listen."

It couldn't be worse than earlier. If he confirmed Gemma's story, I wasn't sure I'd survive the guilt of what our mother went through.

"Do you think she hated us? For being reminders of what she sacrificed to end the war?"

"No, she loved us, Ari. So much. There is no faking that

kind of love. I'm sure we were a reminder of exactly why she made the sacrifice. When I look at Phina, I know what a mother's love makes me want to do to keep her safe."

My heart was heavy. Perhaps what she said was true. "I still miss her. Seeing you, Gemma, lessens the grief, but it hangs in my heart like a missing piece filled with darkness."

Sadness shadowed her face. "There will always be a missing piece of her in us, but we can honor her by making the world better for our children and their children."

I swallowed hard, remembering how Mother took us out into the villages to aid and cook for our people.

"Do you know what they called our court in the old times, before the war?"

"The Court of Love and Prosper."

Gemma snorted. "No, that was something implanted after the war when the population was low enough that it didn't require much to reframe it."

Each piece of my life was being reduced to a lie or a mismatched version of the truth I was raised to believe. "Do you know what the real name was?"

"The Court of Curses," she said quietly. "We lived in a court known for cursing others to increase their power and wealth. Father had been from there, and that's why the cursed court was chosen for him to live out his days."

"And Mother used her own form of a curse to contain it."

Gemma pressed her lips into a thin line and nodded.

I didn't want to believe it, but yet, it was true to my mother's sacrifices. To her love of us and the people. She thought of others above herself. Always. Could she have been older than we realized? Father too?

"Go with me to talk to him?" I wanted to hear from our father what the truth was from his point of view.

Gemma chewed her lip like she was debating an answer. If this was too difficult for my sister, I wouldn't pressure her any further.

"I can go by myself. It's fine. I know the way now." I'd been with him until a few weeks ago, so he might act differently if I was alone with him. I didn't know what to expect from this version of my father.

"No, you can't. The guards will not let you pass," she said. "But they will if you're with me."

"Well, I can at least try." I stood up and walked toward the door. My determination to know the truth from our father drove me forward.

A few steps away, I heard the soft scrape of wood against the rug. "I'll take you."

We passed through both sets of guards to find Father lounging on the couch. His demeanor hadn't changed from earlier. "My whoring daughters have arrived."

I kept my distance. My expectations were lower for how the conversation would go.

"Might I remind you, *Father*," Gemma snarled, dragging his name out. "Your treachery is the reason we are all here. Our saint of a mother was with you, gave up her life for the good of all fae."

"Have you come to remind me that I fathered two disgusting creatures with a noble fae of a court on this side of the empire?"

Gemma cut her gaze to me. Goddesses and gods. Our mother was highborn in this court. "We're not related to them. I'll explain later, but she was from a different court and worked with renowned king here."

Rainier and Laurel. That's who she meant.

"So, we mean nothing to you?" I asked, hoping I'd misunderstood his actions.

"Not as long as you serve this court like a harlot fool."

I moved closer wanting a better look at his eyes. They were wild and unrecognizable. I searched for any reminder of who he had been our entire lives, but there was none. The man we knew as our father didn't exist. "What would you do if we freed you?"

A wicked smile crossed his face. "I'd rain down the curses that were prevented before and exterminate those who oppose me."

Gemma gripped my wrist and coaxed me away from the barrier.

I bit down on the inside of my lip to think about a different kind of pain. I'd lost my mother years ago. I'd temporarily lost Gemma but had her back. I'd lost the father I'd held so dear, but that person never existed. "We're done."

I turned away, and Gemma linked her arm in mine. The doors closed behind us, and they slammed in my mind as the final chapter of my old life had come to an end. Whatever the future held started here, but I couldn't stay like Gemma had. I'd return to the Court of Love and Prosper one day. I couldn't leave it to return to a court known for curses. We'd been happy there. The people were happy there.

"I'm sorry, Ari." Gemma hugged me close. "I know you wanted to see the man who was our father. I did, too, and I already knew the truth. Had years to adjust to what seeing him like this would be like. Yet, I still hoped to find our father there. But you still have me."

I heard her, and she was trying to help me like our mother would have. She was so much like Mother that it made me wonder if I was more like our father. Was she the goodness of our mother? And if so, what did that make me?

Arianna! Marius's voice was a shout in my head. I grabbed my temple.

Marius? My call back to him was shaky from my panic. *Is everything okay? How are you reaching me?*

We've maneuvered close enough, but it's still a great distance.

Is Drew okay? Why did you risk coming close?

Drew is fine and happy with Leana. I needed to warn you.

I let out a long sigh. *You knew, didn't you? About my father?*

A long pause filled my head with silence. At first, I thought the connection was broken, but it hit me that he didn't want to say his betrayal out loud.

Is that why you bonded with me? To make sure I didn't turn out like him?

No. Another shout and my knees buckled, but I steadied myself against the wall. *While it did grant me access to him, I bonded you for another reason.*

And what was that, Marius? The flatness of my voice carried through my thoughts.

I can't tell you.

The duplicity from those I cared about was all around

me. How could I trust any of them? My heart fractured in a million directions, and I wanted to shut them all out.

Don't you dare, Ari.

Oh, I'm not. Not until we got Drew.

"Is there somewhere we can meet, Marius, to get Drew?"

"I can get us into the forest if he agrees to it." Gemma paused. "I'd love nothing more than for our brother to join us, but maybe you should feel safe here first. I know you don't yet, and that's okay. It took me six months before I wasn't looking over my shoulder constantly, and Laurel barely left my side."

Get Drew close to the edge of the forest on your side and let me know when you're there. We can discuss it then.

I shut him out, molding my shield against him specifically. I'd let it back down in a few minutes when I didn't feel him pressing on my mind.

"Did he agree?"

"Marius will never deny me," I said, turning toward my quarters. Rainier's suite. I would not let anyone decide for me nor would I acquiesce to them. Was I strong enough to break the bond with Marius? He'd been in my head since I was a child, but maybe that was part of the problem. I'd become dependent on having him there, and for Gemma always being there before she left. But maybe alone was exactly what I needed. Maybe it was time to stand on my own...no, no maybe about that. It was time.

"Has your power changed since you've been here, Gemma?"

She blinked a couple of times. "Yes, I'm stronger, but

I've practiced more here than I ever did in our lands. Are you worried about your magic?"

"Despite Marius's constant training, it's still as unpredictable as it was before you left." There were a couple of times with Rainier that I was able to focus it, but no one else needed to know that.

"And since you've been here?"

"It hasn't responded. It's like this place dampens it." My agitation over it annoyed me like an itch I couldn't reach.

She stopped and turned to me. "It's not this place. We can't go into the forest for Drew without our magic to protect us." She tugged on my arm in a different direction. "Come on. I have an idea."

CHAPTER 36

ARI

Gemma opened the double doors and ushered me inside the room. The doors echoed around the space as they shut. A dozen mats covered the floor along with weights, training weapons, small child-sized pools of water, and several clear chambers lined along the wall. A training center for sure, but I didn't see anything geared specifically for magic.

My sister scurried around the room gathering items from the various stations. She inclined her head toward one of the chambers. As if she sensed my apprehension, Gemma entered the chamber first. I followed her in, and she pressed her hand against a panel. The door closed, and the breath lodged in my chest. The room seemed smaller inside, and it was like catching a bug in glass.

"Let it out, Ari," she said over her shoulder as she set up the things she'd gathered on a long narrow table. "You did the same thing when you were scared when we were kids."

I let the breath out. "What are we doing, Gemma?"

"These chambers allow us to practice our magic without being a hazard to the court or kingdom. If the power reaches a certain level and becomes a threat, the technology in the chamber counters it and extinguishes the hazard."

Gemma made it sound so simple, but I'd never heard of anything like it. I gulped, scanning for how the clear room could eliminate threats. "And what if we're the danger?"

She shook her head. "It's focused on the magic and will not harm a fae."

"You're sure of that?"

"I'm positive."

"How are you so certain?"

"Because I was angry when I first arrived here, and I came here to vent my magic." My sister waited by the narrow-width, waist-high table. "I triggered the tech so many times in one day, that I caused a temporary power outage to contain it."

Shit. Gemma's magic had always been strong—stronger than mine. I wasn't surprised she would break the system.

"Come on." She waved me over to the table. There were knives and small swords like I preferred, dirt, rope, a gold bowl with water, and some other objects that seemed random. "Choose one. Don't think too hard. Choose the one that connects with you."

I held my hand out, skimming over the table. I stopped over the twin swords. I preferred the type because they were lightweight and easier for me to wield. Opponents tended to underestimate their deadliness and that of those who carry them. These were dark metal and intricately etched with the moon and stars of the goddess Nyx. I ran a finger down the hilt over the symbols. They seem to hum to me. I closed my hand over the base and spun them in my hand.

"These feel right." I turned.

Gemma clapped her hands together. "I knew it."

"Knew what?"

"That you would choose them, and they would choose you. No one has been able to touch them but me and I can't use them. They are heavy and awkward when I try."

Gemma was skilled with a sword. In all the times I'd watched her train, even before I was allowed to, she never made a move that wasn't as elegant as a dance. I flicked my wrists whirling the blades around again. "But they feel so light to me."

"They have been waiting for the one worthy to possess them. Let me go find a belt for you to sheath them." She pressed her hand on the pad, and it lit up. The door opened and she dashed out.

Dark mist clouded my vision. Please don't let me pass out.

I studied the swords in my hands, and the emblem glowed silver, but what caught my eye was the symbols glowing on the blades themselves. I recognized all of them. The mist. The owl. The moon. The night sky. All pointed to one goddess. Nyx. Another symbol formed and glinted into the metal as if to emphasize its importance.

The Triple Moon. The most divine of Nyx's symbols, it meant innocence, strength, and wisdom or in some interpretations, the cycle of life.

The mist cleared from my sight, but the emblems were permanently etched on both. *Thank you for this blessing, Nyx. I don't know why you have chosen me for it, but I will endeavor to be worthy.*

Gemma returned and fastened the leather around my hips. It looked odd against the finery of the pants and sweater. I tried to stifle a laugh, but I couldn't. She stood back and doubled over laughing.

"That is a fashion statement." Her eyes fell to the blades and her face sobered. "Ari…"

"I know. What does it mean?"

My sister lifted the blades with care and examined them. "I'm not sure other than Nyx has blessed your journey. Some of the scholars might be able to provide more insight, but to me, I think she's chosen you to be her warrioress."

"But I'm not a soldier, Gemma." The confession went against my very confidence. I was well trained, but I'd never been in a battle. While Marius had made sure I could stand on my own in sparring, my skills had never been tested in real combat.

"Our goddess thinks otherwise." She smiled. "There is something I want you to see, but we should catch up with the guys before I take you there. They'll want to go with us, and we need to change clothes."

"What about training with my magic?" I asked, disappointed to leave so soon. "And where can I find the scholars?"

"We'll tackle those tomorrow. What I have to show you is exactly what you need to see right now."

"Lead the way," I said, sheathing the blades in the awkward leather belt.

"I think you're the one who will be leading." She grinned.

Like the empire would let a foreign queen regent lead anything. But if Nyx had chosen me for a task, maybe I could have an impact on our world. Maybe I could restore the seat of my empire. The blades hummed at my sides, but the response didn't feel like an agreement.

The four of us traveled through the city with our cloaks concealing our identities. There wasn't much risk in me being recognized, but Rainier, Laurel, and Gemma were known figures. No guards watching our every move...at least that I could see. I stepped off a curb and one of the motorized things honked at me. Rainier yanked me back and held me against his chest. My heart hammered so hard I wasn't sure I could slow it down. Concern creased his face, but it gave way to the tiniest inkling of amusement.

"Careful," he said, letting me go. "You need to look both ways before crossing the street."

I immediately missed the warmth of his body pressed against mine. When I was near him, safety radiated around me, which confused me since he had lied to me. "Mmmhmm." I turned back around, following Gemma and Laurel to the other side.

Our group emerged from the street, Rainier at my side,

to a large circle where many streets, twelve of them if my quick count was correct, seemed to dead-end at a statue. Flowers encircled the bottom, moonflowers, and in front of them were random bouquets as if others had paid respects at a grave. Passerbies paused to pay reverence before moving on. My gaze traveled up as Gemma took my hand and led me across. Rainier and Laurel stayed behind us a few steps. I gasped as I made out the face. My mother.

"This is the proof," Gemma said, softly, her voice rough with unshed tears. "We were warrior-born, Ari, like our mother."

I slid the hood of my cloak back to take in the entirety of the representation of my mother. It was her just as she looked my entire life. The plaque on the base didn't just read Daphina but General Daphina and under her moniker was *Chosen by Nyx*. She'd given up the life she'd known to save her people, this city, and no telling how many others in this land. Grief. Respect. Love. They all mixed in my heart. My mother was the reason this city stood intact.

"Look here," Gemma said, pointing to the panels. Stories of how courageous she had been came to life. Families she had saved. Her sacrifice. There were so many filling the base.

"These were only the ones that were selected," Rainier said. "There were more than could fit on the statue. Look down."

My gaze drifted down to the cobblestone, and indeed, there were hundreds more worked in with the stones to make an intricate design. My knees hit the cold ground, and I ran my fingers over the stones. Mother's sacrifice would fill volumes in history. This was her legacy. A legacy I'd never live up to, but I'd do everything in my power to be worthy of being her daughter.

Rainier knelt in front of me. His thumbs brushed across my cheeks, and dampness smeared. I hadn't even realized I was crying.

"She was always my hero, but I never knew this part of her life and how she was a hero to so many others."

"This isn't the only memorial to her, but this one is special because the main streets of the city were rerouted to end here with her. She allowed the city and the empire to keep moving forward. There is a garden I want to show you when you are up to it. It was hers, and it has been tended by keepers loyal to her since she made her decision."

A garden...Mother and I'd shared my garden before she passed. A moment of grief gripped my heart and let go. Mother loved the cultivating and nurturing of plants. It was the perfect way to keep her memory.

Rainier held out his hand.

I'd avoided contact with him, but as I met his gaze, I saw a vulnerability there I either hadn't noticed or allowed myself to see before. His other hand brushed the hair back from my face.

I slipped my hand in his. The contact was warm and liquified as it ran through my body. He helped me to my feet.

"I think we should head back to check on Phina. I'm

sure Rain can handle the walk to the garden," Gemma said.

Laurel cleared his throat. "Oh, yep. You're right."

Rainier didn't release my hand, but I broke my gaze away from his to look at Gemma.

She glanced at our hands and leaned in to hug me. I flung my free arm around her. Being alone with Rainier sounded like a bad idea. "You two should go with us."

"No, we shouldn't. I visit the garden often, and we can go together on another day," she said, pulling back and smiling. "My daughter is probably using her power on the nanny in order to get more ice cream."

"Ice cream?"

"We're definitely trying that when you get back. Just come knock on the door," Gemma said over her shoulder as they crossed the street.

Night had come swiftly, and I looked up for the stars, but the lights of the city dampened them. "It's unfortunate," I said, breaking the silence.

"What is?"

"That the lights of the city are so pretty but block out the beauty of the night sky."

"Just wait," he said, winking at me.

The smug ass winked at me. I rolled my eyes and glanced down the streets. The city was so quiet. There had been very few people walking in the same direction as us, and even fewer of those motorized things. What had he called them? Cars. Like the first three letters in carriages.

"Where is everyone?"

"Some are worshipping. Others are feasting with their families."

My forehead wrinkled as it sounded like today was a holiday, but unless I'd lost track, we weren't due for a holiday for months. "What are they celebrating?"

"You."

"Me?" I pulled back, studying him and seeing a twinge of amusement mixed with his seriousness. "I thought they didn't know I was here."

"Your arrival means a chance for the empire to see change. Not a guarantee but they have hope." He pointed to the night sky, and there nestled among the constellations was a formation that matched Nyx's blessing on my blades.

I opened my mouth and closed it. Was that what he meant when he said he hoped I'd stay? Not for him but for the people. A twinge of sadness stabbed at my heart even as I knew I'd do the same. According to Gemma, the people here were as much ours as the ones in our lands.

"We're here." He gave me a broad smile as he placed his hand on a panel by the gate, similar to the technology in the training room and throughout the palace.

A large wrought iron gate groaned and swung open. I stepped through and found myself in awe for the second time in one night. An unhindered night sky twinkled above us over a garden like my private one in my empire. I spun around, not believing what I was seeing. It was identical down to the moonflowers and fountain only on a larger scale. There were more night-blooming flowers than just my beloved moonflowers, but it was the purple one I was drawn to.

I reached out to caress the petals. "I've never seen a purple moonflower before. "

"It's rare, like you, Ari," he said. "I had them planted in the garden for your arrival."

I turned to face him. Moonlight danced across his chiseled jaw, accenting his exquisite features—the scar barely visible in the shadows of night. I reached up to trace it. His gaze never left mine. He nuzzled his cheek against my palm.

"The rest of the garden was planted by your mother and those who served with her. King Veran granted the use of the space to your mother when she was in college."

"You still owe me the story of your scar," I whispered.

He lifted a shoulder. "A battle scar from the exchange of power."

"It suits you. You would be too perfect otherwise. Everyone needs a flaw." He cared about his people, and he cared about me. He was so much more than the person I thought was kidnapping me. He wouldn't have even been in my kingdom if my sister hadn't sent him. That was an act of love for his family.

Rainier ran his fingers up my arm, and I shivered as he stopped at my shoulder.

I didn't know if I could get past the deception, but everything he told me since we arrived was true as far as I could tell. Gemma trusted him. If he really did have interest in me, I wanted to find out more. My body agreed from the tingling sensation running down my spine.

"Do you believe in second chances, Rain?"

"You called me Rain." He licked his lips.

I mirrored his actions, willing him to kiss me. "I did."

His mouth claimed mine under the moonlight. My heart begged me to let him in, so I did. I parted my lips to grant him entry, and his tongue explored mine, stroking as if I was the only thing he needed.

He vibrated against me... again in a rhythm. I pulled back. "What is that?"

"A phone." He pulled a rectangle thing that lit up and vibrated in his hand.

"That doesn't look like the phones in our rooms." I narrowed my eyes. "What does it do?"

"It's different technology." He paused as if searching for the words. "Similar to how we communicate through our bond with unicorns, this allows us to communicate with other fae who we share our number with."

The thing lit up and vibrated again. He frowned and flipped it around for me.

"It's Laurel. See the screen," he said, anger in his voice, but I knew when I read the screen it wasn't at me.

LAUREL: ANSWER YOUR PHONE
ALBERT IS LOOSE ON THE GROUNDS

My gut twisted into knots. "My father escaped? How? Where? Goddesses and gods. Marius is on his way with Drew."

"We need to get back to the palace. I need to vanyshen. Hold on." He pulled me close.

Even with my nerves wound tight in my stomach, I

relished the way the wind wrapped around me and the colors bent and blurred as Rain moved us at the speed of magic. I landed just outside the gates of the palace in Rain's arms, and it was a good thing because my legs were weak from the journey.

"Not inside?"

"It's protected," he said. "Can you walk and talk to Marius, or should I carry you?"

"Just lead me by the hand. I can walk but my sight will be unfocused, and I really don't want to die by one of those car things."

"I won't let that happen." Rain took my hand and led us down the street.

Marius? Can you hear me? Father has escaped. Do not bring Drew here. Go back and wait until we can talk again. Did you get that Marius?

We're on the run, Ari. They found us. Marius's voice was faint. Fear for my brother lanced through me.

Don't let him get Drew. Please. Just keep Drew safe.

Trying. His voice faded, and I knew wherever he was, he was out of range.

The further away the safer they would be, but I could relax. Not until I knew for certain Drew never had to fear our Father's actions. My vision cleared. "I can see now."

"Are they okay?" He didn't let go of my hand, and it gave me comfort.

"I'm not sure. I think so." There was no way to know until I heard from Marius again. I'd sacrifice everything to make sure my little brother was safe if it came to it.

We rounded the corner to see Gemma pacing in the hall alone. "Drew?"

I shook my head. "Marius had him and was evading them, but they were far enough away that we lost contact. So, I'm hopeful."

Relief washed over her face. "Laurel is in your situation room, Rain. He's trying to track Albert, but the chip they put in him isn't working. It only gave a few beeps to identify the general direction he was headed."

A door opened and we entered a room with TVs all along the wall.

Laurel was pounding his fingers against something with letters and numbers on it, and they showed up on the TV.

"What do you have?" Rain asked. "Can you flip that screen this way?"

Laurel pushed the closest screen toward Rain. It was on some kind of hinge.

"What is all this?" I whispered to Gemma. "More technology?"

She nodded. "Yes, these screens show the security system and can track certain things. We put a chip, another piece of technology, in dear old Dad that emits a signal we can track. Kind of like those pigeons we had that always came back to the castle."

She pointed to some places on the map where there were red dots. "These are the places the signal pinged, and this was the last one."

"Is that the edge of the forest?" He couldn't be

unleashed on this world. Not after what our mother had sacrificed, and if I had her magic, I was the perfect weapon to stop him.

"Yes," Gemma said.

"I need to get out there." I moved toward the door.

"He could have gone in any direction, Ari."

"But Drew is out there," I said. "I'm not leaving our little brother in his hands. He will not be influenced by him." Or worse...but I pushed what that might mean away.

"Then I'm coming with you." Gemma dropped the jacket she had on over a chair.

"Neither of you should be out there," Rain said. "It could be part of his plans. He could be setting a trap for you."

"He's our father." I gestured between me and Gemma. No one knew Father better than me and my sister. "We can handle him."

"It has to be us. He'll see anyone else as a threat." Gemma was at a wall and pressed her hand against it. The panel flipped open showing an arsenal of swords, knives, and guns. The latter were uncommon in the Court of Love and Prosper...the Court of Curses. There weren't means to make them and so few trades involved them. Luckily, Gemma pulled out two swords and offered me one. I declined, flipping my cape back to show the twin blades secured at my hips. She nodded and reached for two daggers, securing them with straps to her pants.

Gemma crossed the room. Laurel spun in the chair,

and she crushed her lips against his. I looked away. It had been frowned on in our youth to show that kind of affection in public. My gaze landed on Rainier, and he was watching me. I'd moved close enough that I could reach my hand out to him, but I didn't. We weren't my sister and her husband. We'd shared a brief kiss in the garden and still had much to talk through.

I turned away, but a strong hand grasped mine. I slid my gaze back to Rain. His fingers brushed along the tips of mine as he let go. "Come back to me, Ari."

I swallowed down the desire from the intimate contact. He didn't try to stop me, despite his belief I was hope for his people. I nodded and let my hand drop from his.

"Put this in your ear like this." Gemma handed me a soft-tipped thing and showed me how she slipped hers in place. I mimicked her movement. "You got us?"

Laurel punched on the board in front of him and slid a headpiece over his head, covering his ear.

"It's a keyboard," Gemma whispered to me.

That made sense since it unlocked so much information.

She gestured to the thing he'd just put on. "And the contraption on his head is a headset. He'll be able to communicate with us."

Laurel glanced at the TV in front of Rain. Rain scanned the screen. "We've got them."

"Don't send anyone else unless we ask for it," Gemma said.

"We'll keep them back unless we get the signal," Rain said to her, but his eyes found mine. "Are you sure?"

"Yes," I said. "We'll talk when I get back."

Gemma and I darted from the room and out toward our father's last known location.

CHAPTER 38

RAIN

I gritted my teeth until it was painful as I watched her move along the map. Ari and her sister were the only two adult family left with his blood, so they stood a chance of getting closer to him than we would. It was the right call, but I fucking hated it. The way he'd spoken to Ari made me want nothing except death for him. Ari needed to understand her decisions were hers to make, and I wouldn't stand in her way. Ever. She wasn't a prisoner in her real kingdom and never would be. But fucking goddesses and gods, the urge to vanyshen to her and stand between her and her father was like a vise on my chest, squeezing until it was hard to breathe.

"Control your temper, my brother," Laurel warned.

"I am," I grumbled. There was no way I'd lose it with Ari out there and risk dropping a tornado or worse on her and Gemma. My head ached from holding it in, but I'd find another way to let it out.

The monitor flickered, and I banged the side. It went to nothing but static.

"What in all the gods?" Laurel said, looking around the room.

I followed his gaze, and all the screens were static. Fuck this. I scooted my chair back from the desk. "It's him. He knows. We need to get to Ari and Gemma."

The weapons safe opened at the wave of my hand, and I immediately strapped my sword to my back and daggers at both sides. Laurel was on his feet doing the same.

"She's going to be pissed," he said. "They both are."

"You can stay here if you don't want Gemma's wrath, but I'm going," I challenged, knowing he wouldn't back down.

"Not a god's chance," he said opening the door to the hall.

We ran at top speed to the gate where we could vanyshen.

Gemma and I were almost at the gate. She'd opened and closed her mouth several times on the way out of the palace.

"What, Gemma? Just say it."

"I told myself I wouldn't interfere, but Rain likes you. When he's with you, it is the first time I've seen him focus on anything but running the empire."

"Not the time, Gemma." I paused. "I don't know if I could ever fully trust him. Not with my heart anyway."

"Give him a chance. I think you two would be really good together." Gemma faced me and wrapped her arms around me.

"I told him we could talk when you and I get back, but his dick better be some kind of magical peen for all the drama he brought to my life."

Gemma tilted her head back and laughed. "Truth, but he also brought you to me. Ready?"

"Ready." I was ready to reunite with my brother. My

head convinced me my heart could handle what was to become of my father, but my heart, twisting tightly in my chest, contradicted that assessment. I'd do what needed to be done with Father...even if it cost me the good part of me. Even if it made me like what this kingdom believed him to be.

My sister vanyshened us to the last known position. The method of travel was much easier each time. I'm sure I'd enjoy it under other circumstances.

Gemma guided us to a spot several yards away and used her wind magic to shield us so our scents wouldn't travel through the forest.

Arianna... Gemma... The ghosts of the forest started their bullshit using my mother's voice this time, and I couldn't yell at them to shut up without giving us away. The spirits must be cruel to use Mother's voice. Hearing the strong but gentle lilt made my insides hollow and forced me to tune it out despite loving the sound. Control over myself and my power depended on it.

"I hate that," I whispered. "We need to release them."

"Yes, but not tonight," she said, keeping her voice ultra-low. "Try Marius from here and then we can start moving."

I nodded, praying to the goddesses and gods that he was far away from the forest.

Gemma advanced from tree to tree, her affinity for wood allowed her to blend in. She covered me so we could move as one.

Arianna... Gemma...

Chills went down my spine. If it was possible to kick a ghost's ass, that would be on my agenda tonight too.

Gemma froze. I thought for a moment it was from the ghost voice, but it wasn't. Our father was directly in front of us talking to a man with the palest skin I'd ever seen. Father's gestures were lively and animated. For the briefest moment, he reminded me of the man who had sat with us for Yule as we opened our presents. But that man was real. His companion could be a ghost himself. Then, the man smiled at our father, and fangs glinted in the moonlight.

"He's a nosferatu...vampire," Gemma whispered. "I knew he had contacted them, but —

"My daughters are here it seems." Father smiled straight at us.

Bile rose in my throat, and I grabbed for a dagger. Gemma dropped our glamour and stepped out from behind the tree. She reached for her sword.

The vampire hissed at us.

"No." Father smirked. He lifted his hand in the air, and Gemma's weapons were unsheathed and floated away. I tried to grab a dagger, but I couldn't reach it. Mine remained pressed against my hips. There wasn't time to consider why. Father held up two fingers and twisted them. The swords and daggers flipped and pointed at us. My breath froze. I tried to summon my power, but it didn't respond. Goddesses and gods. Why didn't it work when I needed it?

"I'm willing to renegotiate for a taste of them." The vampire licked his lips.

My stomach roiled. I hadn't understood Father's power. Confronting him here like this was a mistake. "We need to go, Gemma."

Wind blew in behind us. I felt Rainier's arrival but didn't turn around. His presence was usually calming, but tension vibrated from him as strong as his magic.

"They are not worth it, and we can end the Court of Storms bloodline with the other two."

My eyes burned. He was not the man who raised us. Not even close.

He thrust a hand towards us, and the swords and knives were coming at us. No time to think. I threw my hands up. The ground rumbled and dirt flew up in front of us followed by a gust of wind. A lightning bolt struck where Father and the vampire had been, but they were gone. If only the storm had shot that bolt a split-second earlier. That would have to be a stroke of luck that didn't seem to be on our side.

I moved to chase them, reaching for the Nyx-blessed blades at my hips.

"Gemma." Rain's pained voice stopped me.

I followed his gaze to find Laurel with my sister in his lap. Blood coated Gemma's shirt around the knife embedded in her chest. No. This wasn't happening. We hadn't changed into leathers. The blade pierced right through her sweater.

"Goddess, please no." I dropped down next to them, taking Gemma's hand in mine. Her grip was weak. "We'll get you to a healer."

"Hold on, my love," Laurel said to her. He grabbed my

shoulder. "Can you help my brother back so I can vanyshen Gemma back to a healer?"

I wanted to go with her, but I glanced at Rainier. A dagger stuck in the top of his leg. I shuddered. He needed help too, and he'd come for me. I couldn't vanyshen but Laurel could. "Go. Save my sister. I've got him."

"If I don't"—she swallowed hard, her skin taking on a grey tinge—"you know...help Laurel with Phina."

"Don't even ask that. You are going to be fine." I squeezed her hand. She would not die. Not today. Not when we had so much to share. Not when she had a daughter who needed her.

"Promise," she said.

I nodded. "I promise. Now go get healed."

Laurel disappeared with her. I scooted over to Rain. His leg with the knife in it was bent at an awkward angle. The blade pierced the inside of his thigh. His color was better than Gemma's but not by much. He needed help from the healers too.

"How do you want to do this?"

"Remove it," he said, his voice a whisper.

"Seriously?"

"Yes."

I gripped the hilt and closed my eyes. Blood coated my fingers, making my hold slippery, but I pulled. Rain cried out. The fleshy sounds were nauseating, but I worked the blade free and opened my eyes. Blood spurted out from the wound. I gagged, tossing the blade to the side. The blood gushed, and I pressed my hands on the open flesh.

"What now?"

"Your belt," he gritted out. "Wrap it around my leg above it and tighten it."

I did as he instructed. He paled and was close to passing out, but the blood slowed. If he lost consciousness here, I wasn't sure I could find my way back to the castle, and I was certain I couldn't carry him. Nor did I think I could fend off my father and the vampire if they returned.

Rain grabbed my hand. "Thank you. I'll try to get us close, but I'll need your help."

Power surged between us. I examined the glow around our hands. It felt like the flow was from me to him, but that wasn't possible. Not like this. But before I could process what it meant, we vanyshened. He got us close to the gate, maybe twenty yards away. I tugged his arm around my shoulders and put mine around his waist, lifting him. He grunted and wobbled as I coaxed him forward.

"Just a little further." I encouraged him, hoping he wouldn't pass out before we got inside. Tugging him through this gravel wouldn't work. I'd have to leave him here and go find help, which would leave him in the open and vulnerable. Not an option.

I half dragged him to the gate, but the metal wouldn't open. Where were all the guards?

"Rain, how do I open the gate?" His eyes were heavy, but he must have understood because he lifted his hand, waving it in front of a panel. The gate groaned open.

There was no time to relish in the relief I felt that we were finally inside the courtyard and near the entrance. I got him up the steps and inside the door, but he collapsed in my arms. I couldn't hold his weight and did my best to guide him down to the floor. "Help," I yelled. "Help!"

"Rain?" I patted his face. He'd worsened in the time it took us to travel. His color was ashen like Gemma's had been. I needed to get to her, but I couldn't leave him. I wasn't even sure where to go. "Rain?"

He can't die. I will not let him die.

The blood had slowed from the belt trick, but it wasn't healing. The wound was worse than I realized. I pressed my hands against it. I wasn't a healer and didn't know how to heal with my magic.

"Help," I screamed again and again. "Goddesses and gods, what do I do?"

A glow spread out from my hands like glamour. I blinked against the light, and we were on the floor of a different room. Dark mist surrounded us and evaporated right away. I heard shouts and jerked around to find Gemma was on a table. Laurel was directing some other fae.

My vision blurred and my throat burned. "Help." My voice was nothing more than a squeak.

Laurel looked up. Concern passed over his face, but he didn't lose focus. "You." He pointed to one of the other fae. "Help my brother."

The dark-skinned fae slid his arms under Rain and lifted him. His blood was on my hands. I wiped it on my clothes, but they were soaked too. The elf turned and placed Rain on a bed in the row across from Gemma. A couple of other fae joined him and started working on Rain.

I stood on shaky legs and made my way over to Gemma. Her color was still tinged grey, and her lips had a bluish tint. She wasn't moving, and my chest constricted. "Is she…" I couldn't finish the sentence and glanced at Laurel.

"She's healing. We have to keep her going until she heals enough."

I nodded, swallowing my fear. "What can I do?"

"If she has blood, familial blood, she will heal faster," he said, his voice soft.

"How do we do it?"

"Hop on that bed next to her." He opened a drawer and pulled out a tube and something silver. "This might sting a little."

"Just do what you need to do."

He ran his fingers over the bend of my elbow and inserted the piece of metal. I closed my eyes but could feel his fingers moving. Then the pressure was gone. The attached tube was filled with my blood and flowing into a bag. From that bag, it flowed down another tube and into a similar setup on Gemma's arm.

Laurel patted my leg. "It shouldn't take much. Blood of blood works fast."

He turned his worried look toward Rain. "I've never seen him go down like that, but he's strong."

I followed his gaze. Rain looked better, his color returning faster than Gemma's.

Laurel sat on the stool between Gemma and me. "Where's the dagger?"

"I don't know. I dropped it on the ground after I extracted it."

"It must have been a fae killer blade," he said, his voice grim.

"A what? Why..." I inhaled and let it out. Could he have died from that wound? "Why in all the goddesses and gods would you have something named that here?"

A new wave of terror rippled through me at what a blade with a name like that was meant to do. Rain had asked for my forgiveness, and he earned it when he came for me and my sister. I didn't want him to die. I wanted him to live, and I wanted to press my lips against his as soon as this tube was out of my arm and as soon as Gemma was awake.

"We retrieved them..." His voice trailed off, and I turned to him. He was staring at Gemma. Her eyes were moving under the lids, and her lashes fluttered.

I sat up and moved to the side of the bed. Laurel inched his stool closer.

"Gemma?" I willed her to open her eyes. There was so much I still wanted us to do.

Laurel took her hand in his. "Open those mesmerizing eyes."

She did as if his voice was a magnet pulling her to him. Her gaze locked on his. "I'm." She paused, swallowing hard. "I made it."

"Yes." Laurel leaned in and pressed his lips to hers.

I blinked back tears. Their love was so strong.

"Where's Phina?"

"She's safe in our room," he said.

She turned her head towards me. "I know, Ari." She slid her hand from Laurel's and found mine. "I know what you went through without me there, and I'm sorry."

The blood. Sometimes it happened when fae exchanged blood. It's why it was discouraged. She had my memories. I pressed my tongue to the roof of my mouth as I tried to hold in a sob.

I looked down at our hands and squeezed. "We'll talk about it later after you are healed."

"Ari?" A rough voice called my name.

I wanted to go comfort him, but I had to finish this blood exchange with Gemma. My heart tore in two pieces.

"He's running a fever, Prince Laurel. We can't use the tea we normally use with the prince unconscious."

Laurel undid the contraption siphoning my blood to Gemma and bandaged my arm.

"Ari..." Rain's eyes were closed but he called my name.

Gemma nodded to me, and I crossed the room to the other person my father nearly killed tonight.

CHAPTER 40
ARI

Blood coated the floor, the sheets, and all four of us. The metallic odor penetrated the air and was so pungent I couldn't smell Rain's minty scent.

"Ari." Rain said my name more as a whisper this time. I scooted a chair from across the room next to him and took his hand in mine.

"I'm here," I said, my voice so soft I almost didn't recognize it as my own.

Laurel was giving instructions to the other healers. "Gather some ice for now. We can use that to keep him cool while the other healers gather the serpent root."

Serpent root couldn't be found on the other side of the forest, but there were tales of what those who gathered it endured. It was only found at the edge of the forest where it met the mountains.

"I'll go with them, Laurel." I knew the area based on the tales and what the root looked like.

"No, I can vanyshen a small group there. Otherwise, it would take days to get there."

I nodded. It wasn't a skill I had, but after how Rain used my power to get us close to the gate, I was confident it was something I could and would learn.

"You'll have to teach me that when you wake up." I caressed his cheek with the backs of my fingers. His skin was so hot to the touch that it was jarring. Several fae rolled carts in the room with rectangular-shaped buckets of ice water. I rose to grab some of them and found towels submerged in the chilled liquid. They planned to wrap him in cold. I'd heard of this technique, but we'd never used it. Fevers like this were so rare on the other side. I reached into the container and pulled one of the towels out, shivering as I squeezed the excess water out.

"Start with the feet and legs. Then the arms. It's better to help the heart adjust to it."

"Thank you," I said with a nod to the man. He was a large elf with kind brown eyes.

He wrapped the opposite foot as I started on mine. "My name is Ari. May I ask yours?"

"Bastian, but most people call me Baz."

"Well, Baz. Thank you for your help."

"Anytime, Your Majesty."

My spine went rigid, and I had to force myself to relax. Surely everyone in the castle knew my story as Gemma's sister. "No need for such formalities. I was a princess in a kingdom made up to be a prison for my father. I believe that makes me just another subject of this kingdom now."

He swallowed and kept working but didn't say anything for a while. Baz stood about the same height as Laurel and had the same light hair color. He had an accent I didn't recognize.

"Your sister is quite brave," Baz said, as we moved to the hands and arms.

I glanced over at her, sleeping as she recovered. Pride swelled in my chest to be related to her. "She is the bravest person I know. More than anyone can imagine."

I studied the strange clock in the room, so different than the large clocks I was used to on the bell tower. If I read it correctly, Laurel and the team had been gone thirty or so minutes. They were searching for the dark root in the nighttime, so it would probably take a bit to find it.

"Have you always lived in this city, Baz?"

"Yes, my family has always resided here. My mother was a cousin to the king."

"So, you are related to Rainier and Laurel?"

His eyes cast down. "No, not really."

He sounded wounded by the memory, so I dropped it and focused on Rain and the wrapping we were doing.

Rain's exposed finger twitched. I slipped my hand into his. "You're not alone. I'm here, Rain. Laurel has gone to get medicine for you. You'll feel better soon."

His hand tightened painfully around mine. I tried to pull it free, but I couldn't. His body stiffened. Our hands glowed, and power licked at me like it had when we vanyshened outside the gate.

Wrong time, power.

I broke out in sweat as I tried to stop it. Rain's arms and legs twitched. The harder they moved, the more power surged between us, and my gut twisted. The bed started to vibrate, and instruments fell from the table next to us. I scanned the room. This was our joined power. I couldn't break Rain's hold on my hand, but maybe I could direct some of my magic around us to protect everyone else.

"Step back." I shot Baz a look. He was wide-eyed but moved away.

I dug deep like Marius had taught me and called for magic that would encase us and shield the others. A dark mist cast around us like a net. Then the room fell away from view, and I was standing in Rain's rooms. But how? He was standing at the window in front of the balcony.

"Rain?" My voice barely worked. "Did you bring us here?"

I made my way across the room to where he was. He turned to look at me. His eyes were an even darker shade of blue, and I wasn't sure how that was possible.

"I'm dreaming. I know I am, but you feel so real." He slid a hand into my hair and caressed my cheek with his thumb.

"It's not a dream. I'm not sure what this is." Maybe it was a dream. Maybe it was my dream. Maybe I passed out from our magic colliding, and this was my subconscious. That had to be it. And if it was, I could give in to this version of Rain...at least until I woke up.

I tentatively placed my hand on his arm. A glow grew around where my skin met his. The touch felt real but not quite completely. As I looked around, a mix of dark mist and golden starlight shrouded us on all sides, but none more noticeable than out the window where most of the city was concealed by it.

Rain crooked his finger under my chin and turned my face gently back to him. He studied my mouth and lowered his to mine. His lips caressed mine so softly, but it electrified me on the inside. My body demanded more. I slid my hand up his arm and around his neck.

The electricity erupted between us as if we were melded together. The sensation like our souls were smelted and then reformed as one. Rain urged my lips apart, and I welcomed him in, meeting his tongue with mine. This was a dream because real life was never this intense.

Rain pulled back, a grin tugging at the corners of his mouth. "It's not a dream."

"Did you read my thoughts?"

"No…" His head tilted. "Maybe. I've never been able to do it before, so don't throw any knives at me."

The knife. The wound. "Are you still hurt?"

He looked down at his leg, and I followed suit. His pants weren't torn or bloody. He kicked his leg as if to emphasize he wasn't injured. "Looks like I'm healed."

"I don't understand." I tried to remember what we were doing before we came here, but the specifics eluded me. "Did you bring us here from the forest?"

He considered my question. "I must have."

"I'm glad you are okay," I said, my hand resting

against his cheek. A flash of a strange room flickered through my mind, but I couldn't latch onto it.

Rain nuzzled into my hand. "There are stories in our history of meetings like this."

"What stories?" I'd never heard of anything like this.

Ari... My name was a whisper around me in a familiar voice. Gemma's. My sister.

"Ari, your eyes look distant."

"I thought I heard Gemma say my name." It must have been Rain. My mind had to be playing tricks on me.

"What were you saying?" Why was my mind so foggy? Like memories were disappearing.

He opened the balcony and coaxed me out there with him. The mist mixed with moonlight was even more beautiful from here. Rain leaned his elbow on the railing and slipped the other arm around my waist, pulling me close to him. His touch warmed and comforted me. "Our origins go back for lifetimes. Many, many lifetimes. There is a story told of one of our goddesses, Nyx. It is said that when her gaze fell upon Erebus, the world was covered in mist and moonlight."

I reached for the blades at my hips, but there was nothing there. What were those blades, and why were they important to me? I lifted my hand and waved it through the air in front of us. The mist and moonlight danced around my fingers. "So, what does it mean now?"

"If the lore is true, it means a union has been blessed by Nyx."

I shivered with delight and fear intertwined in my body. "Us? But I don't even like you."

Rain chuckled and laced his fingers through mine. "Maybe not, but you don't hate me anymore."

I'd never hated him, but before I could give sound to my words, the strange room with the white beds flashed through my eyes, followed by a familiar woman's face. Gemma. My sister. My body jerked, and the balcony rippled. *Ari.* Gemma called my name again.

"Did you hear that?" I peered inside Rain's living room, but no one was there.

He held my hand as I investigated. I walked through the living room and looked down the hall. There wasn't anyone else here with us.

A bright light flashed in my eyes, and I threw my hand up to block. My chest was on fire, burning like hot coals sat on it.

"Ari?" Gemma's voice was close.

I blinked my eyes against the light. "Gemma?"

The healer's room came into view. She'd almost died, but she was standing over me. Rain almost died. The jolt when I held his hand... I tried to sit up.

Gemma pressed a hand on my shoulder holding me down. "Don't sit up just yet."

"Shouldn't you be in bed healing?" I asked, making the sounds was like glass dragging up and down my throat.

"That was two days ago, Ari. I'm healed."

She tugged on my hand, and there was a weight there. A familiar touch. Rain's hand was in mine. I glanced around her to see his head was on the opposite end as mine, but our fingers were still wound with each other's. The dream. It had been a dream, despite how real it felt standing in his rooms and on his balcony. Disappointment coiled in my belly that we weren't a union blessed by Nyx. It was a fabrication of my imagination, and Rain was still out after two days. Did that mean Laurel hadn't returned with the serpent root? Panic slid up my spine and wrenched my heart, because blessed union or not, I wanted Rain to live.

CHAPTER 41

ARI

Laurel came through the door carrying a syringe. "Time for his next dose."

I smiled at him. Laurel had gotten the medicine in his brother, and this was the last of it. Time would tell, but the fever had come down a lot. I'd avoided holding Rain's hand, but I'd only left his side when Gemma insisted I shower. My strength was back within an hour after waking up. There had been no signs of my father, but the patrols were ongoing. I'd managed to reach Marius, and he and Drew were safe after evading some vampires that had come close to their location. Our arrangement to get Drew was postponed until our crew here was healed.

Rain's eyes opened and squinted shut. He peeked through the slits. Relief washed over me like a broken dam.

"Ari." He held his hand out to me. I bypassed the touch

and patted his arm just in case we went to whatever that was while holding hands.

"How are you feeling?" I asked him.

"Better once I get out of this bed." He tried to sit up, but Laurel and I held him down. Rain was strong, but the days and the fever had weakened him. He couldn't fight us and relaxed back to the bed.

"The medicine needs time to work, which means you need to remain still for a while."

"No, I believe things move through our bloodstream faster with exercise." He wagged his eyebrows at me.

"Is it always about sex with you?" I rolled my eyes and laughed. It was a sign he was better.

"I'm going to check on my mate. Glad you didn't die, big brother." Laurel squeezed Rain's shoulder and left us alone.

"It's hard not to think about it when you are taking care of me so well."

I snorted. "I could push you out of that bed with a gust of wind."

His brow quirked up along with the corner of his mouth. "You could try."

I rose to go find the healer, but he grasped my hand as if he was desperate for the touch. No light or dream came this time. "Don't leave."

Staying with him sounded right, but the strange dream thing left me confused. "I'm only going to ask the healer when he will release you."

"We call them doctors here. The ones who don't use technology prefer the title of healer."

I nodded. "I'll be back by the time the *doctor* says you can go home."

He winked at me, and I pressed my hand against my chest fighting the urge to lean against the wall and swoon for him. His ego was already too big. He didn't need to know my heart was beating out of control. I turned away coming face to face with my sister. She'd entered without me realizing it. Rain was a distraction, but I knew that from the first time we met. It was up to me to decide if that was a good or bad thing.

"Ari? I was coming to find you." Gemma said, studying me. The worry in her eyes was a reminder that she still thought I was fragile like the moonflowers in the garden. I wasn't the same girl she left there five years ago, and she was the one wounded a couple of days earlier.

"Hi, Gemma. What for? Shouldn't you be resting?"

"To see if you had eaten. Come have lunch with me?"

I glanced at Rain, hesitant to go too far from the healer's chamber. His smile was like the sun except it heated me from the inside out.

"I promise to have you back before Rain is out of there."

"As the brother of one of the doctors, I can assure you they will not move fast enough to release me before you go eat." Rain was looking down at his phone, but his cheeks were pink from his broad grin.

My stomach growled before I could respond as if it was demanding attention. "Lunch would be great."

Gemma smiled and linked her arm through mine

while guiding me down the hallway, but not in the direction of our rooms.

"We're not going to your apartments?" I asked.

"No, I made friends with the cooks and staff in the kitchen when I was pregnant with Phina. We're going there." Gemma wagged her brows at me.

GEMMA and I perched on the edge of our stools at the countertop. The cook cleared our plates, and mine was spotless. I'd never had roasted meat and vegetables with such delicious gravy in my life.

"Chocolate cake again?" Gemma asked as the cook sat a piece in front of each of us. "Not that I'm complaining it's become a staple, but how about some variety?"

"Prince Rainier has asked that we keep a fresh one ready, but he hasn't eaten any of it."

My cheeks burned even though no one could possibly know what we had done with the cake. I pushed mine away. Embarrassment stole my appetite.

"You have to try it, Ari. It's almost better than..." Gemma's voice trailed off as she took another bite. "Mmm."

I wanted to crawl under the table. "I ate too much already. I don't feel so good. Maybe the walk back to the healer's room, I mean doctor's room, will make me feel better."

Gemma shrugged and thanked the cook. "Can you send a few pieces to my room with dinner tonight?"

My sister couldn't know. He wouldn't have told her... but would he have told his brother? Laurel wouldn't keep anything from Gemma. That was clear. Goddesses and gods, take me now.

"Of course." The cook smiled. "I know your daughter loves chocolate."

"That she does," Gemma said.

When we were in the hall headed back the way we came, she asked what I suspected was coming. "How are you dealing with...everything?"

"It all feels like a dream, not just the weird dream with Rainier from the electrical shock, but all of this."

She nodded. "I understand. I had proof, and I still struggled to comprehend it."

"But look at you now. It's like you have never lived anywhere else. I don't even know the names of half the things I see." I sighed, letting out some of the frustration. My determination to learn all the new technology wavered.

"The knowledge will come with time and repetition. Just like all things we learn. You couldn't wield a blade on the first try." Gemma looped her arm through mine, and we strolled casually down the hall.

The pleasant pace was a nice change. "Speaking of blades—"

"They're in your room. I wouldn't let anyone else touch them. Not that they could."

I smiled. "You are the best big sister a girl could have."

"And don't you forget it." We made the corner to the

infirmary as the sign said above it. "I'm going to leave you here to go check on my husband who probably needs rescuing from our daughter. She has him wrapped around her little finger. Join us for dinner tonight?"

"That sounds perfect." I hugged her and entered the room to find Rain sitting on the edge of the bed.

CHAPTER 42
ARI

Rain's coloring had returned to normal, and he looked like himself even if his strength hadn't fully returned. The doctors gave him strict instructions to rest, and I got him to the couch in his suite of rooms.

"Do you want anything to eat or drink?"

He patted the cushion beside him. "No, come sit. Let's talk. There are lots of things we need to discuss."

Sweat coated my palms, and I wasn't sure why I was nervous. He was offering to answer the questions I had. "Are you sure—"

"Arianna, sit. Please."

I lowered myself to the couch. "Baz helped me wrap you in the towels just before..." I didn't know what to call it and struggled to believe it was even real. "The dream state. He said he is your cousin?"

Rain's eyes narrowed a fraction as he searched mine. "What else did he say?"

I resisted the urge to squirm under his gaze. "Nothing really. What he actually said is his mother was the king's cousin, so that makes you second cousins, right?"

"Not quite." He twirled a strand of my hair between his fingers.

I curled one leg under me and rested my arm on the back of the couch. He mirrored my position and laid his arm on top of mine. I didn't miss the protective nature of it. Gods help me, I relished the contact.

"My father was the brother of the queen. His mother was the cousin of the king. We are of no blood relation. His mother, Laveena, murdered her cousin, King Veran."

My hand slid to my throat. "Murdered?"

"She had good reason. He was mad and executed our people for the smallest infraction. He had my father thrown in a cell that suppresses magic. He almost died in there." Rain's eyes darkened to almost black.

"Where is she now?"

"She drank the same poison she'd given him." His voice lowered to a soft tone as if he were lost in the memories, absently tracing circles on my arm. "Queen Edwina abdicated her rule in favor of my father, because he had two children, and she had no surviving children."

"And your mother?"

"She died giving birth to me, and my father married Laurel's mother. She was a hell of a warrior and died on the battlefield during the war."

"Where the forest is?" His stepmother, Laurel's mother, could be one of the ghosts that haunted the land.

I shivered. It must be horrible to know someone he loved had suffered such a fate.

"Yes." He frowned. His features tightened.

"And where is your father now? The real one …not the duke you claimed at my court."

"He was lost over the border with vampires. He never should have been there. I'd been severely injured." He touched the scar on his face and placed a hand over his chest. I remembered the deep scar just below his breastbone. "He was there to see to me. Familial blood. Something you understand the power of."

His hand stilled on mine, and I laced our fingers together. My heart ached for him and so much tragedy and it didn't escape me how similar his were to my own experiences. "I'm so sorry."

"It's been many decades, but it is still difficult to speak of." He drew the tips of my fingers to his lips and placed the most delicate kiss on my skin.

I worked on a swallow. "Did you know my mother and father? Before the war?"

The corners of his mouth turned up a tiny bit as he looked at his fingers and flattened his hand against my palm. His touch was like fire on my skin. "Your mother's magic was much like yours. Powerful and a bit wild."

"She was always so in command when she was with us. Strong, yes, but I can't imagine her ever being out of control."

His smile grew but it was sad. "What you saw was just a fraction of it. The majority of her magic was used to create the empire you knew. Her power was depleted to keep Albert there."

My mother died to keep my father imprisoned. She deserved honors and accolades, but she was stuck with an evil fae who sucked her magic dry.

"My home was a prison. The home I loved was a cage for him." It wasn't unlike the cage they kept my father in here but a bigger version. My entire life was built around keeping my father from starting another war. A lie. It was all a lie, and anger stole my breath.

He resumed the idle circles on my arm. "It was never meant to be that way for so long, but your mother couldn't keep it in place from a distance. It took a toll on her maintaining it for centuries."

"But it remained after she died."

"Her final gift aided by an ancestor."

"What about the people?" The people I thought were my people who were subjects of this court. People I cared about. Some even my friends.

"The first generation was volunteers, but few of them are left. Volunteers could leave and join as they pleased. Most chose to stay and raise their children there. Many have been born and raised there to continue. Some were aware and others not. We have a team there helping them to adjust and make a choice as to whether to stay there or return here."

But no one saw it necessary to tell me or Gemma. Did Val know? No, she would have told me. Andrews was too young. I shook my head. "Is Val safe?"

"She is. She and her husband are helping with the transition on the other side of the forest."

My friend had decided to stay and help others. Her act of kindness warmed my heart.

"And this ancestor of mine? How did this person help?"

"That is a story Gemma should probably tell."

"Gemma was living in the cursed court with me. I want to hear it from you." I met his gaze. His eyebrows bunched. Concern showed on his face.

He looked down where his fingers touched me. When his gaze drifted back up to mine, his eyes were the deeper dark blue. "It dates back to the time when unicorns began bonding fae. There's a reason the unicorns haven't been bonding with as many. They are a dying breed." He paused, and I watched his throat bob, hyperaware of the tension set in his shoulders now. "The unicorns are going extinct. They have been since before the war. There have only been two born since the end of it, and all their magic will die with them. Nyx's power bound our species together, so our magic will wane with them."

Marius. Leana. Goddess and gods, no. My hand went to my throat. He knew and still bonded me. Why? I had to do something for them. Surely there was a way we could save them, but this kingdom had something they called electricity that it could switch over to and power lights and the technology they called computers. They would survive here, but my unicorn friends would not.

"A world without magic sounds unfathomable." The words tasted foul on my tongue. I chewed on it for a second and realized our magic was a life force. A world without unicorns didn't even seem possible, and I'd do whatever it took to save them.

"Only Nyx's power can save us. Blood of blood. Blood of old."

"So, we need Nyx's blood?" Nyx was ancient and had long since walked this place. There wasn't a way to get her blood unless someone could time travel. Her blessing, yes, but no one could actually walk in her realm and return here.

"In a way."

"Where would we find it? Isn't she out of our reach in a realm of her own?"

"We already have." He paused as if he expected me to say something, but I didn't know what he meant. "It's you, Ari. You are Nyx's descendant, and we have been waiting for one of her direct descendants to manifest all her powers. For her to pass that gift to the one who can undo the bond she created."

I understood then. Why my bond was so strong. Why my training had been important. Why those damn swords had been blessed. Why we saw her triple moon in a constellation. "It's why Marius chose me. Unicorns can sense the power, but he had to know how strong that connection would be. And you're sure it's me? I've never felt particularly powerful, at least not in a meaningful way that I could control."

"Haven't you though? When I returned to your castle, were you not controlling the earth? Do you not know how rare that particular gift is?"

"My mother could do it." I had magic and various kinds. That was true. But none of it was earth-shattering power like he referenced in my mother.

"And I was too weak to bring us here. It was your magic that powered our trip."

The knowledge was too much at once. I couldn't process it all between the strangeness of the city, the technologies, and my magic being more than I realized. *Who am I?* The daughter of a king who slaughtered almost an entire empire, but also, the daughter of a savior of her people. And Nyx's blood ran through me. I stood and walked to the glass door of the balcony. The lights of a city I knew nothing about marked my real home.

Where do I belong? Am I a destructor or rescuer? Or neither?

Rain moved silently, but the heat of his body filled the space between us. My back warmed at his closeness and that damned spot in my lower abdomen tightened. Rain rubbed my upper arms. Comfort was what I needed, and he was giving me that. I reclined back into him, letting my head rest against his chest. His arms slipped around me, caging me in a net of safety. He lowered his chin to the top of my head.

"You belong here, Ari. As General Daphina's daughter. As a descendant of Nyx. I want to help you reach your destiny. And, hopefully, you will allow me to reside in your universe."

It was strange to hear my mother called a general. Hearing her revered was so gratifying, but I wasn't sure I'd get used to it. I saw it more and more in my memories.

What struck me most was Rain asked, not demanded, to be with me. Wished I could have known him growing up, but he probably wouldn't have even known my name if I'd been raised here. I wanted to understand more of my mother's world... more of Rain's world. There was no home for me to return to. I couldn't go back. "I want to stay, Rain, and I'd like to get to know you and your people."

"They are your people too. Why do I hear a but at the end of that statement?" His voice vibrated through me.

"But..." I said, drawing it out. "I don't know that I belong here. That I will ever fit into this kind of world. I don't know anything about TVs or computers or the autos on the streets. Those are scarier than the spirits in the forest, by the way."

His reflection smiled into my hair. "You will become accustomed to those things in time, but you don't have to know everything today. You just have to know what you want. Where you will live. Are you ready to know more?"

I let out a breath and turned in his arms, summoning a bit of courage. There was one thing I had to see. "I know I want to learn more about you."

A crooked smile appeared on his lips. "You do?"

"Yes." I slid my arms around his waist.

"I can help you with that." He lowered his mouth, brushing his lips across mine in a gentle caress. The patience and restraint he showed told me he would follow my lead and go at my pace.

CHAPTER 43
RAIN

Ari looked up at me through her lashes, and my balls tightened. Her gaze filled with trust I didn't deserve, but I wanted to earn. I ruled this kingdom out of duty because, like her, I'd never asked for this either. I'd say fuck it all and go live out our days together in any corner of the kingdom she desired if she ever said she wanted me...chose me.

We have a problem. Casimir's voice echoed in my head. If she was disrupting whatever mission she was on to contact me now, it had to be bad.

What kind of problem?

A vampire problem.

Why hadn't our monitoring or patrols picked them up? I'd be removing guards from posts for this, and if anyone was hurt, they would pay the same price.

And? I asked. *How many?*

Less than twenty. They are saying they are a delegation, and Albert is with them.

Fuck. A shitshow was what it was.

Fuck is right.

Where are they?

At your gate. "My gate" she said. Not the main gate. They'd been watching us and probably saw a weakness I'd missed.

Goddesses and godsdamn it. Let them in with a full escort. Take them to the reception room on the first floor. Guards on full alert.

It was a trick, but having Albert surrounded by my soldiers would make it easy to take him down.

Oh, the goddesses and gods have already damned them, but as you wish.

I leaned back, debating on whether to tell Ari her father was at the door. Not that I didn't believe she could handle it, but because I knew it would cause her pain. Knew she would want to see him if for no other reason but to confront him, and his actions would hurt her. Her trust mattered most to me, and transparency in this situation was a step to earn it.

"Your father is here with a group of emissaries. They just arrived and are being shown to a meeting room where we can maintain security."

Ari's eyes widened. "Was this planned?"

I shook my head. "No, they showed up at the gate. You don't have to see him, but I will make sure you are well-guarded if you want to join the discussion." Anger burned in my gut at how Albert tried to kill Ari. And Gemma. While my good sense might stop me from killing him tonight, his head would be mine for what he tried to do to

Ari. For the trauma he put her through. My phone buzzed, and I retrieved it from my pocket.

"What is that?" Ari asked.

I raised my gaze from Laurel's message to see her pointing at the phone in my hand. I'd flashed the screen to her in the garden, but I hadn't thought to show her how text messages worked. Guess Gemma hadn't either. "These smaller phones can send messages back and forth."

She rolled her eyes. "I know that. I meant what is the message on the pocket phone."

Her tone was so curious I couldn't help but smile despite what waited on the lower floor for us.

"It's my brother." I tapped my reply to Laurel to let him know we knew and were on our way. "And the messages are called texts that we send to each other on them."

"Texts? Got it."

I flipped the screen around so she could see the message I sent to my brother.

"Can I get one?"

"Absolutely. I'll take you to get one after I deal—"

"With my father. I'm going with you." She inhaled a breath and exhaled it.

I extended my hand out to her, and she slipped hers into mine. Touching Ari, a single touch, made me want more from life than to be a warrior or a prince. And more was always dangerous in our world.

Rain released my hand before we entered the room with my father. I understood why, but the lack of contact left an unwelcome chill on my hand. The disgust on my father's face wasn't welcome either. I resisted the urge to return his scowl and kept my face neutral. He wouldn't get a reaction out of me if that was his goal. Marius had trained me well on that for political meetings. Plus, I had the courtier training on how to appear impassive. I'd practiced in the mirror for countless hours.

Father stood, and the men with him stood. No, not men. Vampires. Not long ago I would have been shocked, but no longer.

"No surprise to see my traitorous daughter at your side still." Father sneered, looking me up and down.

Rain moved his body between us as a shield, but I side-stepped him. "Why are you here? To insult me? There is no greater insult you can hurl my way than to call me your daughter. That is the only thing I am ashamed of."

Gemma entered with Laurel, hands intertwined and close together.

A smile spread across his face. "I'm here to claim my right to take both of my daughters with me. As their father, a king, and by fae law, I will be leaving with them."

I'm not property. My sister isn't property. He doesn't own us.

I didn't care whether there was a law I'd never heard of or not.

"That has not been law since before you were imprisoned," Laurel said, his tone steel. "Gemma is my wife by law and my mate. She will not be leaving with you."

Father's expression turned pure evil, a wicked grin spreading across his face. "Without her father's blessing?"

"I do not need your permission," Gemma said. Her hand slipped to the dagger strapped to her waist. "And you are no king."

I hadn't thought to grab any weapons and regret trapped my breath on that decision.

"You've given birth then," he said, his eyes narrowing on her as if he could see the answer, and it wasn't a question.

Gemma's gaze went to Laurel's. It was the movement Father needed for confirmation. His evil grin turned on me.

"You are unwed and unmated still." Another statement and not a question.

I was unsure about the second part. The connection between Rain and me was different. *Mates?* I wasn't sure if that's what it was, but I definitely knew it was different. *Special.*

Rain took my hand as if staking a claim, but I didn't withdraw. I'd choose him this time and every time.

Father studied our entwined hands. "You may keep her if you return my son."

Panic shot up my spine, and if Rain wasn't steadying me my legs might have given out.

"No," Gemma said, her tone terror-filled.

Marius? Can you hear me? I cursed myself for not checking sooner.

"Either Andrews or Arianna will be going with me as my protege. You can choose. Or we can start a war tonight?"

"Why would I give you anything when I could slay you here and be done with it?" Rain sounded every bit a predator. I'd seen that look before in the court of my prison kingdom. He assessed and calculated. I could almost see his mind working out how to draw the important information from my father.

Marius, run. If you are anywhere near this palace, run. If you can hear this, run until you can't.

"Because the vampire legions are ready to lay waste to your city. One of my children for your precious city. It's a fair trade."

I'm coming for you. Marius's voice was a whisper in my head, so he wasn't close. Thank the goddess.

No, get Andrews to safety. Father is here and wants to take him.

He is safe.

A breath threatened to loosen, but showing any reaction to Father could jeopardize them. I worked to keep my face neutral.

Don't come. It's not safe.

You are my charge. I will come.

No, Marius.

"Are you telling that bastard ruler of the unicorns to come save you?" He looked pleased as if I'd played into his hand, but I wasn't the weak child he seemed to think I was.

"No," I said, the single word filled with venom.

The vampire next to him hissed and leaned over to whisper in my father's ear. Father clapped his hands together as if he was excited by what the vampire had told him.

"Excellent. He is here. Shall we meet him outside?"

Panic shot straight down my spine like a spike. *Marius? Tell me you're not here.*

I cannot.

Fuck. "Let him go." *Drew isn't with you, is he?*

No, I left him with Leana. He is safe.

But you're not?

Do not give your father whatever it is he is asking for, Arianna. I am prepared to die. I have been since the day I claimed you as my charge.

Not today, Marius. We protect each other.

Do not—

I closed my mental door on him while I faced my father. "Let my guardian go. You break sacred laws by imprisoning a unicorn, especially Marius."

"Only if you leave here with me."

"We shall see him for confirmation," Rain said, his hand tightening on mine. He gave me one shake of his head, then looked over the top of me to where Laurel and Gemma stood. He wanted my father in the open of the courtyard. It was risky, but a fight outside was better than in these confined quarters. Less risk of injury to others.

"Reach out to him and ask him," Father said, challenging no doubt to see if I had already.

"I cannot." A simple lie to push us forward.

Father let out a disgusted sigh. "You are an embarrassment to not be able to control him."

My anger tipped like water spilling over a dam, and something awakened in me. Since I'd found out who he truly was, a part of me hoped the other him, the one I knew as a child, would return. But it never would. It wasn't the real him. The version of him I loved was a fabrication and never existed. The cruel man before me might be biologically connected, but he wasn't my father. My heart shattered like crystal on a marble floor.

"Very well," he said, gesturing for the door. "You first."

Rain nodded to Laurel, who led the way, followed by Gemma, then me, with Rain at my back. He placed his hand on my hip. The walk to the front door was only a few steps, but with every footfall, a force expanded in me like it craved to erupt. I rolled my head around my shoulders as we crossed the threshold, but the building tension strengthened.

Marius was standing tall in the dim light, but as we plodded closer, shackles came into view—on his ankles, his neck, and around his midsection. Heat rose in me from my magic, and something cool mixed with it. At least twenty vampires surrounded him. I pressed my lips together to keep the utterance of profanity from my brain out of my mouth.

I'll get you free, I said, opening my mind to him once again.

No, I will pay this price. I know what he wants with you. His tone was resigned. The unstoppable leader of the unicorns was willing to sacrifice himself for me, and I finally had the answer that he was more than my bonded. He was my friend...my family.

This is not your choice to make, Marius. It's mine.

"Now, you see he is here. The cost of his freedom is either Andrews or you. Which shall it be?" Father smiled as if he'd already won his prize, and I wanted to throw all my temperamental magic at him. Unfortunately, that risked everyone here.

The intensity inside me thrust as if lashing to get out, and I swayed.

"Arianna?" Gemma's voice drifted from the side.

You are okay. Just hold on. Don't let them see. Do not let yourself go here. It was Rain's voice in my head, not Marius's this time. I looked up to him. *I have a force moving to the wall, but it's surrounded. We'll have to fight here. Stay behind me.*

There are too many outside. Marius's voice now, so distinct from the embrace Rain's was. *Let me take this burden as your bonded guardian.*

I squeezed Rain's hand, letting it go. The power I'd felt slunk away into an abyss as I looked at my father directly in his cold, dark eyes.

CHAPTER 45
ARI

I looked around, taking in the faces of my family. Marius. Gemma. Laurel. And finally, Rain. The lives most important to me. They would be safe. Drew would be safe. I made my decision.

"I'll go with you," I said to my father, stepping away from Rain and the others. "But you must call off your forces outside the wall. Let Marius go. Let them all go."

"No, Ari," Gemma cried out. I didn't turn around, but I knew Laurel was holding her back. Rain would have had to do the same for me. He didn't try to stop me, but his eyes burned into my back like fae fire. I didn't dare look at him. He'd asked me to trust him on this, but I couldn't risk his life or any of the others' for mine. I'd seen my mother's sacrifice to stop my father and end the Great War, and I wasn't the powerful general Mother had been. None of us were. I'd trade my freedom for them and find a way to free myself once they were all safe.

Father came closer. "You must renounce this kingdom

and your bond with Marius. If you come with me, I will let them live... for now. If you stay, you will all die."

He had me. Had all of us. I studied Marius, but his expression was unreadable. I didn't know if a path to stop the extinction of the unicorns existed, but if there was, Marius needed to be part of it. And there was no fucking way I'd let any of my family die today. They would live, and I'd use the time I had to figure out how to kill my father.

I chanced a glance at my family. *Stay strong.* I mouthed to them. My gaze locked on Rain. His jaw clenched so tight it looked painful. He wouldn't stop me, but his eyes pleaded with me not to go. I'd never get a chance to say the words out loud to him. My eyes burned as my lips formed the phrase with so much meaning. *I love you.*

He looked broken beyond words, and that was my fault.

Then, I reached out to my guard and friend, unable to say the words out loud. *Marius, watch over them in my absence.*

Do not do it. I know what you're thinking.

I have to. Thank you for all your protection. Take care of my family. I swallowed against the knot in my throat and closed my eyes.

I, Arianna Alena Christella, release you, Marius of the Guardians, from the bonds of fae and unicorns.

The lights brightened and winked out. Pain splintered through my head and into my chest as if the bond was being ripped physically from my body. I crumpled and hands gripped my arms, but the cool feel of the marble steppingstone pressed against my cheeks.

Shouts of my name were muffled around me. Dark mist crept in around my vision until it consumed me.

LIGHT PIERCED through the slits of my eyes. I threw my arm over to shield them. A rocking motion made it hard to sit up. *Boat. I'm on a boat.* The bed was soft, and the curtains were thrown open wide. There in a chair with his back against the bright sun causing his face to be shadowed sat my father.

"You survived breaking a bond with Erebus's personal guard. His chosen. You are more powerful than I expected."

PART THREE
REBIRTH

The First Year After the Great War
From the personal account of General Daphina's sister archived
at the War Museum

Blood, depravity, and pain were all the blood-thirsty creatures were after. How Albert had sought to strike a deal with them eluded Daphina. He'd been one of the brightest minds in their class at university. She'd even fancied him before she drew the king's affection. He'd become someone else in his pursuit of power. It'd taken the forces a year to push the vampires back to their lands after she trapped Albert in his prison. She'd been trapped with him though, unable to assist her soldiers in the final push to rid their lands of the creatures. Her only contribution was the strategy she provided her direct reports before they left. A piece of her broke knowing she wouldn't be there to finally see freedom in the lands she fought so hard to liberate, because she knew, even if the king hadn't accepted it, this prison would be where she died.

King Veran visited her once to tell her how loved she was by the people since he could no longer profess that for himself. A statue had been commissioned of her at the people's petition, and he had lovingly obliged by donating land in the center of town. She expressed her appreciation when what she wanted was to return to her home. Instead, Daphina wished him well and blessed his choice for marriage as she said her goodbyes, which he refused. He refused to accept she would live out her days next to Albert in a fake world created to keep him in a fantasy. Daphina resigned herself to the fate with Albert that she had once rejected from King Veran. The Fates must have a sense of humor, she thought, to have twisted their lives in such a way.

CHAPTER 46
ARI

The black mist clung in the air and to everything around me. The entirety was out of focus. A friend whose name I couldn't recall, but still a friend, stood next to me. All of us in the room had to pledge ourselves or others would be made to suffer. In the end, I took the blue and white cloth offered to me because I didn't want my friend to be executed.

We were marched down the hall along with his army of guards. Two ladies followed. One carried a box. The other carried another item that was a gift.

We lined the room like his toys ready to be chosen. I glanced at the box the woman next to me held, and it looked soft and warm even though it was black and red. Something ate at my thoughts. She looked at me as if she were curious too.

"Should we peek at it?" she asked.

He'd have our heads. I turned back to tell her no, but she raised the corner. I saw my name on a piece of paper inside and placed my hand on the lid, gently pushing it back down.

"Do you not value your life?"

She cast her eyes down. Panic raked over me. I met my friend's gaze. She was two people away, but it felt like an ocean. She recognized the fear in my eyes. This fucker was going to propose. I should say no, so why did I feel compelled to say yes?

The doors flew open, and he entered with power swirling around him. The mist clouded his features, but I knew it was him by the aura of magic. I hated him and wanted him gone, but saving these people was the priority.

The vampire walked up to me and faced me, his back to the others. Fire blazed in his black eyes. I tried to step back, but I couldn't. He turned his gaze to the two ladies closest to me, and his eyes were like ice on them. "Leave those on the table and return to the line."

The women scurried to leave their gifts on the table, but he skewered me to the wall with his gaze. His eyes danced with amusement. "You are right where you should be."

"What are you doing?" I whispered. If he was about to do what I thought he was, I couldn't reject him. He might not kill me, but others would pay. But he might kill me. He'd certainly killed today as evidenced by the blood on his clothes.

He leaned in next to my ear. His warm breath heated my skin and sent a tingling sensation down my spine. "Do you know why you are here? Why do you hold my sash?"

I glanced down and realized this was his symbol on the soft fabric. Not his country's but his. He was going to propose, and I was torn between saving myself and saving the others.

"Don't do this. You don't really want this."

"You," he said. "I want you. While I fought today, I only thought of returning to you. You might hate me now, but you will grow to love me. Because I will burn this world down and serve you the ashes if that's what it takes to protect you."

"Protect me?" I squeaked out.

"The battle today was because men sought you for what you could do for them, but I want you here with me for what I can do for you."

I should say no. He kidnapped me. But I didn't want to say no. I wanted to say yes. I met his blazing eyes and saw the threat that would burn me if I said yes, but I wanted him to burn me. To burn every inch of my body. "Then ask me. Give me the choice."

His eyes burned hotter through the gray cast shrouding the room. How was that possible? He turned to the people gathered in the room. I noticed the hall outside was packed too. "My people. I asked you here."

I snorted quietly. He didn't ask anything. He commanded.

He shot me a sideways glance that promised a punishment I might enjoy later.

"I asked you here to witness a declaration today." He motioned for me to step forward onto the dais he stood on. I moved through what felt like quicksand, but I made it to his side. He dropped down on one knee in front of me. The emperor was on his knees in front of me and the hundreds of his people. He took my hand between his in a gentle caress. "You brought the sun into my life. Now, let me bring it into yours. Be my wife. Be the empress of our people. Be my sun."

Everything in me said to say no, but my heart screamed yes. "Ask me."

"Will you be my wife?" Tears formed in his eyes, but the heat burned them away.

Fuck me. I should say no, but the way he looked at me turned my insides to molten lava. It was like my freewill was overtaken and there was only one answer I could give. "Yes."

I just agreed to marry the biggest tyrant in the world. Why was I happy? He stood and kissed my cheek, his lips hot against my skin. "I'll show you what it means to be mine later."

He picked up the blue and white sash and draped it around my neck. "The other two presents are for you. I need to wash, but I will see you at the celebration to thank my soldiers for their victory."

Back in my room, I dreaded what he meant about showing me what it meant to be his, but I had a warmth in my belly of anticipation. I wanted to be his. I opened the beautiful black box. It was lacquered wood but carved to look like lace. Inside were red rose petals and a hand-written card. He'd written me a love letter.

The other gift was...

Sweat slicked my body as I woke in a foreign room.

Rain had been in my dream, but he wasn't who he really was. He was a manifestation of my fears for my future. He wasn't here. This wasn't his room or his palace. My bare feet touched a cold floor, and I slapped a hand over my mouth, holding in my gag as I glanced around the room for somewhere to throw up. A small light peeked under a door in the corner, and I threw it open. Blessed goddess. It was a bathing chamber. I knelt in front of the toilet just as my body retched up every last thing from my stomach. Again and again, my body heaved, even when there was nothing left to give. It was like everything from the day had to be purged. My entire body ached as if I were ill with an infection. Only when I sat on the floor with my back against the counter did I allow the memories to flood in. *Goddesses and gods, what have I done?* Had it hurt Marius too? I couldn't even contact him to see if any of them survived. Father had said he would leave them alive, and I had to trust that was true even as my gut rebelled against the notion. My sole task was to make sure he never got the chance to get near them again. I'd play his game until I figured out how to bring him down.

CHAPTER 47

ARI

Another door creaked open, and I scanned the bathing chamber for anything to use as a weapon. There was nothing... not even a glass. I grabbed one of the handcloths like an idiot. A light flicked on.

"I have some food and water or tea, whichever you would like." A soft, sweet voice carried through the room. "Or I could draw you a bath if you prefer."

At least my father wasn't here.

"No," I said. "I just want to be alone."

She let out a long sigh. "If you do not let me do my tasks, he will punish me. Maybe both of us."

He can fucking try to punish me. But I didn't want anyone else to be hurt because of me. The entire reason I came with him centered around preventing harm to others.

The bathroom door wasn't closed all the way, and I toed it open. The woman stood by a small table with chairs on either side of it. Her back was to me, but she had a head full of perfectly coifed dark curls down her back and a slender waist. She stood about my height. A large bay window behind her offered no clues to my location. It was too dark to see what lay beyond that.

"How long was I unconscious?" I asked, moving closer and pulling up short when her scent hit me. It was the decay of vampire, but there was something delicate and lemony, like a moonflower. She was vampire, but not the kind with feral eyes like I'd seen at Rain's palace.

"A few days." She cleared her throat. "I can almost feel you assessing me. I'll save you the trouble. I am vampire and have been for a couple of decades. No, I wasn't born this way."

I nodded, appreciating her candor.

"I think a bath is what is needed most right now," she said, moving towards the bathroom.

"I'm not really in the mood for a bath."

"Mood or not, you stink."

A laugh bubbled up. "That is certainly not what I expected."

"There is a toothbrush and paste in the first drawer beside the sink. You could take care of your oral hygiene while I draw your bath. Would you like to select your clothes, or should I?" She poked her head around the door.

"I can choose my own clothes." I made it to my feet and wandered into the room.

She motioned to a third door, and I opened it to find plenty of dresses.

"Are there any pants? I'm not feeling a dress today."

"Check the lower rack."

There were indeed several pants but no practice leathers. It was clear training was not in my future here, at least not any I was accustomed to. I selected a pair of black pants and a black flowy top I found. If I had to be here, then I'd dress like I was in mourning—because that was exactly how I felt with my family, the real ones, so far away.

"What is your name?" I stood in the doorway of the bathing chamber.

She laid out towels and bathing products while the tub filled. She opened a tall cabinet and pulled a robe out. "Let's see if I survive the day. Then, I'll tell you my name."

"What do you mean?"

"Your father killed the last vampire he assigned to care for you when you didn't immediately wake up."

"Goddesses and gods." I gripped the counter.

"Let's get you presentable and see how it goes. I'll be on the other side of the door. Once you're done and have your robe on, come out and eat. You'll need your strength."

I nodded. I didn't have any more words left in me. The gown was stiff from my sweat. Who had put me in it? The dead vampire? I peeled the garment off and climbed into the tub. As much as I didn't want to be here, the hot water soothed my muscles. Relaxation remained out of reach, but my mind began to clear from the haze.

A sob shuddered through me, and I bit down on my hand to stifle it until I got control of myself. Breaking down here, wherever the fuck that was, wasn't an option.

No weakness here, Ari. Never let them think they have broken you.

That's when they would think they owned me. I scrubbed the stickiness of my perspiration off and washed my hair as quickly as possible.

I emerged from the bathroom in the robe she had laid out for me.

The vampire smiled. Her brown skin was smooth on her kind face. She looked nothing like the vampires in the forest or that were with my father at the palace. In fact, she was stunning.

"Don't you feel better? You certainly smell more acceptable."

"Thanks," I said, not bothering to keep the annoyance out of my voice.

She poured tea in two cups and placed one in front of me and the other in front of the other chair before taking the seat.

"You said you've been vampire for a couple of decades?" I asked.

"Yes." She studied me as if she could assess where I was going with my question. "Do you want to try to eat something? There are scones and jam."

The idea of food made my stomach roil. "Tea for now." I dropped a sugar cube and poured milk into my steaming brew. "You seem different than the other vampires."

"Those are soldiers. Some have been so for centuries," she said, her words coming out slowly as she carefully chose them.

"Were you fae before..."

"I was turned into a vampire?" She smiled, taking a sip of tea, like my half-asked question amused her. "No, I was human, and I chose to be a vampire."

A human who wanted to be a vampire. Goddess and gods, why?

"Your questions are written all over your face. There are expectations for today. Your father wishes to meet with you."

My stomach roiled again. However, a face-to-face with my father would allow me to assess the situation with him and survey my surroundings. I stood. "I'll need five minutes."

"Little elf," she said, gently scolding me. "We must make you presentable."

I didn't want her to be punished. I grabbed the clothes and dressed in the bathroom.

"Sit." She motioned to the chair I'd been in earlier.

I sat down, and she worked on my hair, pulling it back away from my face and securing it. She took a round barrel thing and curled my hair around it. Heat came off of it, but it didn't burn me. When she released it, a perfect spiral curl remained. She continued until my hair hung in shiny, spiral curls around my face. Then, she slid her hands underneath and gave my hair a few shakes to loosen them.

"What do you think?" She studied me in the mirror.

"It's pretty," I said, studying the waves. It was pretty, and if I were anywhere but here, I'd have been excited to have such a good hair day. I didn't care how I looked for this disgusting kingdom.

"Your hair is gorgeous. It's okay to say it." She moved

in front of me and picked up a container from a tray of cosmetics sitting there. "You don't really need makeup, but all women here wear it, so it will help you fit in."

I started to thank her but stopped. My father commanded her to tend to me. She wasn't doing this out of kindness.

She worked quickly and after a few minutes, she stepped back to admire her work. "Perfect."

"I've never felt less than."

She stepped aside where I could see my reflection in the large floor mirror. It wasn't the way my makeup had been done for events before I knew the truth. I looked natural, even with the makeup, but this wasn't the type of party I was used to since I'd be taken to my father next.

CHAPTER 48

RAIN

"It's been three days. Marius can't reach her. We've had no reports. I'm going after her."

Laurel had both hands pressed against my chest as if he could hold me back. "We have scouts on the trail. Let them do their jobs. You can't just barge into a camp of vampires."

"The hell I can't," I said. "I abided by your counsel and waited, but I'm not waiting anymore. I can't feel her, Laurel. She's been under my skin since I laid eyes on her, but I can't feel her now. If he..." I couldn't even finish the sentence. My heart threatened to rip in two. Not finding her wasn't even an option. I'd known I was falling for her since she made me think she'd set fire to my dick, and I would bring her home to torture me any way she wanted.

Laurel gripped my shoulders. "She's not. He wouldn't take her just to kill her. He wants a successor or a pawn. Either way, she is safe."

"She'll never be safe with him." I growled.

The armory door opened, and Gemma entered in her fighting leathers.

Laurel ran a hand through his hair. "Not you too. I can't be good sense for all three of us."

Ari wouldn't forgive me if anything happened to Gemma, who was strapping daggers into place on herself. "I don't need anyone's permission to go after my sister."

"No, you don't need permission, but what about Phina?" Laurel said, his tone pleading.

"I'll go, Gemma," I said. "She wouldn't want you to take the risk."

"Nor I her, but here we are." She reached for her sword and fixed the sheath to her back. "I'm not a fragile flower, nor is she, but she hasn't seen a battle."

"Ari is stronger than you think."

"Don't tell me..." Her words disappeared when she met my gaze. "What do you know?"

I failed to protect her in my own godsdam home. That was what I knew. "She was manifesting Nyx's power in the courtyard. I felt it until our touch broke. Then, I didn't feel it anymore."

"Holy Goddess." Gemma's hand went to her throat. "It is true. You're sure?"

"Yes, it was darkness personified radiating from her. She inherited your ancestor's power just as your mother had suspected. It's why your mother's spell held for so long after her death. Ari has those gifts and maybe even more than General Daphina did."

Gemma reached for a chair and sat down. "I suspected it, but her magic was so untamed when I left."

"It still is, but if your father figures out how powerful she is, she might not live or worse." Because there were worse things than death when someone was living under his control. Albert had butchered elves and staked them along the borders of our kingdom during the Great War. He'd done horrible things out of paranoia to those loyal to him, including draining their power until they withered to nothing. I pushed those memories aside and focused on Ari and rescuing her.

"We need to take her twin blades with us." Gemma held out a leather belt with dual swords in it.

"Her what?"

"Nyx blessed them when I took her to the training center. It's the first time I've ever seen it happen." Gemma unsheathed one to show me.

The blades were as black as a starless night sky and etched with the Triple Moon of Nyx. The swords were the perfect size for Ari to wield in a fight.

"I haven't heard of that happening since stories from long before the war." My brother studied the blade.

"She is the one Nyx chose to save us all, so I have to save her." I took the swords from Gemma and placed the sheathed blades in my pack. "This is my responsibility as the ruler of our kingdom. No one else needs to die because of my duty."

As the vampire led me down the empty corridor, it became apparent that the size of this building rivaled Rain's palace. My life in a prison kingdom limited my knowledge, so I had no idea where I was. What this building was. And worst of all—how far away from Rain, my sister, my brother, and my little niece I was. The best I could hope for was that Phina was far far away from the vampire lands.

My heart ripped into a thousand tiny pieces. I worked a swallow against the knot in my throat.

Father will not break me.

I jutted my chin out and straightened my spine.

"That's it," the vampire said. "Don't let him in."

"I'm sorry?" I glanced in her direction.

"You heard me," she said in a quiet and firm voice.

I had. Was this her attempt to get me to trust her, or was something amiss with my father's alliance with the vampires?

"What is your role here?" I asked as we walked. "Besides my dressmaid."

She huffed and assessed me. "I'm not your dressmaid. I'm to be your companion."

I smirked. She had fire in her, and I related to the fierceness. "If my father doesn't end you," I said. "Isn't that what you said?"

One slow nod was her only acknowledgment of my question. "I have learned the hard way that my life is easier here if I hold my tongue." She paused. "But I've never been one to fall in line." She resumed walking.

While she didn't divulge big secrets, she shared enough for me to recognize the signs Father's rule might not be welcomed by all. "Why tell me this?"

"Because we all need allies, Princess."

"I'm not a princess unless a prison kingdom counts."

"You're right. You are a queen and should remember that."

There was nothing royal about me. She had to know that, so why insist I was… "Even that was just regent."

"I'm not talking about your former kingdom." She stopped in front of large double doors. "We're here."

"Tell me this isn't a throne room."

"I cannot," she said, giving me a wink. "Prepare yourself."

She rapped on the door three times, and the giant wood doors swung open in unison. I pulled my shoulders back and straightened to my full height. The room was dark, even with the lamps lit along the walls, with no windows to let any natural light in. It was more like a dungeon than a throne room. A blood-red rug lined the way to the dais where my father sat on a massive metal throne. The same vampires who had been with him at Rain's palace stood in front of and on the platform close to him. He wore a suit but had a jeweled crown atop his head. Crimson stones peppered the black alloy. The metallic twang of blood wafted around me along with the rotten aroma of death. People had died in this room. A lot of people. I prepared my mental fortitude to face my fate even if that meant I was next, but it didn't make sense for him to bring me here to kill me.

"Come closer, daughter." My father waved a hand. He looked happy to see me on the surface, but the cruel twist of his mouth resembled disgust more than love.

Everything in me said to run, but I was vastly outnumbered and my magic too dampened by something heavy inside the walls to even help me. There was no escape option. I was utterly alone to face whatever fate awaited me at my father's hands.

I made my way down the aisle, and the carpet muffled my already quiet footfalls. Two guards ahead of the steps held out their arms to stop my progression. The vampire who had helped me dress came to a halt beside me. I hadn't even realized she'd walked with me, but I was grateful to have someone at my side even if she wasn't on my side.

"Griselda, you have done well." Father smiled at her, and it looked kind not like the cruel one he'd worn in the other court. I peered over at my companion, Griselda. I surmised this was what she meant by learning her name if she survived the task.

"Thank you, sire," she said, bowing her head. "I hope I've earned the position."

"You have," he said, nodding. "You are dismissed while I speak with my daughter. You may retire to Arianna's chamber and wait for her there."

She didn't turn her head, but I caught how she cut her gaze toward me almost as if she was warning me. "Yes, sire." Griselda curtsied and turned down the aisle. The only sound indicating she was gone was the opening and shutting of the two large doors.

"Clear the room," Father said, his voice low.

The vampire closest to him, who looked about the same age as me, glanced at him. My father raised an eyebrow at the red-haired man as if daring the vampire to say something. The vampire sneered at me but led the others out through a door hidden like a panel in the wall next to the platform. Alone with him might give me an advantage, but Father's history showed his skills included manipulation, so this could be some kind of trick.

"Fun group," I said, turning my gaze back to my father.

He was in front of me a half step before a blur hurled toward me. The back of his hand connected with my cheek. I stumbled to the side, tasting blood on my tongue. Pain splintered across my face. I ground my teeth together to keep from crying out, but I couldn't stop the tears from pooling in my eyes.

"You have embarrassed me."

He'd never hit me once in my entire life. Stunned was

what I was, but not in disbelief. Twice he'd threatened me. I didn't need another sign he wasn't the man who raised me, but he made sure I had plenty. The father I knew died when he crossed the forest. The man before me was an evil tyrant responsible for countless deaths.

"Apologize, and we'll move forward."

I pulled my hand away from my cheek and saw the red staining it. He hadn't hesitated to draw my blood in a building full of vampires.

"Why am I here?"

"Apologize to me," he said with a growl.

Why have me apologize here and without an audience? They had witnessed how I manipulated him for the lives of my real family and the freedom of Marius. He wanted to break me. Perhaps my entire spirit. That was not going to be so easy, and I had no intention of giving him even an inch of my strength.

"Why did you bring me here? What do you wish to use me for?"

He raised his arm again. My fear turned to silent calculation. I anticipated the strike. My reflexes were quick enough to block the blow with my forearm. A force like a gust of wind hit me. My feet lifted from the ground like I was floating away from him. *Thud.* I slammed into a wall with a crack. The breath forced from my lungs came out in a huff. I gasped for air, but a stabbing jolt through my chest made me freeze—every breath a sharp painful dance. I raised my head, and he was looking toward the hidden door.

"Thomas," Father called in the direction he faced.

I took a couple of small steps away from him.

The door opened and the red-haired vampire entered and bowed. "How can I be of service, sire?"

"My daughter needs some lessons. Will you escort her to the interior gallery and show her how we learn obedience here?"

Fear swirled in my chest and dulled the pain of my healing rib. Thomas reached under my arm and lifted me to my feet. I winced and bit down on my lip, determined not to make a sound. His nails dug into my skin with a biting sting.

I ignored the pain and twisted away from him only to be blindsided with a backhand to my other cheek. "You will continue to receive these until you cooperate. Who do you think can last longer at this point? Me or you?"

Me. I kept the word for myself, even as the throbbing made me think a thousand profanities to spew. The man's image blurred as my eye swelled shut.

CHAPTER 50

ARI

The gallery, as viewed through my eye that wasn't swollen closed, stunk of sweat and blood and what was surely human waste. It must have been a ballroom at one time, but judging by the various contraptions, it was used for the viewing of copious acts, from sexual bondage to torture. Thomas chained my arms around a pole in the center.

I forced even breaths because I would survive whatever they did to me here. On my inhales a familiar scent found its way to me—fae. There were elves here. Death had been dealt in the room, but I would survive and deal retribution. The pole smelled like decay, and it wasn't the wood but bits of flesh left in cracks. I focused on a knot at eye level and took myself somewhere other than there. Rain's face came into my mind. The softness of his lips when he was gentle with me. The kindness in his eyes when he looked at Phina. The way he sent strength to me when he held my hand. Strength. I latched onto it and willed it through my body to not break with whatever was to come.

The snap of leather against the wood floor signaled the punishment I would receive. Footsteps, so many pairs, padded lightly into the room both on this level and the levels above. Torture like this was a regular event the people viewed...likely even enjoyed.

The whip slapped against the floor again, and I closed my eyes, looking for the strength from Rain. A whishing sound sliced through the air and a vicious burn slithered across my back tearing the fabric of my shirt. A small grunt stifled in my throat as I tensed and released, preparing for the next strike. The whip whooshed again, and another excruciating burn erupted near the first one. He struck again and again until the fabric shreds stuck in the open wounds of my back. I detached from the event almost like I wasn't in my body. Another crack hissed through the air and connected. I bit down on the inside of my jaw until a metallic taste hit my tongue.

"Enough." My father's voice echoed through the gallery. I sagged against the pole, but I didn't open my eyes to look up at him. What would be the point? No matter what he did to me, I'd never apologize to him. He didn't deserve those words, and I wouldn't tarnish the heritage and sacrifice of my warrior mother by giving in to him.

"Griselda, take her back to her quarters."

I couldn't hear her response, but moments later the shackles fell away from my wrists. My arm was hung across slender shoulders to help me limp from the room.

Every step was like twisting a hot poker of fae fire in my back. I clenched my jaw against the agony.

"Don't let them see you cry," she whispered. "Hold it for the room."

"Not crying," I grunted out through the excruciating pain. No, I wouldn't cry.

"Almost there," she said, as we made a turn. "Keep going."

I envisioned the whip around Thomas's neck and his body swinging from the railing of the upper gallery, but hanging him wouldn't kill him. So, I imagined my swords blessed by the Goddess Nyx cutting in a dual swipe clear through his neck. That gave me the boost I needed to power ahead. My wounds should be healing, but they weren't, and every step was a reminder of what I'd just been through at my father's behest.

I shifted my weight to try to stand on my own. Griselda caught me before I face-planted on the tiled floor.

"The whips are tipped with a poison that prevents healing," Griselda said, keeping her voice low even though I couldn't see anyone else out of my good eye. "It was used during the war, but they perfected it as they prepared to extract Albert."

Marius had told me of this drug, but not how it was made. If I hadn't broken our bond, he'd feel my pain because of the intensity even at this distance, and I was thankful he wasn't suffering. I found strength in the memories of training through injuries with him.

"We're close," she said. "Can you make it? I could carry you."

"Walk," I said through gritted teeth.

She guided me around another corner. "Just at the end."

The distance wasn't far, but the searing steps made it feel like climbing the tallest mountain while being set on fire.

Griselda shoved the door open and helped me inside. I toppled forward, but she held me up by my waist. "I need to take your shirt off to clean the wounds."

"Bathroom."

"Of course." She steadied me and guided me across the room.

My stomach roiled. Bile rose up my throat. "Sick."

"Oh," she said, understanding. "That's going to hurt, so brace yourself."

She helped me kneel, and vomit rose into my mouth from the pain. Griselda held my hair back.

Everything I'd eaten with her this morning emptied. Tears streaked my face from the force and the ripping sensation of my back. My wounded face ached due to the pressure. With nothing else left to expel, I sagged against the toilet seat.

"No, we're not going to lay in our vomit," she said, coaxing me to the edge of the tub. "Lean here, and I'll get scissors to cut what remains of your bodice off."

Her presence was gone in a breeze. The skin tightened as if it was being filleted from my back. I let a single sob loose, afraid I wouldn't stop if I gave myself the freedom to do more. There would be a day when I could let it out, but survival until I could escape was my goal. I started a mental list of those I would kill. My father. Thomas. Anyone who protected them.

A breeze entered the room, and I glanced with the eye that could see. Griselda held a pair of scissors and a jar. "I know that look. Promise not to put me on your kill list after I do this."

Had I said it out loud? I didn't think so.

"Lean forward over the edge." She pointed to the side of the tub.

I did as she said, and I heard the scissors scrape against the fabric. "Here we go. Take a breath and hold it."

The inhale was like prodding embers, and I squeezed my eyes shut. In careful motions, she pulled the fabric from the wounds and cut it away. Her delicate touch was quick. "Can you sit up?

I leaned back into an upright position. "Fuck."

She tugged the top away and slung my hair over the front of my shoulder. "This cream will counteract the poison and allow you to heal. It won't be as fast as you're used to, but it will be faster than without it."

"Just do it." I groaned.

"Take another deep breath," she said.

If the inhale was prodding embers, the ointment was hot coals on bare skin. The room seemed darker and then I was floating above the tub and to the bed.

CHAPTER 51
ARI

I blinked against the light of the room. Not sunlight. Bright bulbs like daylight. I was on my back in a soft bed. Had I dreamed it all? I rolled onto my side and startled at the figure in the chair. Griselda faced me.

Concern lined her perfect vampire face. "How do you feel?"

I stretched in tentative motions, but there was not any intense pain, just some residual tightness in my back. Both of my eyes were open. "Not like I was lashed with a poison-tipped whip."

She smiled, but it didn't reach her eyes. "It's good to see you didn't lose your spunk."

I rubbed my throat. "I could use something to drink." I slid my legs over the side of the bed, my toes burying in the furry rug below.

"Here." She held out a glass to me. "Drink some water, and I'll get you some food. I wasn't sure how long you would be unconscious, so I finally told the servants I would come get a tray for you."

"How long was I out?"

"About a day," she said. "Is there anything in particular you want to eat?"

"I'm not hungry," I said. Another day lost here. How many more would I lose before I got clear of this place? Before I killed the man who was no longer my father?

"You need to eat so the healing can finish."

Nothing sounded good, but I needed hydration. "Are there berries? Fresh berries."

Griselda seemed pleased with my order. "Yes, I can get berries. What else?"

"I don't think I can stomach anything beyond that," I said.

She touched my hand and gave it a gentle squeeze. "Very well. We'll start there. They will lock the door when I leave. Don't panic. I promise I will return."

I nodded, but disquiet skittered up my spine. Being kept as a captive who could move around freely was very different than being confined.

She studied my face, and her brows pinched together like she was concerned. "I won't be gone long and no one else should enter without me. Those were your father's orders."

"Did he order you to be nice to me too?" I asked, a genuine question without venom. Dark misty haze flashed into my vision and disappeared as quickly. I wondered if I hallucinated it.

She sighed. "No, he did not, and he probably would

tell me to be harder on you if he knew what I was doing. If he knew I used the medicine on you I did."

Her compassion for me and my situation touched me, and I wanted to trust her. To have a friend here and someone on my side could help me find a way out.

"He's a—"

"Don't say it," she said. "We'll talk when I get back and dismiss the guards outside the door."

I stood on the rug and swayed, falling back into a seated position on the bed. Not good. I gathered my resolve for another attempt. When I tried again, my footing was stable, and I was able to make it to the bathing chamber. I gazed at my reflection in the mirror. The eye my father had struck was still puffy, and only a small pink mark was left where he'd drawn blood. I turned and lifted the nightgown to examine my back. The flesh was raw with raised pink marks crisscrossing the exposed flesh. I shuddered and let the gown fall back down. The man who raised me and protected me at all costs ordered an unforgivable punishment on me. Mother's magic must have been so strong to have been able to shape him into the man I knew.

Grief hit me in the chest and twisted with more anguish than the whip could ever have done. I slid to the floor and laid my head on my knees. Sobs racked my body, and I didn't fight them. I grieved for my mother who had given up her very existence to save her people. I grieved for the father I knew who wasn't real. I grieved for the life I knew before Rain rescued me. The tears came hard and fast. When they finally dried, I swore to

Nyx they were the last my father would ever get from me.

I pulled myself up off the floor, my body stiff from the awkward position. The person in the mirror with red-rimmed eyes looked different. Dark mist clouded my vision, but I wasn't going to let the darkness take me. I refused to pass out in the bathroom—to lose another day to this place. I splashed cold water my face. A robe of soft silk hung on the door, and I tied it around me before I walked to the window to survey the surroundings.

CHAPTER 52
ARI

Griselda returned with enough strawberries, blueberries, raspberries, and blackberries to feed a dozen people. The sweetness tasted good on my tongue. Something pleasant and normal amongst the evil in my father's palace.

After I ate my fill and pushed the tray away, I steadied myself for answers I was sure I wouldn't like. "How did my father rise to power here so quickly?"

"This was his seat before the war," Griselda said. "I can tell you what I know, but a lot of the history was from before I was made vampire or even born."

"I'm not sure what I was taught was the real history, and I feel like I'm only now learning pieces of the truth." It wasn't out of trust I made my confession. Part of my court training included learning how to give others just the right amount of truth for them to spill secrets. I almost laughed at the thought. My entire life was built on secrets and lies that I never uncovered.

"I can imagine how unsettling that must be. When I became vampire, my life changed. Things I was never aware of before suddenly became my reality."

"The blood-drinking thing?" I cinched the belt of my robe tighter, aware of exactly where it slid over the healing slashes on my back.

She chuckled. "I'd been around vampires my entire life, so not the blood-drinking thing. Although, the thirst was new and very overpowering in the beginning."

"Do you want to drink my blood now?" She'd had plenty of opportunity to drink from me when I was a bloody mess and hadn't.

"No, yours smells..." She paused. "Different than other fae."

"How so?" I tried not to sound offended, because her not wanting my blood was a good thing. How many fae had she drunk from... killed?

"Most fae smell like a sweet spring day, and their blood tastes like honeysuckle. But yours smells..." She paused again. Her face twisted in a look of disgust.

I held in my offense to her expression. Being unlike other fae might have saved me, but it concerned me. "Is mine that different?"

"Yes," she said quietly. "It is."

"And it repulses you?"

"Not so much repels me as it doesn't invite me the way most fae blood does. It's like it's shrouded in a veil of something I cannot name." Her nose scrunched up as if it did repulse her, and if she was afraid that would insult me, she was wrong.

"It's probably because of my father," I said. "How does his blood smell?"

Griselda narrowed her eyes. "He drinks an herb that makes his blood smell like vampire, so it doesn't entice us."

I raised an eyebrow at how freely she gave that information—knowledge an enemy would use to take down their foe. "And he doesn't mind you telling me this?"

"He doesn't know I know." She smiled, and it reached her eyes this time.

"So why tell me?"

"A great question but one I can't quite answer," she said, shifting to look out the window into the darkness.

"Where are we?" The view I'd glimpsed earlier was not a land I'd seen in any books or travels. There had been gravel in a courtyard and a wall with a forest beyond that, so it wasn't dissimilar from the prison kingdom or the Court of Storms.

"I was wondering when you would get around to that question. The answer is a long way from where you were."

My chest tightened. "How far?"

"We are on the far side of this kingdom."

"Can you put that into terms that will help me gauge the distance?" I'd never been anywhere other than my prison kingdom and the real fae empire, so I had no concept of the others.

Her gaze flicked up to the ceiling as she pondered my request. "Think about four of the width of the kingdom you grew up in."

That wasn't a distance I could travel in a day.

"And there are creatures you haven't ever seen before that are dangerous. Fae charms don't necessarily work on them."

She could be making that up, but she'd been upfront with so much other information that seemed unlikely. My only experience outside the prison kingdom was in the city of Rain's kingdom. If there were beasts out there that couldn't be charmed, I'd face them over staying here as my father's captive.

"Don't even think about it," she said as if she read my mind. "You would have to get through the guards inside, the guards outside, and then face those creatures."

I needed to find the power in me that Rain had, so I could vanyshen back. I'd never used it on my own, so it hadn't even occurred to me to try. Was there a limit on how far an elf could make that leap? I should have asked more questions about the power.

"Do you know what my father intends to do with me?"

Griselda pressed her lips together in a tight line. "Unfortunately, I do. He wants your power. All of it."

"I don't have anything helpful to him."

"The power of Nyx is the most powerful in the land." Her tone was grim, and my stomach bottomed out like when Gemma and I leaped off the tall ledge into the pool below the falls.

So, she did know and so did my father. I seemed to be the only one who hadn't known that I was related to Nyx. It did me no good since I didn't know what those powers were or if I even had them. *How did one go about summoning the magic of their... how many greats grandmother would she be for me?*

Even though I'd not only heard but witnessed the deep evil my father was capable of, reconciling that side of him with my childhood memories still proved challenging. I needed to understand how far he would go. "Do you think he will kill me? After he takes my power?"

She let out a long, slow sigh. "I think he will do whatever it takes to be the king of everything."

He didn't need me alive to use my power then. "In the gallery, I smelled other fae."

She turned sad eyes to me. "I doubt you knew them."

"Do they live here?"

"No, they were dessert your father brought as a reward for your capture."

I gasped, unable to hold the reaction inside. "They're dead?"

Griselda stared off and didn't answer. When she turned back to me, her features were set in a grim line.

"You've never seen a vampire drunk on fae blood, have you? For a brief moment, they can even use the power of the fae. It doesn't last long, though...not as long as it makes them drunk."

And she'd drunk fae blood. She'd admitted it. Thank the goddesses and gods my blood was repulsive to them.

RAIN

"Your plan is shit," Casimir said. "Even calling it a plan is being generous."

The rough sound of her voice broke me out of the mind-numbing pain at my back—like a phantom ache that wasn't mine.

"I'm not asking you to go." I prepared my horse in the stables with minimal supplies and weapons. I'd either be in and out of there or... If I were to be caught, the supplies would be wasted. "How is Marius?"

"He's nearly recovered. Their bond is weakened but still intact. However, she is too far away. He can't reach her. Have you injured your back? I feel the throbbing discomfort from you."

I let out a sigh, ignoring the back comment. I'd considered asking Marius to come, but he was the chief of his people. They couldn't afford to lose him with vampires in our lands. I was expendable. Plenty to take my place. "How is it the bond remained after she released him?"

"His magic is strong, and he chose her. As long as he continues to choose her, the bond is unbreakable."

A knot thickened in my throat. Arianna probably thought she was alone, but he was still with her. He'd never left her. Unicorns didn't answer to me, and he was their leader. Marius didn't need me to ask, but I would for Ari. "Does he want to come?"

"Ask him yourself."

"I don't have time to look for him."

Casimir jerked her chin toward the door, bending one front leg while stretching the other out and lowering her head. Marius stood in his true form, solid black with a glimmering gold horn that matched his twin brother's. A streak of grey was in his mane that hadn't been there before the night Ari was taken.

"Yes," he said.

A unicorn was a powerful ally, especially when it was their leader, and I was thankful he valued Ari's safety as much as I did. "You'll come?"

"Yes, to that and the other question you didn't want to ask."

"The grey streak came from that night. Why did it happen?"

"Her magic is older than mine, and although she still doesn't know how to wield it, I had to use a significant piece of mine to hold the bond." A golden tear leaked from his eye.

I stepped forward and held my hand out to catch it. "You have to be careful with these, even here, Marius." I held my hand out to him.

He raised his chin. "Keep it for the journey. If we get separated, you can use it to find me."

"Thank you," I said. A golden tear, particularly from a unicorn as strong as Marius, held value in many ways. I ducked into the tack room for a small jar we used to collect specimens to test the horses. Once the tear was in, I tucked the vial into the inside of my jacket.

"How soon do we leave?" Marius asked.

"At dusk. Traveling by night reduces the prying eyes."

"And do you know where she is?"

"Laurel's scouts picked up her scent crossing the border to the vampire kingdom. They said it was faint but definitely hers." If a vampire drank from her...Thunder rumbled, and I cracked my neck to release some of the tension. If my anger went unchecked, I could bring down a catastrophic storm on the city.

"Did they follow?"

"No, they were under instructions not to follow into vampire territory."

"If Marius is going, so am I," Casimir said.

"And me." Gemma turned the corner. While it meant a lot to see her here, Ari wouldn't want her sister to be in danger, but Gemma wasn't someone who accepted being told no very often.

"No," I said. "We need to keep the group small. The more of us there are, the bigger the risk of being seen or caught."

"But it gives us more ears, eyes, and magic," Gemma said.

"You have a young daughter who needs her mother," I

said, pleading a similar argument to what my brother had with her. If anything happened to Gemma on this rescue mission, Ari would be devastated, and that was unacceptable.

"Then we all better make it back home, because she's going to need this entire family to raise her." She placed her thumb and forefinger in her mouth and whistled. Her grey mare came trotting to her. "Hello, Persephone. Are you ready for a long ride?"

Persephone whinnied and shook her head up and down as if she understood.

"Gemma, can you speak to animals?"

She rubbed the horse's muzzle. "He's asking if I can talk to you?"

Persephone shook her head again and bared her teeth to me in a grin.

"They understand you and you them?" I repeated, realizing I sounded like a blathering idiot.

Gemma chuckled. "Yes, Mother said her grandmother could too."

"It's such a rare gift," Casimir said. "It usually—"

"Skips a generation," Gemma said. "Yes, and it did. Mother couldn't do it, and with my grandmother gone, she didn't know how to teach me about it either." Her gaze fell on Marius. "Cyrus trained me on how to use the gift."

"My brother would do anything for you, Gemma. Even without the bond," Marius said.

"I know," she said. "Phina would not be here without him, but today is not the day to rehash that."

I leaned back against the wall and thought of Ari. *I*

know you can't hear me, but maybe you will get some feeling when I say we are coming for you. I will destroy their kingdom and your father will pay. I love you, Arianna.

The pain in my back had subsided some, but a pain deep in my chest, in my soul, called me to her. She was hurt and needed me. The pull to her was intense. Waiting until dusk was no longer an option. I pushed off the wall and headed for my horse. "I'm leaving now. Whoever wants to ride with me better be prepared to ride hard." I led my horse out of the barn into the late afternoon light and mounted.

My brother grabbed the reins. "You didn't think you could go without me, did you?"

"You better hurry up then, big brother."

Gemma astride Persephone pulled up next to me as did Marius and Casimir. It struck me that this was our family, and the lot of us were riding to face the biggest danger our realm had ever known. The fear of losing them was surpassed by the pride I held in being part of this loyal group. We were going together to bring not only our queen home but a member of our family too. Albert's and the vampires' recompense would be paid in blood. I'd bath their kingdom in crimson.

CHAPTER 54
ARI

A lamp illuminated Griselda where she read a book in the chair that had become hers since I'd been here. She closed the cover. "I could draw you a bath if you are ready for that or get you something to eat."

"What are you reading?" I stood and stretched, hoping it would loosen up some of the tightness in my back. Pain burned through the marks. Tears pricked my eyes, but I blinked them away.

She showed me the cover. "One of those old romance books about a fae prince finding his true love."

"I found some of those in my mother's old books, but it seems odd to think of her reading them now knowing she was a general in the elven army."

Griselda sat the book on the small table. Her shoulders sagged a bit. "It must be very difficult to realize your entire life was a lie."

My heart cracked thinking of what I'd lost and what I found, but I'd be damned if I showed weakness here. "Not all of it but the majority. My sister and my brother and my bonded are what has kept me grounded in this new reality."

"I had a brother," she said. "My parents died when we were in our teen years. But my brother and I had each other. Then, he contracted a fever that ran through our city. I didn't, and that's when I became vampire."

Her openness surprised me, but maybe that was the goal. My father waged a war. He'd most certainly have had spies. She very well could be one of them—sent to be my companion to earn my trust and manipulate me into helping my father.

"What if I told you there was a way out of this house?" Griselda leaned in close.

"I'd say you were a spy for my father who liked to see me tortured." Even as I said the words aloud, a small spark of hope blossomed at the thought of leaving here.

"You are correct in that I'm your father's spy, but I no longer wish to be trapped here myself."

I studied her, unsure whether to trust her. She seemed genuine in her statements, but if she was trained in the arts of deception, her face might not give it away. Why hadn't I been given truth magic? She was a vampire, and everything about them was dangerous. I reminded myself of the fact even as I resolved to take the chance. Whether I accepted her help and she betrayed me or I just existed in this place, I was certain more torturous punishments were coming my way.

"How would someone go about escaping this palace of death?"

"Tomorrow." She lowered her voice. "You should be healed by then, and we'll make our escape."

The top of my priority list was to get out of here, but I didn't want to be sent on a fool's errand either. "Can we put a plan together in such a short time?"

"I've had the plan ready, down to encouraging your father to use this room, from the time I learned who you were and what he planned to do with you." She met my gaze and held it. A dark twinkle glinted in her eye, and it didn't look like bloodlust. Moreover, I believed her.

"What did you do before you became a vampire?"

Her eyes twinkled. "I was an attendant in the temple of Nyx."

Dark mist encroached on my vision as if to confirm what she said. "How long did you serve the goddess?"

"My entire life." The way her eyes danced made me wonder if she still served Nyx. Could a vampire be an acolyte for the Goddess of Night?

"Interesting." I didn't give her more even though I had questions floating through my mind. "I guess I better pick out an outfit for ease of movement."

"With your injuries, no one would think twice about attire to do so." She picked up her book and resumed reading.

I found a pair of boots with sturdy soles, probably for riding, in the back of the closet. There was one pair of pants in a thick material but cut loose enough that I could kick, so I grabbed them and a sweater. I rummaged through a drawer to find gloves.

"Nothing that will look overly suspicious." Griselda

took the gloves and returned them to their rightful place. "I know you've slept a lot, but try to rest now. We might not get to slow down for so much as a nap for days when we leave here."

I climbed into bed, but I knew sleep wouldn't come. The anticipation of my freedom so close pumped adrenaline through my body. My only regret in leaving tomorrow was I'd have to return to kill the man who threatened my family.

CHAPTER 55

ARI

Griselda told me not to pack anything. It would slow us down. She handed me a travel container of water and carried one of her own that I was sure didn't hold the same clear liquid.

"The guards' path hasn't changed in months. We'll be able to avoid them, but you must move exactly with me so the cameras do not catch you."

Cameras. They had those in Court of Storms. The cameras allowed the guards to see in places where they weren't stationed. My impression of the technology differed, and there had been very little missed by the ones at home. Home… that was the first time I'd thought of the Court of Storms as home. "And you can keep from being seen by the devices?"

"Yes, they have blind spots, but they are narrow, so stay with me. If I tell you to move, then make haste."

I nodded and Griselda opened the door of my chamber. She peered left and right. I expected her to fall back and cancel the attempt. She was risking her life. I didn't believe Father would kill me for this, but I did worry about what he would do to her.

"Ready?"

"Ready," I whispered, which was stupid because vampire hearing was nearly identical to elf.

She stuck close to the wall as she led us down the hall. I mimicked her movements including stepping around tables and chairs randomly placed along the long corridor. When we reached the end, I released a breath.

"We have a long way to go yet." She kept her voice low. "Keep the noise to a minimum."

My blood thrummed in my ears, and that seemed like too much sound. I hadn't been summoned, so if we were caught here there would be no excuse. There was no way I was going to get whipped again without a fight. I'd take as many of those bastards down with me as I could.

Griselda continued forward. I stayed in step with her as we navigated more corridors. We descended to a lower floor that was far less opulent than the others I'd seen since my arrival here. What was this area used for?

"Servants floor," Griselda said as if she'd read my mind. "They are all tending to their areas or asleep."

Griselda held up a hand as she stopped in front of a plain door. No glass panels or any light shown around it. She opened it gently and peered around the corner, both ways, before waving me to follow her. It was so dark I could barely see my hand in front of me, and this wasn't the transparent mist I'd had cloud my vision. A guard or anyone might be right next to or behind me, and I wouldn't see them. The space made us vulnerable, and a chill slithered around me. I stepped on the back of Griselda's shoe twice and to her credit, she never faltered. Light came into view, still a distance away, but a sense of freedom washed over me. I could feel how close we were to escape. My neck tingled--the kind of prickle I got when I anticipated something bad was about to happen.

"We need to hurry," she said, quickening her pace. I fell into step with her.

She grasped the knob of the door and turned. We made it. I held my breath, afraid to make any sound, but a rumble came from behind and seemed to get closer. Footfalls. Quick and numerous.

Griselda opened the door wide and hurried me through it. "Run."

I didn't question her command. The footsteps were heavier and faster behind us. She slammed the door shut, but we both knew that wouldn't stop a vampire soldier. A zing flew by me, but I willed myself forward faster. The small gate, probably for the guards to enter and exit for patrols, was close. I could see the forest beyond it, so I understood that was where we were going. Another arrow zipped by me on the same side. Thank Nyx they weren't very good shots. Strange that was who would be after us —soldiers with poor aim and not the best. Another shrill hum missed the mark. Were they deliberately missing us, or did Father not deem me worthy of his best?

A heaviness hit my back, and I almost lost my footing. I realized the weight was Griselda. Everything slowed around me. The arrow hadn't missed. The bolt pierced her back, and the tip poked through her chest near the heart. I twisted to catch her. "Come on. We're almost there."

"Leave me. Go. You need to live."

"No, you are going with me." I looked up to find the guards narrowing the distance between us. They weren't rushing us, but they were so close with their bows and arbalests aimed at me. Nyx, damn them. I wouldn't leave Griselda after she helped me. I called to the wind, and it mercifully answered, pushing back on the soldiers. It wouldn't stop them, but it would slow them down enough to give me a second to think of how to get Griselda out of here.

The ground rattled, and it wasn't me using ground magic. That wouldn't help Griselda. The soldiers inched closer, fighting against the invisible wall I held against them.

This can't be how I die. Not in these lands. Goddesses and gods, please no.

"My time is done. I've served my purpose, and I'm ready to see my family again. Nyx be with you. Praise the goddess." Her skin greyed as she spoke. She turned the color of death. I didn't know much about vampires, but my heart broke at what would come next for her. If Nyx could make an exception for a vampire, I hoped it would be for Griselda.

"Go and remember me as your friend."

"You are my friend. May Nyx grant you passage." I kissed her forehead.

Griselda sagged into the ground. Her hand turned to dust in mine. I used the wind to scatter her ashes toward the forest. Better than this hell. But that released the guards, and they were coming fast for me.

"Arianna?" Rain emerged from the smoke where the wall now gaped open.

He's really here.

I held back the tears burning my eyes and stood. Summoning fire to my fingertips, I shot fireballs at the advancing soldiers. It wasn't enough to stop them, but they dodged the flames, buying me seconds.

I spun and ran toward Rain. Gemma, Laurel, Marius, and Casimir followed him. They were all here for me, and I wished they hadn't come because we were all in danger now. We were outnumbered and needed to move fast. Rain caught me in his arms.

"We need to go," I said. A caustic burn erupted in my side. I reached toward the pain, but Rain stopped me.

He held me close. I felt safe in his arms, but this place wasn't. My head lightened. Rain's lips brushed my temple. "We'll take care of that, but I have to get you somewhere safe first."

Dark mist covered my vision, and a darkness like no other enveloped me, closed in and lifted me. I floated into nothingness. The pain wasn't as agonizing as it had been but still burned. Then, she appeared in front of me. Nyx.

CHAPTER 56

ARI

Nyx floated in front of me, and I realized I was floating too. I studied my hand, and it looked as ethereal as hers. This must be a dream. One very real dream. Something akin to what Rain and I shared when he'd been struck with the fae killer blade. A cloud of dark mist floated around her as if it veiled her. It was the same shroud that had infiltrated my vision numerous times. The goddess was darkness personified as our ancient stories told, but she was more than that. Her beauty eclipsed her power, and her force arched in the air like it couldn't be contained. What struck me most was how much she looked like my mother. There was no denying the relation any longer.

"Hello, Arianna, daughter of Daphina."

I didn't know whether I was supposed to bow or kneel, but I did neither since we were both floating like apparitions. "Hello..."

Do I call her Nyx? Goddess? What?

"You may call me Nyx. We are related after all." Her voice was melodic and soothing. It was a disarming contrast to the obvious power floating like currents around us.

"Nyx," I said. "I'm honored to meet you."

"The honor is mine," she said, resting her hand over her chest and inclining her head. "We don't have much time. You are dying."

Dying? No, I'm not ready. Is everyone else safe?

"The others in your party were not injured, but you have been hit with a poison that has no remedy in your realm," she answered as if she read my mind.

"So, you've come to take me to the afterworld? Will I see my mother?" My heart ached to leave the others, and it broke me knowing there would be no more time with Rain. But they were all safe, and that was what mattered most. I could do this. Not that I had a choice.

"It is not your time to die, Arianna," she said. "There is no cure in your realm, but there is in mine. That is why you are here."

There was a chance to return. I didn't think anyone came back once they crossed over to Nyx's realm. "What is it?"

She cradled my cheek. Her hand was cold but warm at the same time. The smoky mist of her aura wrapped around me like a hug. "Your mate prayed to me. Is still praying to me to save your life. His offer is his own life in trade for yours."

My heartbeat sped up. "No." I shook my head free of her touch. "No, I refuse."

She pressed her hand against my side where the arrow had pierced me. A cold tingle replaced the dull fire. The coolness spread into my chest and out to my limbs. Was this what death felt like? Would I see my mother soon? The only thing I looked forward to in death was seeing her again. Everyone else I loved was still alive. "What's happening to me?"

"You are being made into what you were always meant to be."

A ghost? "I don't understand."

"You will in time. For now, you will return to your realm healed and whole."

"No, I want Rain to live. I refused his offer."

"So did I." Her eyes twinkled. She smiled softly, cupping my cheek once more. "Live long and true." Nyx turned without another word and walked toward a shadowy tree. The mist partially concealed her. Another dark figure emerged and extended a hand. Erebus. He beamed with adoration as Nyx slipped her hand into his. Was that a unicorn horn on his head? I blinked to focus through the mist, but darkness once more filled the space.

I was alone. Nyx refused Rain's offer, so I must have died. That's why I remained in the dark. Disappointment curled in my belly when I wasn't reunited with my mother, but maybe I was being punished for not saving Griselda or being too naïve to realize I grew up in a prison. I drifted in the dark and closed my eyes wondering what was next and whether would I be alone for eternity.

"Open your fucking eyes, Arianna." Rain's voice gritted out in the dark.

It must have been my imagination. He wasn't here—wherever in Nyx's realm I was.

"Please, Ari." That was Gemma's voice. Apparently, hallucinations were normal in Nyx's realm, and my destiny was to be haunted by all those I loved.

Something wet landed on my face. The droplet beaded and rolled down my cheek. *Rain? Here?*

"I love you, Ari, and I refuse to live in this world without you." Definitely Rain but not the wet kind. It was the elf kind. His voice was so rough, and he sounded so close like he was right in my face. "If you don't come back, I will march to your father to avenge you. Once he has paid, I'll join you. I don't relish the idea of death though. I'd rather live a long life with you."

"Live long and true," I whispered to him the words Nyx had said to me.

His choked laugh rumbled over me. *This feels real.* His voice. His laugh. They all felt authentic. I tried to open my eyes but only met pure darkness.

"Open your eyes, Ari." Gemma's voice floated around me. My hair was stroked at the same time.

This was real. Rain's voice and Gemma's...they were both here. Goddesses and Gods, I was alive. I forced my eyes open and blinked against the light. The forest wasn't as dense as the one I'd grown up near, and sun peeked through the branches making a halo around Rain's head. He looked like a god, and relief to see him waved over me like a gust of wind.

"Thank Nyx." Rain covered his mouth. His eyes were

rimmed in red. Was he crying? My eyes burned as I cradled his cheek in my hand.

"Thanks to Nyx, indeed." I tried to sit up, and he reached behind my back to support me, pulling me into his lap.

Gemma stroked my hair again. "How do you feel?"

"Fine," I said, even as coldness spread inside me like it had while I was in Nyx's realm. "Different but fine."

"You'll be back to yourself soon," she said, kissing the top of my head. "I'm going to get some water for you."

I looked up at Rain. His eyes were damp. "I'm okay."

He pressed his lips together and nodded. The sight of him warmed me and chased away the coldness.

I sat up to face him. He reached for my face, but I grabbed his hands. Blood coated them. His leathers too. *No. No. No.* I reached for his chest, but he brought my hand to his lips, placing a soft kiss on the tips.

"It's all yours," he said, tucking some loose hair behind my ear.

"All of it?" There was so much.

"The arrow was poisoned, and you weren't healing." His jaw tightened and his voice grew rough. "You were bleeding out. I thought you died."

"I think I did." Realization hit me like a unicorn horn, sharp and swift. "Nyx saved me. I don't know why, but she said live long and true like I had something to do."

"That would explain the weird dark cloud that wrapped around you. I thought it was death coming to claim you, and I refused to let you go. Then, you just stopped bleeding and healed." His eyes locked on my gaze, and I saw the promise he'd sworn to the Goddess in them. The truth of the words she had spoken was now a bond between us. I'd refused to trade my life for his and so had Nyx.

I leaned my head against his. "Don't you ever offer your life for mine again. Promise me."

He inhaled a long breath and slowly let it out. "You can ask anything of me, Ari. I mean anything, but that request is the one thing I will never promise you. If the day came to lay down my life for you, I would walk toward my fate and embrace it with both arms. Not that I want to leave you, but I would so that the kingdom would still shine with your presence."

Tears spilled down my cheeks, and I couldn't stifle my sob. "You are a stupid, stupid man."

"I might be stupid, but I know that there will never be another love in this realm greater than when the fates brought me you. I love you, Ari."

"I love you too."

His lips brushed mine. Nyx called Rain my mate. An endearment usually reserved for Nyx and her consort—gods and goddesses. Maybe it was a slip of the tongue, but I didn't dare think anything Nyx did was a mistake. Mate. As if acknowledging what that kind of term meant, the desire pooling in my lower belly magnified. I sank my fingers into Rain's hair. Needed him closer. Wanted all of him. My lips crashed into his with all the emotions I'd had pent up.

"Huh hmm."

Rain brushed his lips over mine. His eyes cooled as he

turned his gaze toward our interruption. "Brother, your timing sucks as always."

Laurel's laugh was warm. "We brought some water back for you two to wash the blood off."

"Where are we?" I asked, taking in the lush trees, and trying to get my bearings.

"We are just over the border." Gemma let go of Laurel's hand and reached for me. She helped me to my feet and wrapped her arms around me in a tight embrace. "We were afraid to go too far...that you wouldn't make it."

My heart cratered at what they must have felt in those minutes I was out. Maybe it was longer judging by the position of the sun in the sky. The light danced through the leaves to the forest floor over familiar hooves. My gaze moved up to meet the obsidian orbs of my majestic guardian. He let out a huff. I released Gemma and slung my arms around Marius's neck. He didn't bother to glamour into human form.

"See how foolish you are when I'm not at your side? Did he hurt you?" He pulled back and studied me with the same scrutiny he used during training exercises. "I mean other than the arrow from one of his abhorrent soldiers."

"We'll talk about that later." I choked out the words. The memories of the beating were still too fresh. Coldness crept into my chest. Anger slid down our bond. *I can't talk about it yet.* A soothing caress like a hug came back. No words. Just love from my friend.

A warm hand splayed across my back, and I leaned into Rain's arms. The pain was gone from my wounds.

They may have healed, but I gave the credit to his touch and relished the connection. "Let's go home."

"I'd like nothing more." He placed two fingers in his mouth and whistled. Horses came galloping towards us. "Do you feel like riding?"

"It's like I was never injured." Nyx had healed me, and I wasn't tired or sore or weak. The way my body had been repaired seemed nothing short of a miracle.

We rode for hours through the forest. There was a cacophony of sounds, from birds singing to small animals rustling in the leaves. Teaming with life, it was so different from the Forgotten Forest near my doorstep growing up.

An ache in my side drew my attention—like a phantom pain of the now-absent injury. I rubbed the spot where the arrow had pierced me. The skin felt cooler there as if Nyx's touch remained. What had she intended to convey to me when she said I was being made into what I was meant to be? Coldness chilled my extremities despite the warm temperatures. Darkness edged around my vision.

What is happening to me?

CHAPTER 57
RAIN

No one said anything if they noticed how the faint hints of dark, smoky mist clung to Ari. It had to be Nyx's touch. I wasn't aware of anything else that could heal the way Ari had been. Only the goddess herself could have done that, and I'd be forever grateful no matter how long or short my life might be.

I trotted my horse up next to hers, and Ari smiled up at me. The darkness evaporated as if her simple gesture radiated so brightly nothing else could remain.

Gemma and Laurel had doubled up on Persephone when Ari asked if she could have her own steed to show she was indeed fine. I would have preferred her nestled in front of me where I could protect her, but I wouldn't stand between her and this decision. My brother and sister-in-law trailed behind us with Casimir and Marius.

"We're not far now," I said, returning her smile.

She looked over her shoulder as if noting everyone in

our party's position a good distance away. "Good. I can't wait to get you alone with walls around us."

My cock responded and pressed against my zipper. "I like the sound of that. What will you do to me when you have me all to yourself?"

"After I remove all your clothing, I'll take your…" She gave another glance, making sure no one could hear, I assumed. "I'll grab your length in my hand and stroke it up and down."

The sweetness in her voice when she told me her plans gave me a full, raging hard on. The saddle was uncomfortable, and I wanted to take Ari—feel her quiver when I thrust inside her. Our audience prevented me from satisfying my fantasy.

"Anything else?" I drank in the relaxed way she sat in the saddle and how she would look astride me the same way.

She licked her lips and smiled. The corners of her mouth turned up with a wicked promise. "You first."

"Oh, are we playing a game, my love?" I nudged my horse into a trot to add some space between us and the rest of the group.

Ari fell into stride beside me on her horse. "Tell me the first thing you'll do to me when we're alone."

I couldn't hold back my smile. "Undress you."

She scoffed. "Hmm. Maybe I don't want to be alone with you."

I chuckled and let out a long sigh, staring forward. "I'd slide your clothing from you, licking the exposed skin along the way. Every inch of your flesh." I gazed her direction. Ari's eyes had widened slightly. "And I do mean all of it."

Her mouth formed a small "O." I winked at her, content with the reaction on her face.

She coaxed her horse into a gallop.

"Come on," I said to mine. We caught up to Ari. "Where are you going?"

"Home. We have plans to tend to."

I grabbed her reins and pulled her horse to a stop next to mine.

"What?" She simpered.

I waited for the horses to settle, so I could position them side by side. "We're in no hurry."

She ogled me up and down. "Speak for yourself."

A chuckle rumbled from me. I leaned in and brushed my lips over hers. She sighed against me. My free hand landed on one half of her twin blades, securely fastened around her waist where they belonged. "We have others to consider."

Marius caught up to us first. "Did something happen?" He looked around as if there was danger.

"Ari's horse got spooked. We're fine." The horse snorted and shook her head. *Traitor.*

Laurel and Gemma rode up next to us.

Gemma focused on her sister. "What happened? Are you okay?"

"Yes, I'm fine." Ari smiled at her. "I'm sorry if we scared you."

"Too soon for another fright, Sis." Gemma gave her a

smile. "I'd prefer we stay close together until we get back to familiar territory."

"Better to be safe in a group," Marius said.

"I'm just ready to get home." Ari winked at me. "We'll slow down per my guardian's advisement."

I turned my head to hide my smirk from the others, but I didn't miss Gemma's raised eyebrow.

"Home," Gemma repeated quietly as if she latched onto the word the same way I had when Ari said it.

Ari slipped her hand in mine, drawing my attention back to the group. "Yes, home."

My heart swelled that she wanted a home with all of us—with me. Her hand was cold, and I circled my thumb over the smooth skin. Had something changed with her since her near-death experience? There was no denying Nyx had touched her. Nothing else could explain what we had witnessed. My only prayer was that it hadn't changed Ari at the core because that was the person I'd fallen in love with—the fierce fighter, the resilience in her perseverance, the love for others she showed, the protector of those she loved, the way she matched me. She was a part of me, and I wouldn't let anyone, even Nyx, steal the most precious parts of her.

CHAPTER 58

ARI

Laurel looped his arm around Gemma's shoulders in the entry of the palace. "Who's hungry? We can get Phina and meet you in the dining hall."

I peered down at my bloody clothes. Rain laced his fingers with mine, and I massaged the palm of his hand with my thumb. Marius had gone to retrieve Drew and bring him to the palace. My father hadn't shown any interest in him, and my brother should be here where we could keep him safe. My bonded suggested we not draw attention by going. It would be two days there and back provided the weather stayed mild.

"We're going to get cleaned up." Rain regarded me with a lustful gaze but there was more there. Love. My heart pounded as if it sought out the rhythm of his. "If that's what you want."

I nodded and looked at my sister. "Maybe we meet up later."

Gemma rubbed my arm and smiled. "Or maybe tomorrow."

"Tomorrow," I said, looking at my sister first and then my brother-in-law. "Thank you. Both of you. Give my niece lots of love."

Gemma leaned into Laurel as they turned and walked down the hall. I watched them stroll away for a moment, and the word Nyx had used to describe Rain to me came to mind. *Mate.* If Rain was that for me, then surely Gemma and Laurel were for each other too. I couldn't imagine anyone loving anyone more than they loved each other. But in my heart, I knew what I felt for Rain was equally abundant if not greater. Mate. I should talk to Rain about Nyx's matter-of-fact use of the term. Because if he was my mate and I his, he should know. Why did it feel so awkward to think about telling him this? He'd said he loved me. Of course, I was near death or just returned from it at the time. And there was another person we had to consider in this complicated situation—Drew. He was going to have to be where Gemma and I were, and I didn't want him growing up away from us. He needed to get to know Gemma again, but I was the only person he would know here. Rain might not want to raise a child who wasn't his. He might not want children at all.

A gentle finger lifted my chin until I gazed into Rain's eyes. "What are you thinking in that beautiful head of yours?"

"Just that I'm happy we are all safe. And...we should talk about my little brother's living arrangements."

Rain tugged me down the hall. "It's up to you and your

sister where you want him to live. He can stay with us or Laurel and Gemma or have his own quarters."

"He's too young for his own suite," I said, even though he'd had his own in our prison kingdom. After being separated from my little brother for so long, I needed him close so I could make sure he was adjusting okay. "Selfishly, I want him with me...us, but if he stayed with my sister and your brother, he'd grow up with Phina. He deserves a bond like me and Gemma and you and your brother."

"He will play with and learn with Phina regardless of which living quarters are considered his permanent residence." Rain navigated us toward the final turn to our hall.

"I could take up a separate suite for Drew and me. It's a lot to raise someone else's child, especially the child of your enemy. There are three of us in the palace after all..." I couldn't seem to suppress my ramblings. "Your people might not—"

Rain stopped and studied me. His face was full of love and assurance. "Our people, Ari. They are as much yours as mine, and I don't want you in any other suite than this one."

I stared at the door and then at him. He'd accepted me from the beginning. The people in his kingdom remembered my mother as the hero, not me, and Rain had ruled for a long time. I was no one here. They might never accept me. "Are you sure?"

He traced a finger down my cheek and across my lips. "Never more sure of anything."

"Thank you," I whispered against his jaw.

He caressed my mouth with his. I leaned into him until

our bodies pressed firmly against each other. Rain elbowed the door open and backed me into the room without breaking the kiss. He scooped me up in his arms. His mouth never left mine, even as he sat me on the counter in the bathroom.

"Shower?" he asked, brushing his lips along my earlobe. A shiver ran down my neck and all the way to my center.

"Yes." I undid the sheath at his back, and the weapon clattered to the ground. He pressed his hand to a panel on the wall and the water flowed from the two shower heads.

I reached for the leather holding my blades in place and unbuckled it. Rain removed all his weapons, and the lot formed an impressive stack on the counter. "How did you...never mind. We'll talk about that later."

I yanked the bloody sweater over my head. Rain ripped his shirt open and tossed it aside.

"Ari?" His eyes were on the mirror...not me.

I peered over my shoulder into the reflection. "Oh, my goddess."

"That's the triple moon." Rain's eyes were wide.

"Nyx's blessing." It was like she'd inked a tattoo over where the poison arrow had claimed me.

Rain knelt before me and kissed the tattoo and blazed a trail with his lips to my stomach. He worked the thick pants off for me. I reached for his waistband and slid off the counter, taking his pants down with me. He stepped out of them.

With no shame, I drank in every inch of him, running a finger over the scar on his jaw and down his throat to the center of his chest. I licked his nipple and bent to kiss the scar below his pec. Rain sucked in a breath. My mate was an incredible feast, including the impressive member between his legs. He cupped my chin and forced me to look up. A smirk greeted me with all the smugness that was him...and that smugness was well-earned. His eyes ablaze with fierce desire. My mate was my perfect match.

I grasped the back of his neck and pulled his mouth to mine. The hunger in his embrace sent sparks down to my most intimate parts. Rain lifted me, and I wrapped my legs around him. He inched into the shower until he stood between the two streams of water, my back against a wall. The water slipped over both of us. He pushed his leg between my thighs, rubbing against my throbbing center. My desire spiked with anticipation of his cock inside me. His chest brushed against mine, and my nipples pebbled. The friction ratcheted up my desire. He reached between us and circled my clit. My hips bucked against him, and I gasped.

"Rain..."

He slid two fingers inside me, and my core tightened. "Were you this wet when you hated me?"

I ground myself against his fingers. "Yes. I still hate you, but I love you."

His cock jerked against my leg, and he bit down on my shoulder. "Is this what you want?"

My breath came in little pants. "Yes."

He swirled his thumb over my clit. I moved my hips in time. "What about this?"

"I want you." I whimpered, hoping it was clear I meant all of him as my mate.

"Tell me you're mine and you can have me."

"I'm yours."

His mouth covered mine, and he positioned himself at my entrance. He pushed in a fraction. I murmured praises, wanting more. The anticipation was both torture and pleasure.

"Once we do this, I am yours and you are mine."

I tried to take him in, but he held my hips in place. Was he stopping? I squirmed, needing relief.

"Say it, Ari."

Oh, he wants it all so I can have it all. I took his lip between my teeth, applying just enough pressure. His cock twitched in me—the answer I wanted. "I am yours, and you are mine."

"I love you." He thrust in until he was seated fully. My chest expanded, overwhelmed with him inside me and in my heart. I loved him, but I couldn't form the words. Only incoherent sounds trickled from my lips. His forehead rested against mine. My walls tightened around him.

Rain moved in slow strokes, drawing pleasure with every slick slide of his dick.

"Ari..." He pumped faster, the rhythm erratic.

My pussy contracted around him. I moaned a garbled string of curses and called the gods. My vision fractured, and I spiraled into euphoria. Rain grunted and called out my name as his warm seed filled me. The connection between us had never been so powerful, and as if to reinforce the depth, our bodies were bathed in a gentle glow similar to when he was injured.

Rain shook against me, and I trailed my fingers up and down his spine. "I love you," I whispered into his ear.

Rain released my legs and steadied me, my back still against the wall. His hands cupped my cheeks. "I love you far more."

I slapped his shoulder and scooted out of his hold so I could tilt my head back under the water. His hands covered my breasts, thumbs swirling over my peaks until they hardened again. "Who said I was done with you?"

"At least let me clean up. I did die...I think."

His hands were on my face again, and I opened my eyes.

There was love and fear and revenge in his gaze, and I understood what the look was.

"I will never forget."

THE NIGHT HAD long since set, and Rain and I had only made it as far as the bed after our shower. The bliss inside of me butted up against my trepidation for telling him what Nyx had said. "I need to tell you something, but I don't know how you will feel about it." I twisted my fingers into the sheet.

Rain propped himself up on an elbow. "Whatever it is I will listen with an open mind, Ari."

His reassurance gave me up, and I inhaled and let it

out slowly to steady myself. "When I was...with Nyx." I didn't know what to call that time. Was it death? I pushed the thought away. "She told me of your offer, and I refused it, and she refused it."

He nodded, hurt flickering across his face.

"Not because it wasn't the worthiest gift you could offer me, but because I wasn't willing to trade your life for mine. I wanted you to live too."

Rain caressed my cheek. "I understand. I wanted the same for you."

I wrapped my hand around his and tucked it against my chest. "Nyx referred to you as my mate. I know the term isn't used much in our realm and is usually for goddesses and gods. And Gemma and Laurel are mates, but we're different from them. Why do you think Nyx used that term?" I wanted to hear him say he understood and that it felt that way to him...something more than love.

He reached for my waist and pulled me closer. "Because that is what we are. I didn't have the word for what I felt until you said mate. It clicked in place, and it makes sense now. I've had a sense of knowing you were important to me from the first time I met you. You are my mate, and I am yours. No light shines brighter than the fire burning in my soul for you, Ari."

Rain lowered his head to mine and kissed me with light, feathery touches.

I never felt more alive as if my body awoke by us just uttering it to each other. Desire tightened in my belly, and I deepened the kiss, darting my tongue in to meet Rain's.

He rolled, positioning me astride him. "I've been thinking about you in this position since that ride home."

I wiggled on his lap. My slicked center rubbed against his satin-like flesh that was hardening. "What?"

"You spread across my lap like you were in that saddle has occupied too many of my thoughts." He ran his hands up my arms and down my breasts, over my belly to rest on my hips.

The apex between my thighs tightened. I moved faster. A moan drifted out of me, and a similar sound echoed from Rain. The contact was intimate, but the friction wasn't enough. I needed him inside me. I shifted to guide him in, but his hands tightened on my hips.

"No, take yours first. I want to watch you pleasure yourself against me." A wicked smile ghosted over his lips, daring me.

CHAPTER 59

RAIN

My dick was painfully hard watching Ari slide back and forth. The most exquisite night with all the stars and a full moon couldn't compare to her. My love, my mate, a fierce force…she was mine. Ari was everything I wanted and didn't know to ask for from the goddesses and gods. She moved faster, my cock so slick from her there was no resistance. No, it was smooth strokes of soft skin against me, and I held my orgasm back. I could have come, but I wanted to study every moment and memorize what ecstasy looked like on her.

She moved in wild motions, and I knew she was close. I dug my fingers into her hips, helping her along. Her thighs tightened around the outside of mine. A string of curses or promises, I couldn't decipher which, tumbled from her lips. I flipped her over and drove deep in her. Goddesses and gods, she was wet. I wanted to spend every moment we had together buried in her to show how bottomless my love was for her. Her pussy clenched around me still in the throes of her orgasm, soft and tight. I wouldn't last long.

"Rain…" Her voice was both pleading and lilted with pleasure.

"Your mate." I stroked in and out of her as her walls milked me. Stars exploded in my vision, and my seed spilled in her for what seemed like an eternity. I rested my head in the bend of her neck, placing soft kisses as I tried to slow my erratic breaths. She meant everything to me. I'd never expected to find love much less one blessed by the goddess herself, but then, Ari was a goddess in her own right to me.

"My mate." She panted against my temple.

At that moment, I knew anything I had was hers—my heart, my life, my soul, and my kingdom.

CHAPTER 60

ARI

Rain's minty scent mixed with the aroma of tea. I opened my eyes to find him on his side, head resting on his arm, studying me.

I reached out and caressed his cheek. "Good morning."

"Good morning, my love." His gaze dipped down to my bare breasts and back to my face.

"What's on your mind?" My hand drifted to his chest. He caught my hand and brought my fingers to his lips.

"We should talk about..." He paused like he searched for the right words.

"Everything." There were so many things we needed to talk about.

"I was referring to us being mates."

"Oh," I said, looking down at the bedsheets.

He crooked a finger under my chin and tilted it up, so I was looking him in the eyes. "Oh? That's all you have to say?"

Did he just want to see me squirm? I tried to look away, but he held my chin in a gentle but firm grasp.

Whatever was between us, Nyx had seen fit to label it with something reserved for her and Erebus and a select few. She'd blessed the union between me and Rain with one word, and it changed the entire world for me.

"My heart was yours before I knew we were mates, Ari. Before I even admitted to myself what this was, I would have risked my kingdom for a stolen moment with you."

"I wouldn't have asked that kind of sacrifice of you."

"No, you wouldn't, but my choice is you. Nothing in this realm means more to me than my mate, and I love you with my soul."

My heart ached and swelled for the depth of what he said. He deserved so much more than to be with the daughter of a traitor and murderer, but I was more than that. I was the daughter of a great warrior and descendant of Nyx. Would his people see that though? Would they accept me for my mother's side or reject me for my father's? And if they rejected me for my father, what would that do for Rain and his ability to lead?

"Talk to me," he whispered. "I can almost see the thoughts flowing through your head, but there is no argument that would make me not want to be with you."

"If I wasn't your mate, would you still want this? The challenges? Me? Us?"

He swept a piece of loose hair behind my ear. "I loved you before I knew you were my mate, and I'll love you if some seer says it's not true. I've known I wanted to be with you from the moment you spoke the first day we met."

I don't know what I expected, but I'd never felt more loved.

"We can always go ask Nyx to take it back if you don't like being called mates." He lifted a shoulder and fought back a smile. He chuckled.

"I love you, you jerk." I leaned in to kiss him, and he leaned back with a hair's width between us. "Well, I'll just get dressed then." I moved to get out of bed.

He snaked his arm around my waist, and his lips crashed down on mine.

I sighed against his mouth.

"We're not going anywhere right now."

"My heart is yours, Rain."

He rolled over and sat on the edge of the bed. I scooted up behind him and slipped my arms around his waist. "Are you okay?"

Rain laughed and pulled me onto his lap. He pressed his lips to my forehead. "I'm perfect, but we do need to get dressed. I'll shower first, so you can drink your tea." He tilted his head to the little table beside the bed.

The aroma wafted up to me. "Smells good."

He leaned down and took my nipple in his mouth, swirling his tongue. I gasped and pressed my thighs together.

"You are lecherous."

He raised his head and wagged his eyebrows. "I can be if you want."

I slid off of his lap with a laugh and wrapped the sheet around me. "Go clean up."

"Only because you asked so nicely." He walked across the room in the nude, his ass on full display...so perfect. "Hope you enjoyed the view."

I tossed a pillow and hit him. He laughed until I froze.

"Rain...is that?" I crossed the room and touched the mark on his side. He had a mark like mine—the perfect twin.

"Fucking hell. That must have been what I felt last night."

Nyx hadn't just blessed me. She had blessed us. "Does that make us official mates?"

"I've never heard of this happening, but I'm going to say yes." He tilted my head up and brought our lips together in a soft dance. "I'm going to take my shower now, my mate."

I shoved my hands against him and sauntered toward the bed.

He let out a whistle as he disappeared into the bathroom.

I picked up the cup of tea and walked to the window with the sheet held tight by my other hand. The tint of the sky was the most beautiful I remembered seeing. I watched as it crested the top of the buildings. The oranges, pinks, and golds disappeared, leaving only the bright sun against the azure blue sky. Residents of the city walked along the sidewalks. Life teemed at every corner of Rain's city, and I wanted to be a part of that. I wanted to live near my sister and family, and most of all, I wanted to make a life with Rain, my mate.

The water cutoff and Rain emerged a few minutes later with a towel draped around his hips. His wet hair laid around his face, and it made him look far younger than his actual years. I crossed the room and dropped the sheet in front of me. Standing on my tiptoes, I pressed my lips to his. "Are you sure you're clean?"

"Hmm." He pulled me against him. "I feel very dirty again."

I giggled. "Maybe you could use another shower."

"Excellent suggestion." His hands slipped over my rear until he grasped my thighs and lifted me. My legs wrapped around his waist like they were magnets encasing him. He carried me to the shower. I couldn't think of a more perfect way to start the day.

CHAPTER 61
ARI

Rain was on the mobile phone while I finished my toast and bacon. The late morning light drifted in through the large window and covered the floor in gold, dancing as if music guided it. A thin line of shadow seemed to be glued to me, and I wasn't sure if anyone saw it but me. Nyx's touch was what I assumed it was. A healing gift I only needed because of my father's psychotic ideas. Revenge would come in time for my father, but I refused to let him steal any more joy from not only my life but that of the lives of my family. Time with those most important to me was what we would have today. I wasn't foolish enough to think we were completely safe, but Rain and Laurel had fortified the boundaries, increased patrols, and set up more early warning systems. We were as secure as we could be.

The heavy days were not behind us.

Rain held his hand out to me. "I want to take you somewhere. Show you how I have fun."

I slid my hand into his. "As long as it doesn't involve sparring or weapons.

He threw his head back and laughed. "No sparring or weapons, but there are occasional injuries."

I let out a big breath. I'd seen enough fighting for a while.

"Trust me," he said and winked at me.

The casual gesture made me trust him less. I narrowed my eyes at him.

When we were outside the palace, my internal guard lit up for my father. Rain's calm demeanor notched my anxiety down. He vanyshened us to a finely manicured field. Groups of people sat in stands on either side of the line marked green. Poles with a crossbar were erected at each end like the letter H, but the adjoining bar was lower.

"Is this a game?"

"Yes, did you ever play keep away as a child?"

"Of course," I said, my curiosity piqued.

"We have a sport that many of us participate in that is similar to that. Those are the teams." He pointed to the groups in matching clothes on either side—all males.

I counted fifteen on each.

"Today is the men's league. There is a women's league and a mixed league too."

"What are the uniforms they are wearing?" I'd never seen anyone in those types of clothes. Hell, I'd never seen so many bare fae legs at one time.

"The jerseys and shorts?" His face looked confused.

"Shorts?" I chewed on the word. "Those are the pants.

He smiled at me. "Yes. Let's go find a seat before they start."

A man in a striped shirt came running towards us. I stepped back, but Rain's hand tightened around us. The fae had broad shoulders and dark, curly hair. He stood slightly taller than Rain, and there weren't many who did.

The man glanced between us and bowed. "Prince Rainier, will you be joining us?"

"As a spectator today, Joshua."

"If you change your mind, the Blue Stallions could use another player."

Rain's hand went over his heart. "You know I could never play for another team other than my own."

Joshua nodded, his curls bouncing. "The Dark Storms will be happy to hear that."

"I'll be cheering from the front row. Have you met Princess Arianna? Princess Gemma is her sister."

I wasn't technically a princess. The empire never really existed outside the glamoured little bubble of the prison kingdom. I'd never been queen regent either. It was time to let the formality I'd never enjoyed go.

Joshua bowed again. "Princess."

I held my hand out as I'd seen Rain do. "Just Arianna, please."

Joshua gave my hand a firm shake and let go, mirroring the gesture he'd shared with Rain.

"Shall I walk you to your box?" Joshua asked.

"No, I'm taking Arianna to the center field seats."

"It should be a good game today." Joshua bowed and turned to jog off to the two other men in striped shirts.

"He's a referee for the game, so he'll point out penalties."

I felt my face scrunch up as I thought of his words.

"The rules will make more sense as the gameplay starts."

Rain led us to front-row seats behind the team in the midnight blue and grey jerseys. As I took in the players standing in front of us, I was shocked to realize all of the men were about the size of Rain. The team turned to him. None of them bowed, and that was a pleasant surprise. Instead, hands waved in the air to greet their prince. They all had similarly cropped hair and neatly trimmed facial hair, like it was part of their uniform. Rain waved them off.

I leaned close to him. "If you want to go do whatever this is, it's fine."

He wrapped an arm around my shoulders. "I'm right where I want to be. Besides, who would explain Moirai to you?"

"You call this game after the ancient name of the Fates?"

"It predates our generation, but that is the name."

"Do you cut your hair and wear the beard when you play?" I wagged my eyebrows at him.

His lips brushed my ear. "I'll wear the beard and cut my hair or go play in the nude if it pleases you."

I smashed my lips together. "Let's keep that particular gift between us."

He kissed my temple. "As you wish."

A man stood in the center of the field. "Welcome to the first Moirai match of the day between the Blue Stallions and the Dark Storms." The wind carried his voice around the stands. The crowd got to their feet and cheered. Rain stood, and I followed his lead, clapping.

The players were introduced one by one, and some garnered more yells than others. By the time the introductions were done, the excitement of the event bled into me.

"The Dark Storms have won the coin toss and have chosen to kick."

The team positioned themselves in various spots behind the man with the ball. He dropped the odd-shaped ball and kicked it away from them. Then, what looked like chaos ensued.

Rain was on his feet cheering. I glanced around to see that everyone in the stands appeared to be on their feet. I tamped down my awkwardness and stood along with them.

A few minutes in, and with the help of Rain, I started to understand how the match worked.

"No magic is allowed to be used in the game."

"So, it's all..." I glanced out to see one of the Dark Storm players tackle a Blue Stallion player and waited for the cheers to quiet down. "It's all just brute force?"

One side of Rain's mouth quirked up. "Something like that."

"The game is up to fate instead of power."

Rain winked at me. "That's why they called it Moirai."

By the time they called the half, I was engrossed in the game. I hadn't seen anything like it before today. Growing up, our games were far tamer, and adults were usually training or working, so they didn't participate. One of the

Dark Storm players limped off the field and dropped into a chair. Rain had pointed him out earlier and told me he was not only the best player but the captain. It didn't bode well for the tied game.

"I'm out," the player said. "I need a healer for my knee."

A large man with rich, dark skin approached Rain. "We need you, my friend." His voice was sonorous, and he radiated calm. The handsome man inclined his head toward me. "If you can spare him, my lady."

Gemma and Laurel strolled up minus my niece. I missed her sweet hugs as much as I missed my little brother's.

"Go help your team," I said. "They need you, and I've got company."

"We've got her. Save the day. It's what you do." Laurel patted Rain on the back.

Rain studied me for a moment, and I saw the debate in his eyes.

"I'd like to see you play," I said.

A grin broke his serious expression as he leaned forward, placing a soft kiss on my cheek. He whispered in my ear, "That blush looks good on you."

Then, he turned and ran toward a small door, pulling his shirt over his head. The defined muscles in his back rippled, and I couldn't help but lick my lips.

CHAPTER 62
ARI

My sister and brother-in-law dropped into the seats next to me. "I didn't expect to see you here."

Gemma pulled me into a hug. "We come when we can. Phina has a friend over for a playdate, and the nanny is with them."

"Playdate?"

"Two friends playing together." She turned to Laurel. "Get us some drinks, love."

Laurel kissed Gemma's temple and rose from the chair. "Anything for you."

"And no fae folk specials," she called after him. "He'll bring back the most potent thing they have if I don't tell him."

I laughed, but my laughter died when my eyes caught on a figure jogging from the door I'd seen Rain enter a few minutes ago. He was wearing a form-fitting jersey and shorts. My gaze was drawn to the massive bulge in his pants. He joined his teammates, and I couldn't help but glance at the others. None were as large as his.

"Ari, are you staring at his...package?" Gemma asked. Of course, she knew where I was looking. The task of telling me about sex and attraction had fallen on her, and to her credit, she'd been honest and candid answering my questions, even when my fourteen-year-old self giggled every time she mentioned penis and vagina. She was there when I lost my virginity to a jerk of a boy, too. I'd cried on her shoulder for what seemed like days, and she listened and soothed my broken heart until I had no more tears to shed. From that point on, I'd sworn off love until I was ready to marry, not for sex but for love... until Rain.

I didn't look at her, but my cheeks burned.

"You are," my sister whisper-yelled at me and burst out laughing.

I shot her a death stare. "Shut up, Gemma." I looked back to where Rain huddled with his team. He raised his gaze to mine and winked.

"You are in for a treat."

"I have seen..."

She laughed harder. "Not that. Him in the game."

"Why?" I asked.

"Rain doesn't play very often, but when he does, it's something to watch."

"Does Laurel participate too?"

"Oh, he has his own team. They would rather face each other on the field. In the best brotherly way, of course."

The other team drop kicked the ball again to kickoff the second half. One of the Dark Storm players caught the ball and was swarmed by the Blue Stallions. He passed the ball to Rain. His feet moved so fast. No magic. Those were the rules. The speed that propelled him was natural and unlike any I'd witnessed before. He scored, and the crowd erupted. They began to chant his name.

"Close your mouth, little sister. I told you he was good."

He held his hands up and waved at the crowd as the teams got back into position.

The play resumed and Rain tackled a player. I was vaguely aware of the other players, but I only saw him and his smooth, strategic movements. He caught the ball and ran it for another score. The crowd grew louder.

By the end of the game, the crowd was worked up, and so was I. The stand emptied into the field surrounding the team. I couldn't see Rainier, but I could sense him. My eyes closed, and I turned around. When I opened them, he was standing in front of me.

"That was..." I couldn't stop from glancing down at his large bulge and glancing back up. "Impressive."

He chuckled and wrapped his arms around me. "How about we get out of here? I need a shower, and I think you do too."

"Yes," I said, hearing how breathless my own voice was. "It was hot out here."

He pulled me close to vanyshen. A shrill noise stopped me in my tracks. I covered my ears. "What is that?"

He pulled out his phone. "We're under attack." His finger jammed against his phone. "Where are you? What do you see?"

Fae scattered out through the archways. Panic radiated around me.

Rain listened with the phone pressed against one ear and his hand covering the other. "We'll meet you in the war room."

Rain grabbed my hand and jerked me toward him.

My stomach dropped. It had to be my father. "What's going on?"

"The vampires are here."

"We're going to get Phina," Gemma shouted over the alarm. "We'll meet you at the palace." They vanyshened out of the stadium, and I was relieved they would be safe.

The vampires were looking for me. I was the prize my father wanted.

"We need to go." Rain held his hand out for me, not forcing me to go.

I slid my hand into his. "If the one who hit me is among them, he's mine."

"Only if you get to him first. If I find him before you, he'll be a pile of charred lightning dust."

The ground shook, and a deafening boom vibrated around me. Pieces of the stadium came down on top of fae. Panic coiled around my spine and spiked when I saw a line being cut through the elves. Vampires poured into the space. An entire section of seating was gone, crumpled on the stadium floor. Unmoving fae, bleeding and some drained, piled up on either side of the wall of vampires. It was hard to look at. I reached for my blades blessed by Nyx, but I hadn't worn them. I scanned the area, and there was only one viable way out. A way that wasn't an option for most fae.

Rain barked orders to someone on the phone. I glanced in his direction, and his face was a mask of rage and terror.

"We need to go." His voice shook as he pulled me close.

"We have to help them," I said, spinning toward the crowd.

"They have Laurel and Gemma cornered."

Fuck. My heart dropped. "How do we get out of here?"

I scanned the stadium as we backed toward the center of the field. The crowd pushed forward as the fae fought back with all the magic at their disposal. The vampires gained fae powers as they fed. Even briefly obtaining those gifts tipped the scale. There would be no survivors if we didn't do something now. Rain grasped my arm. "I have an idea."

CHAPTER 63

ARI

Rain studied my face as if he was memorizing it. "Remember how we converged our powers in the forest?"

Converged... oh, when he used my power to bring us back to the palace. "Yes."

"We're going to use it to channel my storms over the vampires. We need to get high up to see, though."

Rain vanyshened us to a rooftop as close as possible to where the guards said the most concentration was—where Gemma and Laurel were last seen. The ugly sounds of elves and vampires clashing permeated the air. The people, my people, his people, were in full-on warfare.

Nyx, give me strength because I'm fucking terrified—for myself, for Rain, for my family, and for the elves in the middle of the siege my father brought to this city.

Rain wrapped his fingers around mine. He lifted my trembling hand and pressed his lips to my knuckles. With his free hand, he pointed to a tower—the height exactly what we needed to see the square where Gemma and Laurel were.

Nyx, please let them be okay.

I closed my eyes as Rain pulled me into his arms. Air breezed around me as Rain whisked us up. I opened my eyes and peered down from the ledge of the tower.

Rain slipped his arm around my waist and pulled me back. "There's no rail."

"Do you see them?" I asked, staring at the space filled by vampires. So many. Down the streets, to the stadium we were just in, and back to the statue of my mother. Where were the elves who had been there? Where were Gemma and Laurel? The scent of blood—fresh blood and death drifted up around me, and my stomach roiled.

"There."

I followed where he pointed, and Gemma and Laurel were trapped at the statue. No viable path for escape. No way for us to fight through so many vampires. No way to save them. My heart tightened in my chest.

"Relax. I just need your power boost to stop them."

"There are too many."

"Not for me... with your help," he said, his voice quiet, focused. I glanced over at him, and his eyes were closed. When he opened them, silver streaked across them like lightning. His hand entwined with mine. "When I give you the signal, charge me up just like you did in the forest."

The time in the forest barely got us to the gates. It was going to take something a hell of a lot more powerful. "We need to at least go try."

"Trust me."

I swallowed against the knot in my throat and gripped his hand.

He extended his other arm up toward the sky, and clouds swirled as if at his command. Thunder rumbled and shook us where we stood. I squeezed his hand tighter. Rain's eyes glowed. He reached for the sky like he could pull it to him. His jaw tightened. A loud clap sounded around us. My heart stammered.

"Now," he said through gritted teeth.

I mirrored what we did in the forest, and our joined hands had an aura around them. The color expanded and enveloped Rain. Warmth pulsed between us in an all-consuming connection. My mate. His love for me flowed across, and mine back to him. There was no time to rejoice in the tie. Another loud clap shook the space, and then bolts of blinding silver light erupted from the sky. One after another, they hit the space beneath us with precision. I stared below and saw swaths of vampires turn to ash. I reached for my power and sent a wall of protection to Gemma and Laurel. To my surprise, it responded without much effort.

Rain's lightning struck again and again, instantly vaporizing dozens of the vampires at a time. I wanted to look back at him, in awe of his power, but I didn't dare take my eyes off my sister and her husband. Never had I seen someone command lightning like Rain was. Heat radiated like the sun between our hands, and I ground my teeth to keep our tether tight and the shield up I'd put around Gemma and Laurel.

Mounds of grey ash piled up around my mother's statue. The lightning bolts danced in a methodical, rapid cadence. At last, there was nothing left of the vampires except the dust floating away on the wind. Rain's grip on my hand loosened, and I turned in time to witness the hard thud of his knees on the stone.

My heart fell into my stomach. I dropped down next to him. His breathing was shallow. He'd given too much.

Nyx, help me heal him. Please.

A shadow enclosed me, and power coursed through me. Nyx's power. I placed my hands over him and let the force pour out of me and into Rain. I embraced the strength of what Nyx had given me and what it meant. I'd be someone different. An heir from a forgotten time. A force in me that wouldn't be contained. I'd saved Rain, but I'd damned myself to an isolated existence. Darkness, Nyx's darkness, was a part of me. Dominated me with power not meant for our time. This was the end of the me he'd known.

Rain was the storm, and I was the night.

Rain's long lashes fluttered, and I packed Nyx's power back into me like bricks of a castle. When his eyes opened, the darkness had been swept away as if it was never there, but the abyss in me told me its hold was as tight as my grip had been on Rain's hands moments ago. I helped him sit up.

"How do you feel?"

He cradled my face with his palms. "I thought...how am I here?" His deep blue eyes searched mine, but he'd find no answers. None I could give anyway.

"Let me help you up," I said, moving to slide an arm around him.

"I've got it," he said, rising to his feet. Rain swayed, and I steadied him.

"Are you sure?" His jaw tightened, and I followed his gaze.

My father found me up in the tower and smiled as his men led Gemma and Laurel away. I gasped. "No."

Their hands were bound. Then they just disappeared, and I knew without a doubt he'd taken them away to the vampire kingdom. Terror slashed across my chest like the lashes of the whip I'd endured at my father's command, and I'd lay down my own freedom to protect my sister from that agony.

I fought back tears as I looked at Rain. We'd obliterated more vampires than I could count, and my father still won the battle. I should have been on the ground with my sister. I was the one my father wanted. Gemma would be safe. "If you had let me go down there, I—"

"Would be dead or in the same position as Gemma and Laurel, and I will never let your father harm you again." His words held a promise I couldn't process until my family was whole once more. He looked away and back to me. "My brother...your sister..." He was stumbling over his words. I'd never seen him like that.

I rested a hand against his cheek, understanding that raw emotion on his face. "We're going to get them back." I leaned in and kissed him with all the fierceness of my love for him, knowing the probability of meeting again was slight. My father did this, and it was my problem to solve. I knew that meant I would have to tap into a force beyond Nyx's power. I'd tried to ignore the part of me that was my father, but that was the exact piece I needed to defeat him. Like to like. "I'm going to get them back."

Rain was too weak from using his power to stop me, and taking him to this fight would be a death sentence in his current state. Suddenly, I was ten years old again and watching my mother wither away. Her abilities drained her, but I could feel her using them. I'd begged her to stop when she became bedridden. She'd cradled my cheek and smiled for the last time. *You will understand one day. Never be afraid of what you are. Of what you are capable of.* She'd said as light had filled the space around us. Then, her hand fell away.

Dampness blurred my vision. I blinked to clear my sight as Mother's voice drifted away. I saw Rain's face again, still struggling to remain upright.

He reached for me as I stepped onto the ledge.

"I love you," I whispered to my mate. Never more sure since Nyx first said that was who Rain was to me, I stood just out of his reach when I vanyshened away. The tears and fear in his eyes haunted me as I landed on the edge of my father's lands. My task taunted me. I had to stop the man responsible for the pain generations had endured. I was the daughter of perhaps the greatest general to walk this realm. I was the descendant of Nyx and called on all the power afforded to me. My fingertips tingled as darkness, pregnant with unyielding power, shrouded around me. I was coming for my father, and I wanted him to feel the force of my ancestors as I approached. But I was his daughter, and I let that putrid, rancid part that was him take over as I crossed the border into his vampire kingdom.

To be continued...

Ready for more? Read Gemma's story in the prequel.

CRAVING MORE PASSION AND MAGIC?

The magic you've experienced in these pages is just the beginning of the Empire of Curses and Dreams world. Join my newsletter family for exclusive content—from deleted scenes to sneak peeks of upcoming releases. I share writing updates, behind-the-scenes views, and magical surprises with my most devoted readers first. Let's continue this journey together

ACKNOWLEDGMENTS

To my editors, Dawn and Lisa, thank you for the invaluable notes, chats, and edits on this series. You have both been completely supportive as I decided to dive into this subgenre with both feet. This series wouldn't exist without your brainstorming, thoughts, and discussions.

To my incredible cover designer, Laura, you are undeniably a phenomenal artist. I am in awe at how you make the important elements of the story come to life for the cover. I treasure our creative sessions!

To my sister and my nieces, you remind me to have perseverance every day. Thank you for hopping on the ride for this journey by attending events, decorating tables, giving me honest feedback, celebrating the wins with me, and sharing my books with your friends. It means more to me than I can convey that you support me and my writing.

To my friend, Lizzie, you encouraged me to keep going when I thought it would be impossible to create this series in the abbreviated window I had. You were there, talking me through the oopsies and when things just didn't go right. Most of all, you made me laugh when I needed it most. Thank you for supporting my ideas, no matter how crazy they get, and for telling me an elote cup from one of our favorite places will make me feel better.

To my beta readers, ARC readers, and fans, you are the reason I write, and I'm so honored that you have joined me for this new series. Thank you for sharing the excitement with me over the launch of my Empire of Curses and Dreams world. I would be remiss if I didn't take this opportunity to recognize those who actively seek out indie authors to support, whether that is on BookTok, Bookstagram, or any other platform. You help indie authors so much, and I appreciate you.

About the Author

Susan Person is an award-winning author of fantasy and dark paranormal romance. After years in the business world, she returned to college to pursue a degree in anthropology and graduated in 2021. Susan enjoys meeting writers and readers alike at conferences and events. She knew at an early age she wanted to write powerful heroines and fulfills that dream by writing badass empowered heroines who take charge in their paranormal worlds.

Susan grew up on a thoroughbred horse farm before moving to the big city of Dallas. She considers herself a Texan but is loyal to her home state of Arkansas. A lover of travel, she has visited several countries with many more to go on her list. She particularly loved dowsing at Stonehenge and seeing the Parthenon in Athens. The outdoors is a place where Susan finds inspiration and can often be found in a park, at the lake, or on a road trip. She especially loves the mountains. Furry animals hold a special place in her heart, and dogs tend to seek her out as a friend.

Connect with her at susanperson.com

WANT TO LEARN MORE ABOUT SUSAN PERSON?

Scan the QR code below to see where you find more of Susan's book or see what reader events she is attending.

ALSO BY SUSAN PERSON

The Falling From Hell Series

Fallen, Book 1

Reverie, Book 2

Marred, Book 3

The Blood Moon Prophecy

Queen of Sacrifice, Book 1

Queen of Darkness Book 2

Queen of Moons Book 3

A Vampire Ice Age Series

In Blood & Ice, Book 1

Reclamation In Ice, Book 2

Book 3: TBA in 2025

Enchanted Rock Immortals World

Fae Undone, The Enchanted Rock Immortals Clan Fae 1

Fae Redone, The Enchanted Rock Immortals Clan Fae 2

www.ingramcontent.com/pod-product-compliance
Lightning Source LLC
Chambersburg PA
CBHW051427190726
48289CB00001B/88